WOUNDS *in the* RAIN

WOUNDS IN THE RAIN

War Stories

BY
STEPHEN CRANE

Short Story Index Reprint Series

BOOKS FOR LIBRARIES PRESS
PLAINVIEW, NEW YORK

First Published 1900
Reprinted 1976

Library of Congress Cataloging in Publication Data

Crane, Stephen, 1871-1900.
   Wounds in the rain.

   (Short story index reprint series)
   CONTENTS: The price of the harness.--The lone
charge of William B. Perkins.--The clan of No-name.
[etc.]
   I. Title.
PZ3.C852Wo5 [PS1449.C85]   813'.4   72-3294
ISBN 0-8369-4145-4

TO

Moreton Frewen

THIS SMALL TOKEN OF THINGS

WELL REMEMBERED BY

HIS FRIEND

STEPHEN CRANE.

BREDE PLACE, SUSSEX, *April*, 1900.

CONTENTS

THE PRICE OF THE HARNESS.................. 1

THE LONE CHARGE OF WILLIAM B. PERKINS.... 33

THE CLAN OF NO-NAME..................... 42

GOD REST YE, MERRY GENTLEMEN............ 74

THE REVENGE OF THE ADOLPHUS.............. 107

THE SERGEANT'S PRIVATE MADHOUSE.......... 138

VIRTUE IN WAR........................... 152

MARINES SIGNALLING UNDER FIRE AT GUANTANAMO. 178

THIS MAJESTIC LIE........................ 190

WAR MEMORIES........................... 229

THE SECOND GENERATION.................... 309

WOUNDS IN THE RAIN

THE PRICE OF THE HARNESS

I

TWENTY-FIVE men were making a road out of
a path up the hillside. The light batteries in the
rear were impatient to advance, but first must be
done all that digging and smoothing which gains
no encrusted medals from war. The men worked
like gardeners, and a road was growing from the
old pack-animal trail.

Trees arched from a field of guinea-grass which
resembled young wild corn. The day was still
and dry. The men working were dressed in the
consistent blue of United States regulars. They
looked indifferent, almost stolid, despite the
heat and the labour. There was little talking.
From time to time a Government pack-train, led
by a sleek-sided tender bell-mare, come from one
way or the other way, and the men stood aside

as the strong, hard, black-and-tan animals crowded eagerly after their curious little feminine leader.

A volunteer staff-officer appeared, and, sitting on his horse in the middle of the work, asked the sergeant in command some questions which were apparently not relevant to any military business. Men straggling along on various duties almost invariably spun some kind of a joke as they passed.

A corporal and four men were guarding boxes of spare ammunition at the top of the hill, and one of the number often went to the foot of the hill swinging canteens.

The day wore down to the Cuban dusk, in which the shadows are all grim and of ghostly shape. The men began to lift their eyes from the shovels and picks, and glance in the direction of their camp. The sun threw his last lance through the foliage. The steep mountain-range on the right turned blue and as without detail as a curtain. The tiny ruby of light ahead meant that the ammunition-guard were cooking their supper. From somewhere in the world came a single rifle-shot.

Figures appeared, dim in the shadow of the trees. A murmur, a sigh of quiet relief, arose from the working party. Later, they swung up the hill in an unformed formation, being always like soldiers, and unable even to carry a spade save like United States regular soldiers. As they passed through some fields, the bland white light of the end of the day feebly touched each hard bronze profile.

"Wonder if we'll git anythin' to eat," said Watkins, in a low voice.

"Should think so," said Nolan, in the same tone. They betrayed no impatience; they seemed to feel a kind of awe of the situation.

The sergeant turned. One could see the cool grey eye flashing under the brim of the campaign hat. "What in hell you fellers kickin' about?" he asked. They made no reply, understanding that they were being suppressed.

As they moved on, a murmur arose from the tall grass on either hand. It was the noise from the bivouac of ten thousand men, although one saw practically nothing from the low-cart road-way. The sergeant led his party up a wet clay bank and into a trampled field. Here were scattered tiny white shelter tents, and in the darkness they were luminous like the rearing stones in a graveyard. A few fires burned blood-red, and the shadowy figures of men moved with no more expression of detail than there is in the swaying of foliage on a windy night.

The working party felt their way to where their tents were pitched. A man suddenly cursed; he had mislaid something, and he knew he was not going to find it that night. Watkins spoke again with the monotony of a clock, "Wonder if we'll git anythin' to eat."

Martin, with eyes turned pensively to the stars, began a treatise. "Them Spaniards——"

"Oh, quit it," cried Nolan. "What th' piper do you know about th' Spaniards, you fat-headed Dutchman? Better think of your belly, you blunderin' swine, an' what you're goin' to put in it, grass or dirt."

A laugh, a sort of a deep growl, arose from the prostrate men. In the meantime the sergeant had reappeared and was standing over them. "No rations to-night," he said gruffly, and turning on his heel, walked away.

This announcement was received in silence. But Watkins had flung himself face downward, and putting his lips close to a tuft of grass, he formulated oaths. Martin arose and, going to his shelter, crawled in sulkily. After a long interval Nolan said aloud, "Hell!" Grierson, enlisted for the war, raised a querulous voice. "Well, I wonder when we *will* git fed?"

From the ground about him came a low chuckle,

full of ironical comment upon Grierson's lack of certain qualities which the other men felt them-selves to possess.

II

In the cold light of dawn the men were on their knees, packing, strapping, and buckling. The comic toy hamlet of shelter-tents had been wiped out as if by a cyclone. Through the trees could be seen the crimson of a light battery's blankets, and the wheels creaked like the sound of a musketry fight. Nolan, well gripped by his shelter tent, his blanket, and his cartridge-belt, and bearing his rifle, advanced upon a small group of men who were hastily finishing a can of coffee.

"Say, give us a drink, will yeh?" he asked, wistfully. He was as sad-eyed as an orphan beggar.

Every man in the group turned to look him straight in the face. He had asked for the prin-cipal ruby out of each one's crown. There was a grim silence. Then one said, "What fer?" Nolan cast his glance to the ground, and went away abashed.

But he espied Watkins and Martin surrounding Grierson, who had gained three pieces of hard-tack by mere force of his audacious inexperience. Grierson was fending his comrades off tearfully. " Now, don't be damn pigs," he cried. " Hold on a minute." Here Nolan asserted a claim. Grierson groaned. Kneeling piously, he divided the hard-tack with minute care into four portions. The men, who had had their heads together like players watching a wheel of fortune, arose suddenly, each chewing. Nolan interpolated a drink of water, and sighed contentedly.

The whole forest seemed to be moving. From the field on the other side of the road a column of men in blue was slowly pouring; the battery had creaked on ahead; from the rear came a hum of advancing regiments. Then from a mile away rang the noise of a shot; then another shot; in a moment the rifles there were drumming, drumming, drumming. The artillery boomed out suddenly. A day of battle was begun.

The men made no exclamations. They rolled their eyes in the direction of the sound, and then swept with a calm glance the forests and the hills which surrounded them, implacably mysterious forests and hills which lent to every rifle-shot the ominous quality which belongs to secret assassination. The whole scene would have spoken to the private soldiers of ambushes, sudden flank attacks, terrible disasters, if it were not for those cool gentlemen with shoulder-straps and swords who, the private soldiers knew, were of another world and omnipotent for the business.

The battalions moved out into the mud and began a leisurely march in the damp shade of the trees. The advance of two batteries had churned the black soil into a formidable paste. The brown leggings of the men, stained with the mud of other days, took on a deeper colour. Perspiration broke gently out on the reddish faces. With his heavy roll of blanket and the half of a shelter-tent crossing his right shoulder and under his left arm, each man presented the appearance of being clasped from behind, wrestler fashion, by a pair of thick white arms.

There was something distinctive in the way they carried their rifles. There was the grace of an old hunter somewhere in it, the grace of a man whose rifle has become absolutely a part of himself. Furthermore, almost every blue shirt sleeve was rolled to the elbow, disclosing fore-arms of almost incredible brawn. The rifles seemed light, almost fragile, in the hands that were at the end of these arms, never fat but always with rolling muscles and veins that seemed on the point of bursting. And another thing was the silence and the marvellous impassivity of the faces as the column made its slow way toward where the whole forest spluttered and fluttered with battle.

Opportunely, the battalion was halted a-straddle of a stream, and before it again moved, most of the men had filled their canteens. The firing increased. Ahead and to the left a battery was booming at methodical intervals, while the infantry racket was that continual drumming which, after all, often sounds like rain on a roof. Directly ahead one could hear the deep voices of field-pieces.

Some wounded Cubans were carried by in litters improvised from hammocks swung on poles. One had a ghastly cut in the throat, probably from a fragment of shell, and his head was turned as if Providence particularly wished to display this wide and lapping gash to the long column that was winding toward the front. And another Cuban, shot through the groin, kept up a continual wail as he swung from the tread of his bearers. " Ay—ee! Ay—ee! Madre mia! Madre mia!" He sang this bitter ballad into the ears of at least three thousand men as they slowly made way for his bearers on the narrow wood-

path. These wounded insurgents were, then, to
a large part of the advancing army, the visible
messengers of bloodshed and death, and the men
regarded them with thoughtful awe. This dole-
ful sobbing cry—" Madre mia "—was a tangible
consequent misery of all that firing on in front
into which the men knew they were soon to be
plunged. Some of them wished to inquire of the
bearers the details of what had happened ; but
they could not speak Spanish, and so it was as if
fate had intentionally sealed the lips of all in
order that even meagre information might not
leak out concerning this mystery—battle. On
the other hand, many unversed private soldiers
looked upon the unfortunate as men who had
seen thousands maimed and bleeding, and absolutely could not conjure any further interest in
such scenes.

A young staff-officer passed on horseback. The
vocal Cuban was always wailing, but the officer
wheeled past the bearers without heeding anything. And yet he never before had seen such a
sight. His case was different from that of the
private soldiers. He heeded nothing because he
was busy—immensely busy and hurried with a
multitude of reasons and desires for doing his
duty perfectly. His whole life had been a mere

period of preliminary reflection for this situation, and he had no clear idea of anything save his obligation as an officer. A man of this kind might be stupid; it is conceivable that in remote cases certain bumps on his head might be composed entirely of wood ; but those traditions of fidelity and courage which have been handed to him from generation to generation, and which he has tenaciously preserved despite the persecution of legislators and the indifference of his country, make it incredible that in battle he should ever fail to give his best blood and his best thought for his general, for his men, and for himself. And so this young officer in the shapeless hat and the torn and dirty shirt failed to heed the wails of the wounded man, even as the pilgrim fails to heed the world as he raises his illumined face toward his purpose—rightly or wrongly, his purpose—his sky of the ideal of duty ; and the wonderful part of it is, that he is guided by an ideal which he has himself created, and has alone protected from attack. The young man was merely an officer in the United States regular army.

The column swung across a shallow ford and took a road which passed the right flank of one of the American batteries. On a hill it was booming

and belching great clouds of white smoke.   The
infantry looked up with interest.   Arrayed below
the hill and behind the battery were the horses
and limbers, the riders checking their pawing
mounts, and behind each rider a red blanket
flamed against the fervent green of the bushes.
As the infantry moved along the road, some of
the battery horses turned at the noise of the
trampling feet and surveyed the men with eyes as
deep as wells, serene, mournful, generous eyes,
lit heart-breakingly with something that was akin
to a philosophy, a religion of self-sacrifice—oh,
gallant, gallant horses!

"I know a feller in that battery," said Nolan,
musingly.   "A driver."

"Dam sight rather be a gunner," said Martin.

"Why would ye?" said Nolan, opposingly.

"Well, I'd take my chances as a gunner b'fore
I'd sit way up in th' air on a raw-boned plug an'
git shot at."

"Aw——" began Nolan.

"They've had some losses t'-day all right." interrupted Grierson.

"Horses?" asked Watkins.

"Horses and men too," said Grierson.

"How d'yeh know ?"

"A feller told me there by the ford."

They kept only a part of their minds bearing on this discussion because they could already hear high in the air the wire-string note of the enemy's bullets.

———

III

The road taken by this battalion as it followed other battalions is something less than a mile long in its journey across a heavily-wooded plain. It is greatly changed now,—in fact it was metamorphosed in two days ; but at that time it was a mere track through dense shrubbery, from which rose great dignified arching trees. It was, in fact, a path through a jungle.

The battalion had no sooner left the battery in rear when bullets began to drive overhead. They made several different sounds, but as these were mainly high shots it was usual for them to make the faint note of a vibrant string, touched elusively, half-dreamily.

The military balloon, a fat, wavering, yellow thing, was leading the advance like some new conception of war-god. Its bloated mass shone above the trees, and served incidentally to indicate to the men at the rear that comrades were in advance.

The track itself exhibited for all its visible length
a closely-knit procession of soldiers in blue with
breasts crossed with white shelter-tents. The first
ominous order of battle came down the line.
"Use the cut-off. Don't use the magazine until
you're ordered." Non-commissioned officers repeated the command gruffly. A sound of clicking
locks rattled along the columns. All men knew
that the time had come.

The front had burst out with a roar like a brush-
fire. The balloon was dying, dying a gigantic and
public death before the eyes of two armies. It
quivered, sank, faded into the trees amid the flurry
of a battle that was suddenly and tremendously
like a storm.

The American battery thundered behind the
men with a shock that seemed likely to tear the
backs of their heads off. The Spanish shrapnel
fled on a line to their left, swirling and swishing
in supernatural velocity. The noise of the rifle
bullets broke in their faces like the noise of so
many lamp-chimneys or sped overhead in swift
cruel spitting. And at the front the battle-sound,
as if it were simply music, was beginning to swell
and swell until the volleys rolled like a surf.

The officers shouted hoarsely, " Come on,
men ! Hurry up, boys ! Come on now ! Hurry

up!" The soldiers, running heavily in their accoutrements, dashed forward. A baggage guard
was swiftly detailed; the men tore their rolls
from their shoulders as if the things were afire.
The battalion, stripped for action, again dashed
forward.

"Come on, men! Come on!" To them the
battle was as yet merely a road through the woods
crowded with troops, who lowered their heads
anxiously as the bullets fled high. But a moment
later the column wheeled abruptly to the left and
entered a field of tall green grass. The line scattered to a skirmish formation. In front was a
series of knolls treed sparsely like orchards; and
although no enemy was visible, these knolls were
all popping and spitting with rifle-fire. In some
places there were to be seen long grey lines of
dirt, intrenchments. The American shells were
kicking up reddish clouds of dust from the brow
of one of the knolls, where stood a pagoda-like
house. It was not much like a battle with men;
it was a battle with a bit of charming scenery,
enigmatically potent for death.

Nolan knew that Martin had suddenly fallen.
"What——" he began.

"They've hit me," said Martin.

"Jesus!" said Nolan.

Martin lay on the ground, clutching his left forearm just below the elbow with all the strength of his right hand. His lips were pursed ruefully. He did not seem to know what to do. He continued to stare at his arm.

Then suddenly the bullets drove at them low and hard. The men flung themselves face downward in the grass. Nolan lost all thought of his friend. Oddly enough, he felt somewhat like a man hiding under a bed, and he was just as sure that he could not raise his head high without being shot as a man hiding under a bed is sure that he cannot raise his head without bumping it.

A lieutenant was seated in the grass just behind him. He was in the careless and yet rigid pose of a man balancing a loaded plate on his knee at a picnic. He was talking in soothing paternal tones.

" Now, don't get rattled. We're all right here. Just as safe as being in church. . . . They're all going high. Don't mind them. . . . Don't mind them. . . . They're all going high. We've got them rattled and they can't shoot straight. Don't mind them."

The sun burned down steadily from a pale blue sky upon the crackling woods and knolls and fields. From the roar of musketry it might have been that the celestial heat was frying this part of the world.

Nolan snuggled close to the grass. He watched a grey line of intrenchments, above which floated the veriest gossamer of smoke. A flag lolled on a staff behind it. The men in the trench volleyed whenever an American shell exploded near them. It was some kind of infantile defiance. Frequently a bullet came from the woods directly behind Nolan and his comrades. They thought at the time that these bullets were from the rifle of some incompetent soldier of their own side.

There was no cheering. The men would have looked about them, wondering where was the army, if it were not that the crash of the fighting for the distance of a mile denoted plainly enough where was the army.

Officially, the battalion had not yet fired a shot; there had been merely some irresponsible popping by men on the extreme left flank. But it was known that the lieutenant-colonel who had been in command was dead—shot through the heart— and that the captains were thinned down to two. At the rear went on a long tragedy, in which men, bent and hasty, hurried to shelter with other men, helpless, dazed, and bloody. Nolan knew of it all from the hoarse and affrighted voices which he heard as he lay flattened in the grass. There came to him a sense of exultation. Here, then, was one of those dread and lurid situations, which in a nation's history stand out in crimson letters, becoming a tale of blood to stir generation after generation. And he was in it, and unharmed. If he lived through the battle, he would be a hero of the desperate fight at —·—; and here he wondered for a second what fate would be pleased to bestow as a name for this battle.

But it is quite sure that hardly another man in the battalion was engaged in any thoughts concerning the historic. On the contrary, they deemed it ill that they were being badly cut up on a most unimportant occasion. It would have benefited the conduct of whoever were weak if they had known that they were engaged in a battle that would be famous for ever.

————

IV

Martin had picked himself up from where the bullet had knocked him and addressed the lieutenant. "I'm hit, sir," he said.

The lieutenant was very busy. "All right, all right," he said, just heeding the man enough to

2

learn where he was wounded. "Go over that way. You ought to see a dressing-station under those trees."

Martin found himself dizzy and sick. The sensation in his arm was distinctly galvanic. The feeling was so strange that he could wonder at times if a wound was really what ailed him. Once, in this dazed way, he examined his arm ; he saw the hole. Yes, he was shot; that was it. And more than in any other way it affected him with a profound sadness.

As directed by the lieutenant, he went to the clump of trees, but he found no dressing-station there. He found only a dead soldier lying with his face buried in his arms and with his shoulders humped high as if he were convulsively sobbing. Martin decided to make his way to the road, deeming that he thus would better his chances of getting to a surgeon. But he suddenly found his way blocked by a fence of barbed wire. Such was his mental condition that he brought up at a rigid halt before this fence, and stared stupidly at it. It did not seem to him possible that this obstacle could be defeated by any means. The fence was there, and it stopped his progress. He could not go in that direction.

But as he turned he espied that procession of

wounded men, strange pilgrims, that had already worn a path in the tall grass. They were passing through a gap in the fence. Martin joined them. The bullets were flying over them in sheets, but many of them bore themselves as men who had now exacted from fate a singular immunity. Generally there were no outcries, no kicking, no talk at all. They too, like Martin, seemed buried in a vague but profound melancholy.

But there was one who cried out loudly. A man shot in the head was being carried arduously by four comrades, and he continually yelled one word that was terrible in its primitive strength,— "Bread! Bread! Bread!" Following him and his bearers were a limping crowd of men less cruelly wounded, who kept their eyes always fixed on him, as if they gained from his extreme agony some balm for their own sufferings.

"Bread! Give me bread!"

Martin plucked a man by the sleeve. The man had been shot in the foot, and was making his way with the help of a curved, incompetent stick. It is an axiom of war that wounded men can never find straight sticks.

"What's the matter with that feller?" asked Martin.

"Nutty," said the man.

"Why is he ?"

"Shot in th' head," answered the other, impatiently.

The wail of the sufferer arose in the field amid the swift rasp of bullets and the boom and shatter of shrapnel. " Bread ! Bread ! Oh, God, can't you give me bread ? Bread !" The bearers of him were suffering exquisite agony, and often they exchanged glances which exhibited their despair of ever getting free of this tragedy. It seemed endless.

" Bread ! Bread ! Bread !"

But despite the fact that there was always in the way of this crowd a wistful melancholy, one must know that there were plenty of men who laughed, laughed at their wounds whimsically, quaintly inventing odd humours concerning bicycles and cabs, extracting from this shedding of their blood a wonderful amount of material for cheerful badinage, and, with their faces twisted from pain as they stepped, they often joked like music-hall stars. And perhaps this was the most tearful part of all.

They trudged along a road until they reached a ford. Here under the eave of the bank lay a dismal company. In the mud and in the damp shade of some bushes were a half-hundred pale-faced

men prostrate.   Two or three surgeons were working there.   Also, there was a chaplain, grim-
mouthed, resolute, his surtout discarded.   Overhead always was that incessant maddening wail of
bullets.

Martin was standing gazing drowsily at the
scene when a surgeon grabbed him.   " Here, what's
the matter with you?"   Martin was daunted.
He wondered what he had done that the surgeon
should be so angry with him.

" In the arm," he muttered, half-shamefacedly.

After the surgeon had hastily and irritably bandaged the injured member he glared at Martin
and said, " You can walk all right, can't you?"

"Yes, sir," said Martin.

"Well, now, you just make tracks down that
road."

"Yes, sir."   Martin went meekly off.   The doctor had seemed exasperated almost to the point of
madness.

The road was at this time swept with the fire of
a body of Spanish sharpshooters who had come
cunningly around the flanks of the American
army, and were now hidden in the dense foliage
that lined both sides of the road.   They were
shooting at everything.   The road was as crowded
as a street in a city, and at an absurdly short range

they emptied their rifles at the passing people. They were aided always by the over-sweep from the regular Spanish line of battle.

Martin was sleepy from his wound. He saw tragedy follow tragedy, but they created in him no feeling of horror.

A man with a red cross on his arm was leaning against a great tree. Suddenly he tumbled to the ground, and writhed for a moment in the way of a child oppressed with colic. A comrade immediately began to bustle importantly. "Here," he called to Martin, "help me carry this man, will you?"

Martin looked at him with dull scorn. "I'll be damned if I do," he said. "Can't carry myself, let alone somebody else."

This answer, which rings now so inhuman, pitiless, did not affect the other man. "Well, all right," he said. "Here comes some other fellers." The wounded man had now turned blue-grey; his eyes were closed; his body shook in a gentle, persistent chill.

Occasionally Martin came upon dead horses, their limbs sticking out and up like stakes. One beast mortally shot, was besieged by three or four men who were trying to push it into the bushes, where it could live its brief time of anguish without thrashing to death any of the wounded men in the gloomy procession.

The mule train, with extra ammunition, charged toward the front, still led by the tinkling bell-mare.

An ambulance was stuck momentarily in the mud, and above the crack of battle one could hear the familiar objurgations of the driver as he whirled his lash.

Two privates were having a hard time with a wounded captain, whom they were supporting to the rear, He was half cursing, half wailing out the information that he not only would not go another step toward the rear, but that he was certainly going to return at once to the front. They begged, pleaded at great length as they continually headed him off. They were not un-like two nurses with an exceptionally bad and headstrong little duke.

The wounded soldiers paused to look impas-sively upon this struggle. They were always like men who could not be aroused by anything further.

The visible hospital was mainly straggling thickets intersected with narrow paths, the ground being covered with men. Martin saw a busy person with a book and a pencil, but he did

not approach him to become officially a member
of the hospital. All he desired was rest and immunity from nagging. He took seat painfully
under a bush and leaned his back upon the trunk.
There he remained thinking, his face wooden.

V

"My Gawd," said Nolan, squirming on his
belly in the grass, "I can't stand this much
longer."

Then suddenly every rifle in the firing line
seemed to go off of its own accord. It was
the result of an order, but few men heard the
order; in the main they had fired because they
heard others fire, and their sense was so quick that
the volley did not sound too ragged. These
marksmen had been lying for nearly an hour in
stony silence, their sights adjusted, their fingers
fondling their rifles, their eyes staring at the intrenchments of the enemy. The battalion had
suffered heavy losses, and these losses had been
hard to bear, for a soldier always reasons that men
lost during a period of inaction are men badly
lost.

The line now sounded like a great machine

set to running frantically in the open air, the
bright sunshine of a green field,   To the prut of
the magazine rifles was added the under-chorus of
the clicking mechanism, steady and swift, as if the
hand of one operator was controlling it all.   It
reminds one always of a loom, a great grand steel
loom, clinking, clanking, plunking, plinking, to
weave a woof of thin red threads, the cloth of
death.   By the men's shoulders under their eager
hands dropped continually the yellow empty
shells, spinning into the crushed grass blades to
remain there and mark for the belated eye the
line of a battalion's fight.

All impatience, all rebellious feeling, had
passed out of the men as soon as they had been
allowed to use their weapons against the enemy.
They now were absorbed in this business of hitting something, and all the long training at the
rifle ranges, all the pride of the marksman
which had been so long alive in them, made them
forget for the time everything but shooting.
They were as deliberate and exact as so many
watchmakers.

A new sense of safety was rightfully upon
them.   They knew that those mysterious men in
the high far trenches in front were having the
bullets sping in their faces with relentless and

remarkable precision ; they knew, in fact, that they were now doing the thing which they had been trained endlessly to do, and they knew they were doing it well.   Nolan, for instance, was overjoyed. "Plug 'em," he said :   "Plug 'em."   He laid his face to his rifle as if it were his mistress.   He was aiming under the shadow of a certain portico of a fortified house : there he could faintly see a long black line which he knew to be a loop-hole cut for riflemen, and he knew that every shot of his was going there under the portico, may-hap through the loop-hole to the brain of an-other man like himself.   He loaded the awkward magazine of his rifle again and again.   He was so intent that he did not know of new orders until he saw the men about him scrambling to their feet and running forward, crouching low as they ran.

He heard a shout.   "Come on, boys !   We can't be last !   We're going up !   We're going up."   He sprang to his feet and, stooping, ran with the others.   Something fine, soft, gentle, touched his heart as he ran.   He had loved the regiment. the army, because the regiment, the army, was his life,—he had no other outlook ; and now these men, his comrades, were performing his dream-scenes for him ; they were doing as he had ordained in his visions. It is curious that in this charge he considered himself as rather unworthy. Although he himself was in the assault with the rest of them, it seemed to him that his comrades were dazzlingly courageous. His part, to his mind, was merely that of a man who was going along with the crowd.

He saw Grierson biting madly with his pincers at a barbed-wire fence. They were half-way up the beautiful sylvan slope; there was no enemy to be seen, and yet the landscape rained bullets. Somebody punched him violently in the stomach. He thought dully to lie down and rest, but instead he fell with a crash.

The sparse line of men in blue shirts and dirty slouch hats swept on up the hill. He decided to shut his eyes for a moment because he felt very dreamy and peaceful. It seemed only a minute before he heard a voice say, " There he is." Grierson and Watkins had come to look for him. He searched their faces at once and keenly, for he had a thought that the line might be driven down the hill and leave him in Spanish hands. But he saw that everything was secure, and he prepared no questions.

" Nolan," said Grierson clumsily, " do you know me ? "

The man on the ground smiled softly. " Of
course I know you, you chowder-faced monkey.
Why wouldn't I know you?"

Watkins knelt beside him. " Where did they
plug you, old boy ? "

Nolan was somewhat dubious. " It ain't much.
I don't think but it's somewheres there." He
laid a finger on the pit of his stomach. They
lifted his shirt, and then privately they exchanged
a glance of horror.

" Does it hurt, Jimmie ?" said Grierson, hoarsely.

" No," said Nolan, " it don't hurt any, but I
feel sort of dead-to-the-world and numb all over.
I don't think it's very bad."

" Oh, it's all right," said Watkins.

" What I need is a drink," said Nolan, grinning
at them. " I'm chilly—lying on this damp ground."

" It ain't very damp, Jimmie," said Grierson.

" Well, it is damp," said Nolan, with sudden
irritability. " I can feel it. I'm wet, I tell you—
wet through—just from lying here."

They answered hastily. " Yes, that's so, Jimmie. It *is* damp. That's so."

" Just put your hand under my back and see
how wet the ground is," he said.

" No," they answered. " That's all right, Jimmie. We know it's wet."

"Well, put your hand under and see," he cried, stubbornly.

"Oh, never mind, Jimmie."

"No," he said, in a temper. "See for yourself." Grierson seemed to be afraid of Nolan's agitation, and so he slipped a hand under the prostrate man, and presently withdrew it covered with blood. "Yes," he said, hiding his hand carefully from Nolan's eyes, " you were right, Jimmie."

"Of course I was," said Nolan, contentedly closing his eyes. "This hillside holds water like a swamp." After a moment he said, "Guess I ought to know. I'm flat here on it, and you fellers are standing up."

He did not know he was dying. He thought he was holding an argument on the condition of the turf.

VI.

"Cover his face," said Grierson, in a low and husky voice afterwards.

"What'll I cover it with?" said Watkins.

They looked at themselves. They stood in their shirts, trousers, leggings, shoes; they had nothing.

"Oh," said Grierson, "here's his hat." He brought it and laid it on the face of the dead man. They stood for a time. It was apparent that they thought it essential and decent to say or do something. Finally Watkins said in a broken voice, "Aw, it's a dam shame." They moved slowly off toward the firing line.

.   .   .   .   .   .

In the blue gloom of evening, in one of the fever-tents, the two rows of still figures became hideous, charnel. The languid movement of a hand was surrounded with spectral mystery, and the occasional painful twisting of a body under a blanket was terrifying, as if dead men were moving in their graves under the sod. A heavy odour of sickness and medicine hung in the air.

"What regiment are you in?" said a feeble voice.

"Twenty-ninth Infantry," answered another voice.

"Twenty-ninth! Why, the man on the other side of me is in the Twenty-ninth."

"He is? . . . Hey, there, partner, are you in the Twenty-ninth?"

A third voice merely answered wearily. "Martin of C Company."

"What? Jack, is that you?"

" It's part of me. . . . Who are you ? "

" Grierson, you fat-head. I thought you were wounded."

There was the noise of a man gulping a great drink of water, and at its conclusion Martin said, " I am."

" Well, what you doin' in the fever-place, then ? "

Martin replied with drowsy impatience. " Got the fever too."

" Gee! " said Grierson.

Thereafter there was silence in the fever-tent, save for the noise made by a man over in a corner—a kind of man always found in an American crowd—a heroic, implacable comedian and patriot, of a humour that has bitterness and ferocity and love in it, and he was wringing from the situation a grim meaning by singing the " Star-Spangled Banner " with all the ardour which could be procured from his fever-stricken body.

" Billie," called Martin in a low voice, " where's Jimmy Nolan ? "

" He's dead," said Grierson.

A triangle of raw gold light shone on a side of the tent. Somewhere in the valley an engine's bell was ringing, and it sounded of peace and home as if it hung on a cow's neck.

" And where's Ike Watkins ? "

" Well, he ain't dead, but he got shot through the lungs. They say he ain't got much show."

Through the clouded odours of sickness and medicine rang the dauntless voice of the man in the corner.

THE LONE CHARGE OF WILLIAM B. PERKINS

HE could not distinguish between a five-inch quick-firing gun and a nickle-plated ice-pick, and so, naturally, he had been elected to fill the position of war-correspondent. The responsible party was the editor of the " Minnesota Herald." Perkins had no information of war, and no particular rapidity of mind for acquiring it, but he had that rank and fibrous quality of courage which springs from the thick soil of Western America.

It was morning in Guantanamo Bay. If the marines encamped on the hill had had time to turn their gaze seaward, they might have seen a small newspaper despatch-boat wending its way toward the entrance of the harbour over the blue, sunlit waters of the Caribbean. In the stern of this tug Perkins was seated upon some coal bags, while the breeze gently ruffled his greasy pajamas. He was staring at a brown line of entrenchments surmounted by a flag, which was Camp McCalla. In the harbour were anchored two or three

3   33

grim, grey cruisers and a transport. As the tug steamed up the radiant channel, Perkins could see men moving on shore near the charred ruins of a village. Perkins was deeply moved ; here already was more war than he had ever known in Minnesota. Presently he, clothed in the essential garments of a war-correspondent, was rowed to the sandy beach. Marines in yellow linen were handling an ammunition supply. They paid no attention to the visitor, being morose from the inconveniences of two days and nights of fighting. Perkins toiled up the zigzag path to the top of the hill, and looked with eager eyes at the trenches, the field-pieces, the funny little Colts, the flag, the grim marines lying wearily on their arms. And still more, he looked through the clear air over 1,000 yards of mysterious woods from which emanated at inopportune times repeated flocks of Mauser bullets.

Perkins was delighted. He was filled with admiration for these jaded and smoky men who lay so quietly in the trenches waiting for a resumption of guerilla enterprise. But he wished they would heed him. He wanted to talk about it. Save for sharp inquiring glances, no one acknowledged his existence.

Finally he approached two young lieutenants,

and in his innocent Western way he asked them if they would like a drink. The effect on the two young lieutenants was immediate and astonishing. With one voice they answered, " Yes, we would." Perkins almost wept with joy at this amiable response, and he exclaimed that he would immediately board the tug and bring off a bottle of Scotch. This attracted the officers, and in a burst of confidence one explained that there had not been a drop in camp. Perkins lunged down the hill, and fled to his boat, where in his exuberance he engaged in a preliminary altercation with some whisky. Consequently he toiled again up the hill in the blasting sun with his enthusiasm in no ways abated. The parched officers were very gracious, and such was the state of mind of Perkins that he did not note properly how serious and solemn was his engagement with the whisky. And because of this fact, and because of his antecedents, there happened the lone charge of William B. Perkins.

Now, as Perkins went down the hill, something happened. A private in those high trenches found that a cartridge was clogged in his rifle. It then becomes necessary with most kinds of rifles to explode the cartridge. The private took the rifle to his captain, and explained the case.

But it would not do in that camp to fire a rifle
for mechanical purposes and without warning,
because the eloquent sound would bring six hundred tired marines to tension and high expectancy.
So the captain turned, and in a loud voice announced to the camp that he found it necessary
to shoot into the air. The communication rang
sharply from voice to voice. Then the captain
raised the weapon and fired. Whereupon—and
whereupon—a large line of guerillas lying in the
bushes decided swiftly that their presence and
position were discovered, and swiftly they
volleyed.

In a moment the woods and the hills were
alive with the crack and sputter of rifles. Men
on the warships in the harbour heard the old
familiar flut-flut-fluttery-fluttery-flut-flut-flut from
the entrenchments. Incidentally the launch of
the "Marblehead," commanded by one of our
headlong American ensigns, streaked for the
strategic woods like a galloping marine dragoon,
peppering away with its blunderbuss in the bow.

Perkins had arrived at the foot of the hill,
where began the arrangement of 150 marines that
protected the short line of communication between the main body and the beach. These men
had all swarmed into line behind fortifications

improvised from the boxes of provisions. And to them were gathering naked men who had been bathing, naked men who arrayed themselves speedily in cartridge belts and rifles. The woods and the hills went flut-flut-flut-fluttery-fluttery-flut-fllllluttery-flut. Under the boughs of a beautiful tree lay five wounded men thinking vividly.

And now it befell Perkins to discover a Spaniard in the bush. The distance was some five hundred yards. In a loud voice he announced his perception. He also declared hoarsely, that if he only had a rifle, he would go and possess himself of this particular enemy. Immediately an amiable lad shot in the arm said : " Well, take mine." Perkins thus acquired a rifle and a clip of five cartridges.

"Come on!" he shouted. This part of the battalion was lying very tight, not yet being engaged, but not knowing when the business would swirl around to them.

To Perkins they replied with a roar. " Come back here, you —— fool. Do you want to get shot by your own crowd? Come back, —— ——!" As a detail, it might be mentioned that the fire from a part of the hill swept the journey upon which Perkins had started.

Now behold the solitary Perkins adrift in the

storm of fighting, even as a champagne jacket of
straw is lost in a great surf. He found it out
quickly. Four seconds elapsed before he discovered that he was an almshouse idiot plunging
through hot, crackling thickets on a June morning in Cuba. Sss-s-swing-sing-ing-pop went the
lightning-swift metal grasshoppers over him and
beside him. The beauties of rural Minnesota
illuminated his conscience with the gold of lazy
corn, with the sleeping green of meadows, with
the cathedral gloom of pine forests. Sshsh-swing-
pop! Perkins decided that if he cared to extract
himself from a tangle of imbecility he must shoot.
The entire situation was that he must shoot.
It was necessary that he should shoot. Nothing
would save him but shooting. It is a law that
men thus decide when the waters of battle close
over their minds. So with a prayer that the
Americans would not hit him in the back nor the
left side, and that the Spaniards would not hit
him in the front, he knelt like a supplicant alone
in the desert of chaparral, and emptied his magazine at his Spaniard before he discovered that his
Spaniard was a bit of dried palm branch.

Then Perkins flurried like a fish. His reason
for being was a Spaniard in the bush. When the
Spaniard turned into a dried palm branch, he

could no longer furnish himself with one adequate reason.

Then did he dream frantically of some anthracite hiding-place, some profound dungeon of peace where blind mules live placidly chewing the far-gathered hay.

" Sss-swing-win-pop ! Prut-prut-prrrut ! " Then a field-gun spoke. " *Boom*-ra-swow-ow-ow-ow-*pum.*" Then a Colt automatic began to bark. " Crack-crk-crk-crk-crk-crk " endlessly. Raked, enfiladed, flanked, surrounded, and overwhelmed, what hope was there for William B. Perkins of the " Minnesota Herald ? "

But war is a spirit. War provides for those that it loves. It provides sometimes death and sometimes a singular and incredible safety. There were few ways in which it was possible to preserve Perkins. One way was by means of a steam-boiler.

Perkins espied near him an old, rusty steam-boiler lying in the bushes. War only knows how it was there, but there it was, a temple shining resplendent with safety. With a moan of haste, Perkins flung himself through that hole which expressed the absence of the steam-pipe.

Then ensconced in his boiler, Perkins comfortably listened to the ring of a fight which seemed

to be in the air above him. Sometimes bullets
struck their strong, swift blow against the boiler's
sides, but none entered to interfere with Perkins's
rest.

Time passed. The fight, short anyhow, dwin-
dled to prut . . . prut . . . prut-prut . . . prut.
And when the silence came, Perkins might have
been seen cautiously protruding from the boiler.
Presently he strolled back toward the marine lines
with his hat not able to fit his head for the new
bumps of wisdom that were on it.

The marines, with an annoyed air, were settling
down again when an apparitional figure came
from the bushes. There was great excitement.

" It's that crazy man," they shouted, and as
he drew near they gathered tumultuously about
him and demanded to know how he had accomp-
lished it.

Perkins made a gesture, the gesture of a man
escaping from an unintentional mud-bath, the
gesture of a man coming out of battle, and then
he told them.

The incredulity was immediate and general.
" Yes, you did ! What? In an old boiler? An
old boiler? Out in that brush? Well, we guess
not." They did not believe him until two days
later, when a patrol happened to find the rusty

boiler, relic of some curious transaction in the ruin of the Cuban sugar industry. The patrol then marvelled at the truthfulness of war-correspondents until they were almost blind.

Soon after his adventure Perkins boarded the tug, wearing a countenance of poignant thoughtfulness.

THE CLAN OF NO-NAME

Unwind my riddle.
Cruel as hawks the hours fly;
Wounded men seldom come home to die;
The hard waves see an arm flung high;
Scorn hits strong because of a lie;
Yet there exists a mystic tie.
Unwind my riddle.

SHE was out in the garden. Her mother came
to her rapidly. " Margharita ! Margharita, Mister
Smith is here ! Come ! " Her mother was fat
and commercially excited. Mister Smith was a
matter of some importance to all Tampa people,
and since he was really in love with Margharita
he was distinctly of more importance to this particular household.

Palm trees tossed their sprays over the fence
toward the rutted sand of the street. A little
foolish fish-pond in the centre of the garden
emitted a sound of red-fins flipping, flipping.
" No, mamma," said the girl, " let Mr. Smith wait.
I like the garden in the moonlight."

Her mother threw herself into that state of
42

virtuous astonishment which is the weapon of her kind. " Margharita ! "

The girl evidently considered herself to be a privileged belle, for she answered quite carelessly, " Oh, let him wait."

The mother threw abroad her arms with a semblance of great high-minded suffering and withdrew. Margharita walked alone in the moonlit garden. Also an electric light threw its shivering gleam over part of her parade.

There was peace for a time. Then suddenly through the faint brown palings was struck an envelope white and square. Margharita approached this envelope with an indifferent stride. She hummed a silly air, she bore herself casually, but there was something that made her grasp it hard, a peculiar muscular exhibition, not discernible to indifferent eyes. She did not clutch it, but she took it—simply took it in a way that meant everything, and, to measure it by vision, it was a picture of the most complete disregard.

She stood straight for a moment ; then she drew from her bosom a photograph and thrust it through the palings. She walked rapidly into the house.

II

A man in garb of blue and white—someth.ng relating to what we call bed-ticking—was seated in a curious little cupola on the top of a Spanish blockhouse. The blockhouse sided a white military road that curved away from the man's sight into a blur of trees. On all sides of him were fields of tall grass, studded with palms and lined with fences of barbed wire. The sun beat aslant through the trees and the man sped his eyes deep into the dark tropical shadows that seemed velvet with coolness. These tranquil vistas resembled painted scenery in a theatre, and, moreover, a hot, heavy silence lay upon the land.

The soldier in the watching place leaned an unclean Mauser rifle in a corner, and, reaching down, took a glowing coal on a bit of palm bark handed up to him by a comrade. The men below were mainly asleep. The sergeant in command drowsed near the open door, the arm above his head, showing his long keen-angled chevrons attached carelessly with safety-pins. The sentry lit his cigarette and puffed languorously.

Suddenly he heard from the air around him the querulous, deadly-swift spit of rifle-bullets, and, an instant later, the poppety-pop of a small volley sounded in his face, close, as if it were fired only ten feet away. Involuntarily he threw back his head quickly as if he were protecting his nose from a falling tile. He screamed an alarm and fell into the blockhouse. In the gloom of it, men with their breaths coming sharply between their teeth, were tumbling wildly for positions at the loop-holes. The door had been slammed, but the sergeant lay just within, propped up as when he drowsed, but now with blood flowing steadily over the hand that he pressed flatly to his chest. His face was in stark yellow agony ; he chokingly repeated : "Fuego! Por Dios, hombres!"

The men's ill-conditioned weapons were jammed through the loop-holes and they began to fire from all four sides of the blockhouse from the simple data, apparently, that the enemy were in the vicinity. The fumes of burnt powder grew stronger and stronger in the little square fortress. The rattling of the magazine locks was incessant, and the interior might have been that of a gloomy manufactory if it were not for the sergeant down under the feet of the men, coughing out : " Por Dios, hombres ! Per Dios ! Fuego ! "

III

A string of five Cubans, in linen that had turned earthy brown in colour, slid through the woods at a pace that was neither a walk nor a run. It was a kind of rack. In fact the whole manner of the men, as they thus moved, bore a rather comic resemblance to the American pacing horse. But they had come many miles since sun-up over mountainous and half-marked paths, and were plainly still fresh. The men were all practicos— guides. They made no sound in their swift travel, but moved their half-shod feet with the skill of cats. The woods lay around them in a deep silence, such as one might find at the bottom of a lake.

Suddenly the leading practico raised his hand. The others pulled up short and dropped the butts of their weapons calmly and noiselessly to the ground. The leader whistled a low note a. d immediately another practico appeared from the bushes. He moved close to the leader without a word, and then they spoke in whispers.

"There are twenty men and a sergeant in the blockhouse."

"And the road?"

"One company of cavalry passed to the east this morning at seven o'clock. They were escorting four carts. An hour later, one horseman rode swiftly to the westward. About noon, ten infantry soldiers with a corporal were taken from the big fort and put in the first blockhouse, to the east of the fort. There were already twelve men there. We saw a Spanish column moving off toward Mariel."

"No more?"

"No more."

"Good. But the cavalry?"

"It is all right. They were going a long march."

"The expedition is a half league behind. Go and tell the general."

The scout disappeared. The five other men lifted their guns and resumed their rapid and noiseless progress. A moment later no sound broke the stillness save the thump of a mango, as it dropped lazily from its tree to the grass. So strange had been the apparition of these men, their dress had been so allied in colour to the soil, their passing had so little disturbed the solemn rumination of the forest, and their going had been so like a spectral dissolution, that a witness could have wondered if he dreamed.

IV

A small expedition had landed with arms from the United States, and had now come out of the hills and to the edge of a wood. Before them was a long-grassed rolling prairie marked with palms. A half-mile away was the military road, and they could see the top of a blockhouse. The insurgent scouts were moving somewhere off in the grass. The general sat comfortably under a tree, while his staff of three young officers stood about him chatting. Their linen clothing was notable from being distinctly whiter than those of the men who, one hundred and fifty in number, lay on the ground in a long brown fringe, ragged —indeed, bare in many places—but singularly reposeful, unworried, veteran-like.

The general, however, was thoughtful. He pulled continually at his little thin moustache. As far as the heavily patrolled and guarded military road was concerned, the insurgents had been in the habit of dashing across it in small bodies whenever they pleased, but to safely scoot over it with a valuable convoy of arms, was decidedly a more important thing. So the general awaited the return of his practicos with anxiety. The still pampas betrayed no sign of their existence.

The general gave some orders and an officer counted off twenty men to go with him, and delay any attempt of the troop of cavalry to return from the eastward. It was not an easy task, but it was a familiar task—checking the advance of a greatly superior force by a very hard fire from conceal-ment. A few rifles had often bayed a strong column for sufficient length of time for all stra-tegic purposes. The twenty men pulled them-selves together tranquilly. They looked quite indifferent. Indeed, they had the supremely cas-ual manner of old soldiers, hardened to battle as a condition of existence.

Thirty men were then told off, whose function it was to worry and rag at the blockhouse, and check any advance from the westward. A hun-dred men, carrying precious burdens—besides their own equipment—were to pass in as much of a rush as possible between these two wings, cross the road and skip for the hills, their retreat being covered by a combination of the two firing parties. It was a trick that needed both luck and neat ar-rangement. Spanish columns were for ever prowl-ing through this province in all directions and at all times. Insurgent bands—the lightest of light

4

infantry—were kept on the jump, even when
they were not incommoded by fifty boxes, each
one large enough for the coffin of a little man,
and heavier than if the little man were in it; and
fifty small but formidable boxes of ammunition.

The carriers stood to their boxes and the firing
parties leaned on their rifles. The general arose
and strolled to and fro, his hands behind him.
Two of his staff were jesting at the third, a young
man with a face less bronzed, and with very new
accoutrements. On the strap of his cartouche
were a gold star and a silver star, placed in a hor-
izontal line, denoting that he was a second lieutenant. He seemed very happy; he laughed at
all their jests, although his eye roved continually
over the sunny grass-lands, where was going to
happen his first fight. One of his stars was bright,
like his hopes, the other was pale, like death.

Two practicos came racking out of the grass.
They spoke rapidly to the general; he turned and
nodded to his officers. The two firing parties
filed out and diverged toward their positions.
The general watched them through his glasses.
It was strange to note how soon they were dim to
the unaided eye. The little patches of brown in
the green grass did not look like men at all.

Practicos continually ambled up to the general.

Finally he turned and made a sign to the bearers
The first twenty men in line picked up their boxes,
and this movement rapidly spread to the tail of
the line.   The weighted procession moved painfully out upon the sunny prairie.   The general,
marching at the head of it, glanced continually
back as if he were compelled to drag behind him
some ponderous iron chain.   Besides the obvious
mental worry, his face bore an expression of intense physical strain, and he even bent his shoulders, unconsciously tugging at the chain to hurry
it through this enemy-crowded valley.

V

The fight was opened by eight men who, snug-
gling in the grass, within three hundred yards of
the blockhouse, suddenly blazed away at the bed-
ticking figure in the cupola and at the open door
where they could see vague outlines.   Then they
laughed and yelled insulting language, for they
knew that as far as the Spaniards were concerned,
the surprise was as much as having a diamond
bracelet turn to soap.   It was this volley that
smote the sergeant and caused the man in the
cupola to scream and tumble from his perch.

The eight men, as well as all other insurgents within fair range, had chosen good positions for lying close, and for a time they let the blockhouse rage, although the soldiers therein could occasionally hear, above the clamour of their weapons, shrill and almost wolfish calls, coming from men whose lips were laid against the ground. But it is not in the nature of them of Spanish blood, and armed with rifles, to long endure the sight of anything so tangible as an enemy's blockhouse without shooting at it—other conditions being partly favourable. Presently the steaming soldiers in the little fort could hear the sping and shiver of bullets striking the wood that guarded their bodies.

A perfectly white smoke floated up over each firing Cuban, the penalty of the Remington rifle, but about the blockhouse there was only the lightest gossamer of blue. The blockhouse stood always for some big, clumsy and rather incompetent animal, while the insurgents, scattered on two sides of it, were little enterprising creatures of another species, too wise to come too near, but joyously raging at its easiest flanks and dirling the lead into its sides in a way to make it fume, and spit and rave like the tom-cat when the glad, free-band fox-hound pups catch him in the lane.

The men, outlying in the grass, chuckled deliriously at the fury of the Spanish fire. They howled opprobrium to encourage the Spaniards to fire more ill-used, incapable bullets. Whenever an insurgent was about to fire, he ordinarily prefixed the affair with a speech. " Do you want something to eat? Yes? All right." Bang! " Eat that." The more common expressions of the incredibly foul Spanish tongue were trifles light as air in this badinage, which was shrieked out from the grass during the spin of bullets, and the dull rattle of the shooting.

But at some time there came a series of sounds from the east that began in a few disconnected pruts and ended as if an amateur was trying to play the long roll upon a muffled drum. Those of the insurgents in the blockhouse attacking party, who had neighbours in the grass, turned and looked at them seriously. They knew what the new sound meant. It meant that the twenty men who had gone to the eastward were now engaged. A column of some kind was approaching from that direction, and they knew by the clatter that it was a solemn occasion.

In the first place, they were now on the wrong side of the road. They were obliged to cross it to rejoin the main body, provided of course that the main body succeeded itself in crossing it. To

accomplish this, the party at the blockhouse would
have to move to the eastward, until out of sight
or good range of the maddened little fort. But
judging from the heaviness of the firing, the party
of twenty who protected the east were almost sure
to be driven immediately back. Hence travel in
that direction would become exceedingly hazard-
ous. Hence a man looked seriously at his neighbour. It might easily be that in a moment they
were to become an isolated force and woefully on
the wrong side of the road.

Any retreat to the westward was absurd, since
primarily they would have to widely circle the
blockhouse, and more than that, they could hear,
even now in that direction, Spanish bugle calling
to Spanish bugle, far and near, until one would
think that every man in Cuba was a trumpeter,
and had come forth to parade his talent.

VI

The insurgent general stood in the middle of the
road gnawing his lips. Occasionally, he stamped
a foot and beat his hands passionately together.
The carriers were streaming past him, patient,

sweating fellows, bowed under their burdens, but
they could not move fast enough for him when
others of his men were engaged both to the east
and to the west, and he, too, knew from the sound
that those to the east were in a sore way. Moreover, he could hear that accursed bugling, bugling,
bugling in the west.

He turned suddenly to the new lieutenant who
stood behind him, pale and quiet. " Did you ever
think a hundred men were so many ? " he cried,
incensed to the point of beating them. Then he
said longingly : " Oh, for a half an hour ! Or even
twenty minutes ! "

A practico racked violently up from the east.
It is characteristic of these men that, although they
take a certain roadster gait and hold it for ever,
they cannot really run, sprint, race. " Captain
Rodriguez is attacked by two hundred men, señor,
and the cavalry is behind them. He wishes to
know——"

The general was furious ; he pointed.
" Go ! Tell Rodriguez to hold his place for
twenty minutes, even if he leaves every man
dead."

The practico shambled hastily off.

The last of the carriers were swarming across
the road. The rifle-drumming in the east was

swelling out and out, evidently coming slowly
nearer. The general bit his nails. " He wheeled
suddenly upon the young lieutenant. " Go to
Bas at the blockhouse. Tell him to hold the
devil himself for ten minutes and then bring his
men out of that place."

The long line of bearers was crawling like a dun
worm toward the safety of the foot-hills. High
bullets sang a faint song over the aide as he saluted.
The bugles had in the west ceased, and that was
more ominous than bugling. It meant that the
Spanish troops were about to march, or perhaps
that they had marched.

The young lieutenant ran along the road until
he came to the bend which marked the range of
sight from the blockhouse. He drew his machete,
his stunning new machete, and hacked feverishly
at the barbed wire fence which lined the north
side of the road at that point. The first wire was
obdurate, because it was too high for his stroke,
but two more cut like candy, and he stepped over
the remaining one, tearing his trousers in passing
on the lively serpentine ends of the severed wires.
Once out in the field and bullets seemed to know
him and call for him and speak their wish to kill him.
But he ran on, because it was his duty, and because
he would be shamed before men if he did not do

his duty, and because he was desolate out there all alone in the fields with death.

A man running in this manner from the rear was in immensely greater danger than those who lay snug and close. But he did not know it. He thought because he was five hundred—four hundred and fifty—four hundred yards away from the enemy and the others were only three hundred yards away that they were in far more peril. He ran to join them because of his opinion. He did not care to do it, but he thought that was what men of his kind would do in such a case. There was a standard and he must follow it, obey it, because it was a monarch, the Prince of Conduct.

A bewildered and alarmed face raised itself from the grass and a voice cried to him: " Drop, Manolo! Drop! Drop! He recognised Bas and flung himself to the earth beside him.

" Why," he said panting, " what's the matter? "

" Matter? " said Bas. " You are one of the most desperate and careless officers I know. When I saw you coming I wouldn't have given a peseta for your life."

" Oh, no," said the young aide. Then he repeated his orders rapidly. But he was hugely delighted. He knew Bas well; Bas was a pupil of Macco; Bas invariably led his men; he never was a mere spectator of their battle; he was known for it throughout the western end of the island. The new officer had early achieved a part of his ambition—to be called a brave man by established brave men.

"Well, if we get away from here quickly it will be better for us," said Bas, bitterly. "I've lost six men killed, and more wounded. Rodriguez can't hold his position there, and in a little time more than a thousand men will come from the other direction."

He hissed a low call, and later the young aide saw some of the men sneaking off with the wounded, lugging them on their backs as porters carry sacks. The fire from the blockhouse had become a-weary, and as the insurgent fire also slackened, Bas and the young lieutenant lay in the weeds listening to the approach of the eastern fight, which was sliding toward them like a door to shut them off.

Bas groaned. "I leave my dead. Look there." He swung his hand in a gesture and the lieutenant looking saw a corpse. He was not stricken as he expected; there was very little blood; it was a mere thing.

"Time to travel," said Bas suddenly. His imperative hissing brought his men near him; there

were a few hurried questions and answers ; then,
characteristically, the men turned in the grass,
lifted their rifles, and fired a last volley into the
blockhouse, accompanying it with their shrill
cries. Scrambling low to the ground, they were
off in a winding line for safety. Breathing hard,
the lieutenant stumbled his way forward. Behind
him he could hear the men calling each to each :
" Segue ! Segue ! Segue ! Go on ! Get out !
Git ! " Everybody understood that the peril of
crossing the road was compounding from minute
to minute.

VII

When they reached the gap through which the
expedition had passed, they fled out upon the
road like scared wild-fowl tracking along a sea-
beach. A cloud of blue figures far up this dignified shaded avenue, fired at once. The men already
had begun to laugh as they shied one by one
across the road. " Segue ! Segue ! " The hard
part for the nerves had been the lack of information of the amount of danger. Now that they
could see it, they accounted it all the more lightly
for their previous anxiety.

Over in the other field, Bas and the young lieutenant found Rodriguez, his machete in one hand,
his revolver in the other, smoky, dirty, sweating.
He shrugged his shoulders when he saw them
and pointed disconsolately to the brown thread
of carriers moving toward the foot-hills. His
own men were crouched in line just in front of
him blazing like a prairie fire.

Now began the fight of a scant rear-guard to
hold back the pressing Spaniards until the carriers
could reach the top of the ridge, a mile away.
This ridge by the way was more steep than any
roof ; it conformed, more, to the sides of a French
war-ship. Trees grew vertically from it, however,
and a man burdened only with his rifle usually
pulled himself wheezingly up in a sort of ladder-
climbing process, grabbing the slim trunks above
him. How the loaded carriers were to conquer
it in a hurry, no one knew. Rodriguez shrugged
his shoulders as one who would say with philosophy, smiles, tears, courage : " Isn't this a mess ! "

At an order, the men scattered back for four
hundred yards with the rapidity and mystery of
a handful of pebbles flung in the night. They
left one behind who cried out, but it was now a
game in which some were sure to be left behind to
cry out.

The Spaniards deployed on the road and for twenty minutes remained there pouring into the field such a fire from their magazines as was hardly heard at Gettysburg. As a matter of truth the insurgents were at this time doing very little shooting, being chary of ammunition. But it is possible for the soldier to confuse himself with his own noise and undoubtedly the Spanish troops thought throughout their din that they were being fiercely engaged. Moreover, a firing-line—particularly at night or when opposed to a hidden foe—is nothing less than an emotional chord, a chord of a harp that sings because a puff of air arrives or when a bit of down touches it. This is always true of new troops or stupid troops and these troops were rather stupid troops. But, the way in which they mowed the verdure in the distance was a sight for a farmer.

Presently the insurgents slunk back to another position where they fired enough shots to stir again the Spaniards into an opinion that they were in a heavy fight. But such a misconception could only endure for a number of minutes. Presently it was plain that the Spaniards were about to advance and, moreover, word was brought to Rodriguez that a small band of guerillas were already making an attempt to worm

around the right flank. Rodriguez cursed de-
spairingly ; he sent both Bas and the young lieutenant to that end of the line to hold the men to
their work as long as possible.

In reality the men barely needed the presence
of their officers. The kind of fighting left practically everything to the discretion of the indi-
vidual and they arrived at concert of action
mainly because of the equality of experience, in
the wisdoms of bushwhacking.

The yells of the guerillas could plainly be heard
and the insurgents answered in kind. The young
lieutenant found desperate work on the right
flank. The men were raving mad with it, babbling, tearful, almost frothing at the mouth.
Two terrible bloody creatures passed him, creeping on all fours, and one in a whimper was calling
upon God, his mother, and a saint. The guerillas,
as effectually concealed as the insurgents, were
driving their bullets low through the smoke at
sight of a flame, a movement of the grass or
sight of a patch of dirty brown coat. They were
no column-o'-four soldiers; they were as slinky
and snaky and quick as so many Indians. They
were, moreover, native Cubans and because of
their treachery to the one-star flag, they never
by any chance received quarter if they fell into

the hands of the insurgents. Nor, if the case
was reversed, did they ever give quarter. It was
life and life, death and death ; there was no middle ground, no compromise. If a man's crowd
was rapidly retreating and he was tumbled over
by a slight hit, he should curse the sacred graves
that the wound was not through the precise centre
of his heart. The machete is a fine broad blade but
it is not so nice as a drilled hole in the chest ; no
man wants his death-bed to be a shambles. The
men fighting on the insurgents' right knew that if
they fell they were lost.

On the extreme right, the young lieutenant
found five men in a little saucer-like hollow.
Two were dead, one was wounded and staring
blankly at the sky and two were emptying hot
rifles furiously. Some of the guerillas had
snaked into positions only a hundred yards away.

The young man rolled in among the men in
the saucer. He could hear the barking of the
guerillas and the screams of the two insurgents.
The rifles were popping and spitting in his face,
it seemed, while the whole land was alive with a
noise of rolling and drumming. Men could have
gone drunken in all this flashing and flying and
snarling and din, but at this time he was very
deliberate. He knew that he was thrusting him-

self into a trap whose door, once closed, opened only when the black hand knocked and every part of him seemed to be in panic-stricken revolt. But something controlled him; something moved him inexorably in one direction; he perfectly understood but he was only sad, sad with a serene dignity, with the countenance of a mournful young prince. He was of a kind—that seemed to be it—and the men of his kind, on peak or plain, from the dark northern ice-fields to the hot wet jungles, through all wine and want, through all lies and unfamiliar truth, dark or light, the men of his kind were governed by their gods, and each man knew the law and yet could not give tongue to it, but it was the law and if the spirits of the men of his kind were all sitting in critical judgment upon him even then in the sky, he could not have bettered his conduct; he needs must obey the law and always with the law there is only one way. But from peak and plain, from dark northern icefields and hot wet jungles, through wine and want, through all lies and un-familiar truth, dark or light, he heard breathed to him the approval and the benediction of his brethren.

He stooped and gently took a dead man's rifle and some cartridges. The battle was hurrying,

hurrying, hurrying, but he was in no haste. His glance caught the staring eye of the wounded soldier, and he smiled at him quietly. The man —simple doomed peasant—was not of his kind, but the law on fidelity was clear.

He thrust a cartridge into the Remington and crept up beside the two unhurt men. Even as he did so, three or four bullets cut so close to him that all his flesh tingled. He fired carefully into the smoke. The guerillas were certainly not now more than fifty yards away.

He raised him coolly for his second shot, and almost instantly it was as if some giant had struck him in the chest with a beam. It whirled him in a great spasm back into the saucer. As he put his two hands to his breast, he could hear the guerillas screeching exultantly, every throat vomiting forth all the infamy of a language prolific in the phrasing of infamy.

One of the other men came rolling slowly down the slope, while his rifle followed him, and, striking another rifle, clanged out. Almost immediately the survivor howled and fled wildly. A whole volley missed him and then one or more shots caught him as a bird is caught on the wing.

The young lieutenant's body seemed galvanised from head to foot. He concluded that he was

5

not hurt very badly, but when he tried to move he found that he could not lift his hands from his breast. He had turned to lead. He had had a plan of taking a photograph from his pocket and looking at it.

There was a stir in the grass at the edge of the saucer, and a man appeared there, looking where lay the four insurgents. His negro face was not an eminently ferocious one in its lines, but now it was lit with an illimitable blood-greed. He and the young lieutenant exchanged a singular glance ; then he came stepping eagerly down. The young lieutenant closed his eyes, for he did not want to see the flash of the machete.

———

VIII

The Spanish colonel was in a rage, and yet immensely proud ; immensely proud, and yet in a rage of disappointment. There had been a fight and the insurgents had retreated leaving their dead, but still a valuable expedition had broken through his lines and escaped to the mountains. As a matter of truth, he was not sure whether to be wholly delighted or wholly angry, for well he knew that the importance lay not so much in the truthful account of the action as it did in the heroic prose of the official report, and in the fight itself lay material for a purple splendid poem. The insurgents had run away; no one could deny it; it was plain even to whatever privates had fired with their eyes shut. This was worth a loud blow and splutter. However, when all was said and done, he could not help but reflect that if he had captured this expedition, he would have been a brigadier-general, if not more.

He was a short, heavy man with a beard, who walked in a manner common to all elderly Spanish officers, and to many young ones; that is to say, he walked as if his spine was a stick and a little longer than his body; as if he suffered from some disease of the backbone, which allowed him but scant use of his legs. He toddled along the road, gesticulating disdainfully and muttering: "Ca! Ca! Ca!"

He berated some soldiers for an immaterial thing, and as he approached the men stepped precipitately back as if he were a fire-engine. They were most of them young fellows, who displayed, when under orders, the manner of so many faithful dogs. At present, they were black, tongue-hanging, thirsty boys, bathed in the nervous weariness of the after-battle time.

Whatever he may truly have been in character, the colonel closely resembled a gluttonous and libidinous old pig, filled from head to foot with the pollution of a sinful life. "Ca!" he snarled, as he toddled. "Ca! Ca!" The soldiers saluted as they backed to the side of the road. The air was full of the odour of burnt rags. Over on the prairie guerillas and regulars were rummaging the grass. A few unimportant shots sounded from near the base of the hills.

A guerilla, glad with plunder, came to a Spanish captain. He held in his hand a photograph. "Mira, señor. I took this from the body of an officer whom I killed machete to machete."

The captain shot from the corner of his eye a cynical glance at the guerilla, a glance which commented upon the last part of the statement. "M-m-m," he said. He took the photograph and gazed with a slow faint smile, the smile of a man who knows bloodshed and homes and love, at the face of a girl. He turned the photograph presently, and on the back of it was written: "One lesson in English I will give you—this : I love you, Margharita." The photograph had been taken in Tampa.

The officer was silent for a half-minute, while his face still wore the slow faint smile. " Pobrecetto," he murmured finally, with a philosophic sigh, which was brother to a shrug. Without deigning a word to the guerilla he thrust the photograph in his pocket and walked away.

High over the green earth, in the dizzy blue heights, some great birds were slowly circling with down-turned beaks.

IX

Margharita was in the gardens. The blue electric rays shone through the plumes of the palm and shivered in feathery images on the walk. In the little foolish fish-pond some stalwart fish was apparently bullying the others, for often there sounded a frantic splashing.

Her mother came to her rapidly. " Margharita! Mister Smith is here! Come!"

"Oh, is he?" cried the girl. She followed her mother to the house. She swept into the little parlor with a grand air, the egotism of a savage. Smith had heard the whirl of her skirts in the hall, and his heart, as usual, thumped hard enough to make him gasp. Every time he called, he

would sit waiting with the dull fear in his breast
that her mother would enter and indifferently
announce that she had gone up to heaven or off
to New York, with one of his dream-rivals, and
he would never see her again in this wide world.
And he would conjure up tricks to then escape
from the house without any one observing his
face break up into furrows. It was part of his
love to believe in the absolute treachery of his
adored one. So whenever he heard the whirl of
her skirts in the hall he felt that he had again
leased happiness from a dark fate.

She was rosily beaming and all in white.
"Why, Mister Smith," she exclaimed, as if he
was the last man in the world she expected to
see.

"Good-evenin'," he said, shaking hands nervously. He was always awkward and unlike himself, at the beginning of one of these calls. It
took him some time to get into form.

She posed her figure in operatic style on a
chair before him, and immediately galloped off a
mile of questions, information of herself, gossip
and general outcries which left him no obligation, but to look beamingly intelligent and from
time to time say: "Yes?" His personal joy,
however, was to stare at her beauty.

When she stopped and wandered as if uncertain which way to talk, there was a minute of silence, which each of them had been educated to feel was very incorrect; very incorrect indeed. Polite people always babbled at each other like two brooks.

He knew that the responsibility was upon him, and, although his mind was mainly upon the form of the proposal of marriage which he intended to make later, it was necessary that he should maintain his reputation as a well-bred man by saying something at once. It flashed upon him to ask: "Won't you please play?" But the time for the piano ruse was not yet; it was too early. So he said the first thing that came into his head: "Too bad about young Manolo Prat being killed over there in Cuba, wasn't it?"

"Wasn't it a pity?" she answered.

"They say his mother is heart-broken," he continued. "They're afraid she's goin' to die."

"And wasn't it queer that we didn't hear about it for almost two months?"

"Well, it's no use tryin' to git quick news from there."

Presently they advanced to matters more personal, and she used upon him a series of star-like glances which rumpled him at once to squalid slavery. He gloated upon her, afraid, afraid, yet more avaricious than a thousand misers. She fully comprehended; she laughed and taunted him with her eyes. She impressed upon him that she was like a will-o'-the-wisp, beautiful beyond compare but impossible, almost impossible, at least very difficult; then again, suddenly, impossible—impossible—impossible. He was glum; he would never dare propose to this radiance; it was like asking to be pope.

A moment later, there chimed into the room something that he knew to be a more tender note. The girl became dreamy as she looked at him; her voice lowered to a delicious intimacy of tone. He leaned forward; he was about to outpour his bully-ragged soul in fine words, when—presto—she was the most casual person he had ever laid eyes upon, and was asking him about the route of the proposed trolley line.

But nothing short of a fire could stop him now. He grabbed her hand. " Margharita," he murmured gutturally, " I want you to marry me."

She glared at him in the most perfect lie of astonishment. " What do you say ? "

He arose, and she thereupon arose also and fled back a step. He could only stammer out her

name. And thus they stood, defying the prin-
ciples of the dramatic art.

" I love you," he said at last.

" How—how do I know you really—truly love
me ? " she said, raising her eyes timorously to his
face and this timorous glance, this one timorous
glance, made him the superior person in an instant.
He went forward as confident as a grenadier, and,
taking both her hands, kissed her.

That night she took a stained photograph from
her dressing-table and holding it over the candle
burned it to nothing, her red lips meanwhile
parted with the intentness of her occupation. On
the back of the photograph was written : " One
lesson in English I will give you—this : I love
you."

For the word is clear only to the kind who on
peak or plain, from dark northern ice-fields to the
hot wet jungles, through all wine and want,
through lies and unfamiliar truth, dark or light,
are governed by the unknown gods, and though
each man knows the law, no man may give tongue
to it.

GOD REST YE, MERRY GENTLEMEN

LITTLE NELL, sometimes called the Blessed Damosel, was a war correspondent for the *New York Eclipse*, and at sea on the despatch boats he wore pajamas, and on shore he wore whatever fate allowed him, which clothing was in the main unsuitable to the climate. He had been cruising in the Caribbean on a small tug, awash always, habitable never, wildly looking for Cervera's fleet; although what he was going to do with four armoured cruisers and two destroyers in the event of his really finding them had not been explained by the managing editor. The cable instructions read :—' Take tug ; go find Cervera's fleet." If his unfortunate nine-knot craft should happen to find these great twenty-knot ships, with their two spiteful and faster attendants, Little Nell had wondered how he was going to lose them again. He had marvelled, both publicly and in secret, on the uncompromising asininity of managing editors at odd moments, but he had wasted little time. The *Jefferson G. Johnson* was already coaled, so he passed the word to his skipper, bought some tinned meats, cigars, and beer, and soon the *John-son* sailed on her mission, tooting her whistle in graceful farewell to some friends of hers in the bay.

So the *Johnson* crawled giddily to one wave-height after another, and fell, aslant, into one valley after another for a longer period than was good for the hearts of the men, because the *John-son* was merely a harbour-tug, with no architectural intention of parading the high-seas, and the crew had never seen the decks all white water like a mere sunken reef. As for the cook, he blasphemed hopelessly hour in and hour out, meanwhile pursuing the equipment of his trade frantically from side to side of the galley. Little Nell dealt with a great deal of grumbling, but he knew it was not the real evil grumbling. It was merely the unhappy words of men who wished expression of comradeship for their wet, forlorn, half-starved lives, to which, they explained, they were not accustomed, and for which, they explained, they were not properly paid. Little Nell condoled and condoled without difficulty. He laid words of gentle sympathy before them, and smothered his own misery behind the face of a reporter of the *New York Eclipse*. But they tossed themselves in their cockleshell even as far as Mar-

tinique ; they knew many races and many flags,
but they did not find Cervera's fleet. If they had
found that elusive squadron this timid story would
never have been written ; there would probably
have been a lyric. The *Johnson* limped one morning into the Mole St. Nicholas, and there Little
Nell received this despatch :—" Can't understand
your inaction. What are you doing with the
boat? Report immediately. Fleet transports
already left Tampa. Expected destination near
Santiago. Proceed there immediately. Place
yourself under orders.—ROGERS, *Eclipse*."

One day, steaming along the high, luminous
blue coast of Santiago province, they fetched into
view the fleets, a knot of masts and funnels, looking incredibly inshore, as if they were glued to
the mountains. Then mast left mast, and funnel
left funnel, slowly, slowly, and the shore remained
still, but the fleets seemed to move out toward
the eager *Johnson*. At the speed of nine knots
an hour the scene separated into its parts. On
an easily rolling sea, under a crystal sky, black-
hulled transports—erstwhile packets—lay waiting,
while grey cruisers and gunboats lay near shore,
shelling the beach and some woods. From their
grey sides came thin red flashes, belches of white
smoke, and then over the waters sounded boom—

boom—boom-boom. The crew of the *Jefferson G. Johnson* forgave Little Nell all the suffering of a previous fortnight.

To the westward, about the mouth of Santiago harbour, sat a row of castellated grey battleships, their eyes turned another way, waiting.

The *Johnson* swung past a transport whose decks and rigging were aswarm with black figures, as if a tribe of bees had alighted upon a log. She swung past a cruiser indignant at being left out of the game, her deck thick with white-clothed tars watching the play of their luckier brethren. The cold blue, lifting seas tilted the big ships easily, slowly, and heaved the little ones in the usual sinful way, as if very little babes had surreptitiously mounted sixteen-hand trotting hunters. The *Johnson* leered and tumbled her way through a community of ships. The bombardment ceased, and some of the troopships edged in near the land. Soon boats black with men and towed by launches were almost lost to view in the scintillant mystery of light which appeared where the sea met the land. A disembarkation had begun. The *Johnson* sped on at her nine knots, and Little Nell chafed exceedingly, gloating upon the shore through his glasses, anon glancing irritably over the side to note the efforts of the excited tug.

Then at last they were in a sort of a cove, with troopships, newspaper boats, and cruisers on all sides of them, and over the water came a great hum of human voices, punctuated frequently by the clang of engine-room gongs as the steamers manœuvred to avoid jostling.

In reality it was the great moment—the moment for which men, ships, islands, and continents had been waiting for months; but somehow it did not look it. It was very calm; a certain strip of high, green, rocky shore was being rapidly populated from boat after boat; that was all. Like many preconceived moments, it refused to be supreme.

But nothing lessened Little Nell's frenzy. He knew that the army was landing—he could see it; and little did he care if the great moment did not look its part—it was his virtue as a correspondent to recognise the great moment in any disguise. The *Johnson* lowered a boat for him, and he dropped into it swiftly, forgetting everything. However, the mate, a bearded philanthropist, flung after him a mackintosh and a bottle of whisky. Little Nell's face was turned toward those other boats filled with men, all eyes upon the placid, gentle, noiseless shore. Little Nell saw many soldiers seated stiffly beside upright rifle barrels, their blue breasts crossed with white shel-

ter tent and blanket-rolls. Launches screeched;
jack-tars pushed or pulled with their boathooks;
a beach was alive with working soldiers, some of
them stark naked. Little Nell's boat touched the
shore amid a babble of tongues, dominated at that
time by a single stern voice, which was repeating,
" Fall in, B Company ! "

He took his mackintosh and his bottle of whisky
and invaded Cuba. It was a trifle bewildering.
Companies of those same men in blue and brown
were being rapidly formed and marched off across
a little open space—near a pool—near some palm
trees—near a house—into the hills. At one side,
a mulatto in dirty linen and an old straw hat was
hospitably using a machete to cut open some green
cocoanuts for a group of idle invaders. At the
other side, up a bank, a blockhouse was burning
furiously ; while near it some railway sheds were
smouldering, with a little Roger's engine standing
amid the ruins, grey, almost white, with ashes
until it resembled a ghost. Little Nell dodged
the encrimsoned blockhouse, and proceeded where
he saw a little village street lined with flimsy
wooden cottages. Some ragged Cuban cavalrymen
were tranquilly tending their horses in a shed
which had not yet grown cold of the Spanish
occupation. Three American soldiers were trying

to explain to a Cuban that they wished to buy drinks. A native rode by, clubbing his pony, as always. The sky was blue ; the sea talked with a gravelly accent at the feet of some rocks ; upon its bosom the ships sat quiet as gulls. There was no mention, directly, of invasion—invasion for war—save in the roar of the flames at the block-house; but none even heeded this conflagration, excepting to note that it threw out a great heat. It was warm, very warm. It was really hard for Little Nell to keep from thinking of his own affairs : his debts, other misfortunes, loves, prospects of happiness. Nobody was in a flurry ; the Cubans were not tearfully grateful; the American troops were visibly glad of being released from those ill transports, and the men often asked, with in- terest, "Where's the Spaniards?" And yet it must have been a great moment! It was a *great* moment !

It seemed made to prove that the emphatic time of history is not the emphatic time of the common man, who throughout the change of nations feels an itch on his shin, a pain in his head, hunger, thirst, a lack of sleep ; the influence of his memory of past firesides, glasses of beer, girls, theatres, ideals, religions, parents, faces, hurts, joy.

Little Nell was hailed from a comfortable

veranda, and, looking up, saw Walkley of the *Eclipse*, stretched in a yellow and green hammock, smoking his pipe with an air of having always lived in that house, in that village. " Oh, dear little Nell, how glad I am to see your angel face again ! There ! don't try to hide it ; I can see it. Did you bring a corkscrew too ? You're superseded as master of the slaves. Did you know it ? And by Rogers, too ! Rogers is a Sadducee, a cadaver and a pelican, appointed to the post of chief correspondent, no doubt, because of his rare gift of incapacity. Never mind."

" Where is he now ? " asked Little Nell, taking seat on the steps.

" He is down interfering with the landing of the troops," answered Walkley, swinging a leg. " I hope you have the *Johnson* well stocked with food as well as with cigars, cigarettes and tobaccos, ales, wines and liquors. We shall need them. There is already famine in the house of Walkley. I have discovered that the system of transportation for our gallant soldiery does not strike in me the admiration which I have often felt when viewing the management of an ordinary bun-shop. A hunger, stifling, jammed together amid odours, and everybody irritable—ye gods, how irritable ! And so I—— Look ! look ! "

6

The *Jefferson G. Johnson*, well known to them at an incredible distance, could be seen striding the broad sea, the smoke belching from her funnel, headed for Jamaica. " The Army Lands in Cuba!" shrieked Walkley. "Shafter's Army Lands near Santiago! Special type! Half the front page! Oh, the Sadducee! The cadaver! The pelican! "

Little Nell was dumb with astonishment and fear. Walkley, however, was at least not dumb. " That's the pelican! That's Mr. Rogers making his first impression upon the situation. He has engraved himself upon us. We are tattooed with him. There will be a fight to-morrow, sure, and we will cover it even as you found Cervera's fleet. No food, no horses, no money. I am transport lame; you are sea-weak. We will never see our salaries again. Whereby Rogers is a fool."

" Anybody else here? " asked Little Nell wearily.

" Only young Point." Point was an artist on the *Eclipse*. " But he has nothing. Pity there wasn't an almshouse in this God-forsaken country. Here comes Point now." A sad-faced man came along carrying much luggage. " Hello, Point! lithographer *and* genius, have you food? Food. Well, then, you had better return yourself to

Tampa by wire. You are no good here. Only
one more little mouth to feed."

Point seated himself near Little Nell. "I
haven't had anything to eat since daybreak," he
said gloomily, "and I don't care much, for I am
simply dog-tired."

"Don't tell *me* you are dog-tired, my talented
friend," cried Walkley from his hammock.
"Think of me. And now what's to be done?"

They stared for a time disconsolately at where,
over the rim of the sea, trailed black smoke from
the *Johnson*. From the landing-place below and
to the right came the howls of a man who was
superintending the disembarkation of some mules.
The burning blockhouse still rendered its hollow
roar. Suddenly the men-crowded landing set up
its cheer, and the steamers all whistled long and
raucously. Tiny black figures were raising an
American flag over a blockhouse on the top of
a great hill.

"That's mighty fine Sunday stuff," said Little
Nell. "Well, I'll go and get the order in which
the regiments landed, and who was first ashore,
and all that. Then I'll go and try to find General
Lawton's headquarters. His division has got the
advance, I think."

"And, lo! I will write a burning description

of the raising of the flag," said Walkley. "While the brilliant Point buskies for food—and makes damn sure he gets it," he added fiercely.

Little Nell thereupon wandered over the face of the earth, threading out the story of the landing of the regiments. He only found about fifty men who had been the first American soldier to set foot on Cuba, and of these he took the most probable. The army was going forward in detail, as soon as the pieces were landed. There was a house something like a crude country tavern— the soldiers in it were looking over their rifles and talking. There was a well of water quite hot— more palm trees—an inscrutable background.

When he arrived again at Walkley's mansion he found the verandah crowded with correspondents in khaki, duck, dungaree and flannel. They wore riding-breeches, but that was mainly forethought. They could see now that fate intended them to walk. Some were writing copy, while Walkley discoursed from his hammock. Rhodes —doomed to be shot in action some days later— was trying to borrow a canteen from men who had one, and from men who had none. Young Point, wan, utterly worn out, was asleep on the floor. Walkley pointed to him. "That is how he appears after his foraging journey, during

which he ran all Cuba through a sieve. Oh, yes;
a can of corn and a half-bottle of lime juice."

"Say, does anybody know the name of the
commander of the 26th Infantry?"

"Who commands the first brigade of Kent's
Division?"

"What was the name of the chap that raised the
flag?"

"What time is it?"

And a woeful man was wandering here and
there with a cold pipe, saying plaintively, "Who's
got a match? Anybody here got a match?"

Liftle Nell's left boot hurt him at the heel, and
so he removed it, taking great care and whistling
through his teeth. The heated dust was upon
them all, making everybody feel that bathing was
unknown and shattering their tempers. Young
Point developed a snore which brought grim sar-
casm from all quarters. Always below, hummed
the traffic of the landing-place.

When night came Little Nell thought best not
to go to bed until late, because he recognised the
mackintosh as but a feeble comfort. The evening
was a glory. A breeze came from the sea, fan-
ning spurts of flame out of the ashes and charred
remains of the sheds, while overhead lay a splendid summer-night sky, aflash with great tranquil

stars. In the streets of the village were two or three fires, frequently and suddenly reddening with their glare the figures of low-voiced men who moved here and there. The lights of the transports blinked on the murmuring plain in front of the village; and far to the westward Little Nell could sometimes note a subtle indication of a playing search-light, which alone marked the presence of the invisible battleships, half-mooned about the entrance of Santiago Harbour, waiting—waiting—waiting.

When Little Nell returned to the veranda he stumbled along a man-strewn place, until he came to the spot where he left his mackintosh ; but he found it gone. His curses mingled then with those of the men upon whose bodies he had trodden. Two English correspondents, lying awake to smoke a last pipe, reared and looked at him lazily. " What's wrong, old chap?" murmured one. " Eh? Lost it, eh? Well, look here ; come here and take a bit of my blanket. It's a jolly big one. Oh, no trouble at all, man. There you are. Got enough? Comfy? Good-night."

A sleepy voice arose in the darkness. " If this hammock breaks, I shall hit at least ten of those Indians down there. Never mind. This is war."

The men slept. Once the sound of three or four shots rang across the windy night, and one head uprose swiftly from the verandah, two eyes looked dazedly at nothing, and the head as swiftly sank. Again a sleepy voice was heard. " Usual thing! Nervous sentries!" The men slept. Before dawn a pulseless, penetrating chill came into the air, and the correspondents awakened, shivering, into a blue world. Some of the fires still smouldered. Walkley and Little Nell kicked vigorously into Point's framework. " Come on, brilliance! Wake up, talent! Don't be sodgering. It's too cold to sleep, but it's not too cold to hustle." Point sat up dolefully. Upon his face was a childish expression. " Where are we going to get breakfast?" he asked, sulking.

" There's no breakfast for you, you hound! Get up and hustle." Accordingly they hustled. With exceeding difficulty they learned that nothing emotional had happened during the night, save the killing of two Cubans who were so secure in ignorance that they could not understand the challenge of two American sentries. Then Walkley ran a gamut of commanding officers, and Little Nell pumped privates for their impressions of Cuba. When his indignation at the absence of breakfast allowed him, Point made sketches. At

the full break of day the *Adolphus*, and *Eclipse*
despatch boat, sent a boat ashore with Tailor and
Shackles in it, and Walkley departed tearlessly
for Jamaica, soon after he had bestowed upon his
friends much tinned goods and blankets.

"Well, we've got our stuff off," said Little Nell.
"Now Point and I must breakfast."

Shackles, for some reason, carried a great hunt-
ing-knife, and with it Little Nell opened a tin of
beans.

"Fall to," he said amiably to Point.

There were some hard biscuits. Afterwards
they—the four of them—marched off on the route
of the troops. They were well loaded with luggage, particularly young Point, who had somehow
made a great gathering of unnecessary things.
Hills covered with verdure soon enclosed them.
They heard that the army had advanced some
nine miles with no fighting. Evidences of the
rapid advance were here and there—coats, gaunt-
lets, blanket rolls on the ground. Mule-trains
came herding back along the narrow trail to the
sound of a little tinkling bell. Cubans were ap-
propriating the coats and blanket-rolls.

The four correspondents hurried onward. The
surety of impending battle weighed upon them
always, but there was a score of minor things more

intimate. Little Nell's left heel had chafed until it must have been quite raw, and every moment he wished to take seat by the roadside and console himself from pain. Shackles and Point disliked each other extremely, and often they foolishly quarrelled over something, or nothing. The blanket-rolls and packages for the hand oppressed everybody. It was like being burned out of a boarding-house, and having to carry one's trunk eight miles to the nearest neighbour. Moreover, Point, since he had stupidly overloaded, with great wisdom placed various cameras and other trifles in the hands of his three less-burdened and more sensible friends. This made them fume and gnash, but in complete silence, since he was hideously youthful and innocent and unaware. They all wished to rebel, but none of them saw their way clear, because—they did not understand. But somehow it seemed a barbarous project—no one wanted to say anything—cursed him privately for a little ass, but—said nothing. For instance, Little Nell wished to remark, "Point, you are not a thoroughbred in a half of a way. You are an inconsiderate, thoughtless little swine." But, in truth, he said, "Point, when you started out you looked like a Christmas-tree. If we keep on robbing you of your bundles there soon won't be anything left for the children." Point asked dubiously, "What do you mean?" Little Nell merely laughed with deceptive good-nature.

They were always very thirsty. There was always a howl for the half-bottle of lime juice. Five or six drops from it were simply heavenly in the warm water from the canteens. Point seemed to try to keep the lime juice in his possession, in order that he might get more benefit of it. Before the war was ended the others found themselves declaring vehemently that they loathed Point, and yet when men asked them the reason they grew quite inarticulate. The reasons seemed then so small, so childish, as the reasons of a lot of women. And yet at the time his offences loomed enormous.

The surety of impending battle still weighed upon them. Then it came that Shackles turned seriously ill. Suddenly he dropped his own and much of Point's traps upon the trail, wriggled out of his blanket-roll, flung it away, and took seat heavily at the roadside. They saw with surprise that his face was pale as death, and yet streaming with sweat.

"Boys," he said in his ordinary voice, "I'm clean played out. I can't go another step. You fellows go on, and leave me to come as soon as I am able."

"Oh, no, that wouldn't do at all," said Little Nell and Tailor together.

Point moved over to a soft place, and dropped amid whatever traps he was himself carrying.

"Don't know whether it's ancestral or merely from the — sun — but I've got a stroke," said Shackles, and gently slumped over to a prostrate position before either Little Nell or Tailor could reach him.

Thereafter Shackles was parental ; it was Little Nell and Tailor who were really suffering from a stroke, either ancestral or from the sun.

"Put my blanket-roll under my head, Nell, me son," he said gently. "There now! That is very nice. It is delicious. Why, I'm all right, only— only tired." He closed his eyes, and something like an easy slumber came over him. Once he opened his eyes. "Don't trouble about me," he remarked.

But the two fussed about him, nervous, worried, discussing this plan and that plan. It was Point who first made a business-like statement. Seated carelessly and indifferently upon his soft place, he finally blurted out :

"Say! Look here! Some of us have got to

go on. We can't all stay here. Some of us have got to go on."

It was quite true; the *Eclipse* could take no account of strokes. In the end Point and Tailor went on, leaving Little Nell to bring on Shackles as soon as possible. The latter two spent many hours in the grass by the roadside. They made numerous abrupt acquaintances with passing staff officers, privates, muleteers, many stopping to inquire the wherefore of the death-faced figure on the ground. Favours were done often and often, by peer and peasant—small things, of no consequence, and yet warming.

It was dark when Shackles and Little Nell had come slowly to where they could hear the murmur of the army's bivouac.

"Shack," gasped Little Nell to the man leaning forlornly upon him, "I guess we'd better bunk down here where we stand."

"All right, old boy. Anything you say," replied Shackles, in the bass and hollow voice which arrives with such condition.

They crawled into some bushes, and distributed their belongings upon the ground. Little Nell spread out the blankets, and generally played housemaid. Then they lay down, supperless, being too weary to eat. The men slept.

At dawn Little Nell awakened and looked wildly for Shackles, whose empty blanket was pressed flat like a wet newspaper on the ground. But at nearly the same moment Shackles appeared, elate.

"Come on," he cried; "I've rustled an invitation for breakfast."

Little Nell came on with celerity.

"Where? Who?" he said.

"Oh! some officers," replied Shackles airily. If he had been ill the previous day, he showed it now only in some curious kind of deference he paid to Little Nell.

Shackles conducted his comrade, and soon they arrived at where a captain and his one subaltern arose courteously from where they were squatting near a fire of little sticks. They wore the wide white trouser-stripes of infantry officers, and upon the shoulders of their blue campaign shirts were the little marks of their rank; but otherwise there was little beyond their manners to render them different from the men who were busy with breakfast near them. The captain was old, grizzled—a common type of captain in the tiny American army—overjoyed at the active service, confident of his business, and yet breathing out in some way a note of pathos. The war was come too late

Age was grappling him, and honours were only for his widow and his children—merely a better life insurance policy. He had spent his life policing Indians with much labour, cold and heat, but with no glory for him nor his fellows. All he now could do was to die at the head of his men. If he had youthfully dreamed of a general's stars, they were now impossible to him, and he knew it. He was too old to leap so far ; his sole honour was a new invitation to face death. And yet, with his ambitions lying half-strangled, he was going to take his men into any sort of holocaust, because his traditions were of gentlemen and soldiers, and because—he loved it for itself—the thing itself— the whirl, the unknown. If he had been degraded at that moment to be a pot-wrestler, no power could have starved him from going through the campaign as a spectator. Why, the army ! It was in each drop of his blood.

The lieutenant was very young. Perhaps he had been hurried out of West Point at the last moment, upon a shortage of officers appearing. To him, all was opportunity. He was, in fact, in great luck. Instead of going off in 1898 to grill for an indefinite period on some God-forgotten heap of red-hot sand in New Mexico, he was here in Cuba, on real business, with his regiment.

When the big engagement came he was sure to emerge from it either horizontally or at the head of a company, and what more could a boy ask? He was a very modest lad, and talked nothing of his frame of mind, but an expression of blissful contentment was ever upon his face. He really accounted himself the most fortunate boy of his time ; and he felt almost certain that he would do well. It was necessary to do well. He would do well.

And yet in many ways these two were alike; the grizzled eaptain with his gently mournful countenance—" Too late "—and the elate young second lieutenant, his commission hardly dry. Here again it was the influence of the army. After all they were both children of the army.

It is possible to spring into the future here and chronicle what happened later. The captain, after thirty-five years of waiting for his chance, took his Mauser bullet through the brain at the foot of San Juan Hill in the very beginning of the battle, and the boy arrived on the crest panting, sweating, but unscratched, and not sure whether he commanded one company or a whole battalion. Thus fate dealt to the hosts of Shackles and Little Nell.

The breakfast was of canned tomatoes stewed with hard bread, more hard bread, and coffee. It was very good fare, almost royal. Shackles and Little Nell were absurdly grateful as they felt the hot bitter coffee tingle in them. But they departed joyfully before the sun was fairly up, and passed into Siboney. They never saw the captain again.

The beach at Siboney was furious with traffic, even as had been the beach at Daqueri. Launches shouted, jack-tars prodded with their boathooks, and load of men followed load of men. Straight, parade-like, on the shore stood a trumpeter playing familiar calls to the troop-horses who swam towards him eagerly through the salt seas. Crowding closely into the cove were transports of all sizes and ages. To the left and to the right of the little landing-beach green hills shot upward like the wings in a theatre. They were scarred here and there with blockhouses and rifle-pits. Up one hill a regiment was crawling, seemingly inch by inch. Shackles and Little Nell walked among palms and scrubby bushes, near pools, over spaces of sand holding little monuments of biscuit-boxes, ammunition-boxes, and supplies of all kinds. Some regiment was just collecting itself from the ships, and the men made great patches of blue on the brown sand.

Shackles asked a question of a man accidentally :

" Where's that regiment going to? " He pointed
to the force that was crawling up the hill. The
man grinned, and said, " They're going to look
for a fight ! "

"Looking for a fight ! " said Shackles and
Little Nell together. They stared into each
other's eyes. Then they set off for the foot of
the hill. The hill was long and toilsome. Below
them spread wider and wider a vista of ships quiet
on a grey sea ; a busy, black disembarkation-
place ; tall, still, green hills ; a village of well
separated cottages ; palms ; a bit of road ; soldiers marching. They passed vacant Spanish
trenches ; little twelve-foot blockhouses. Soon
they were on a fine upland near the sea. The
path, under ordinary conditions, must have been
a beautiful wooded way. It wound in the
shade of thickets of fine trees, then through rank
growths of bushes with revealed and fantastic
roots, then through a grassy space which had all
the beauty of a neglected orchard. But always
from under their feet scuttled noisy land-crabs,
demons to the nerves, which in some way possessed a semblance of moon-like faces upon their
blue or red bodies, and these faces were turned
with expressions of deepest horror upon Shackles
and Little Nell as they sped to overtake the

7

pugnacious regiment. The route was paved with
coats, hats, tent and blanket rolls, ration-tins,
haversacks—everything but ammunition belts,
rifles and canteens.

They heard a dull noise of voices in front of
them—men talking too loud for the etiquette of
the forest—and presently they came upon two or
three soldiers lying by the roadside, flame-faced,
utterly spent from the hurried march in the heat.
One man came limping back along the path. He
looked to them anxiously for sympathy and comprehension. " Hurt m' knee. I swear I couldn't
keep up with th' boys. I had to leave 'm. Wasn't
that tough luck?" His collar rolled away from
a red, muscular neck, and his bare forearms were
better than stanchions. Yet he was almost
babyishly tearful in his attempt to make the
two correspondents feel that he had not turned
back because he was afraid. They gave him
scant courtesy, tinctured with one drop of sym-
pathetic yet cynical understanding. Soon they
overtook the hospital squad ; men addressing
chaste language to some pack-mules ; a talkative
sergeant ; two amiable, cool-eyed young surgeons.
Soon they were amid the rear troops of the dis-
mounted volunteer cavalry regiment which was
moving to attack. The men strode easily along,

arguing one to another on ulterior matters. If they were going into battle, they either did not know it or they concealed it well. They were more like men going into a bar at one o'clock in the morning. Their laughter rang through the Cuban woods. And in the meantime, soft, mellow, sweet, sang the voice of the Cuban wood-dove, the Spanish guerilla calling to his mate— forest music ; on the flanks, deep back on both flanks, the adorable wood-dove, singing only of love. Some of the advancing Americans said it was beautiful. It *was* beautiful. The Spanish guerilla calling to his mate. What could be more beautiful ?

Shackles and Little Nell rushed precariously through waist-high bushes until they reached the centre of the single-filed regiment. The firing then broke out in front. All the woods set up a hot sputtering; the bullets sped along the path and across it from both sides. The thickets presented nothing but dense masses of light green foliage, out of which these swift steel things were born supernaturally.

It was a volunteer regiment going into its first action, against an enemy of unknown force, in a country where the vegetation was thicker than fur on a cat. There might have been a dreadful

mess : but in military matters the only way to deal
with a situation of this kind is to take it frankly
by the throat and squeeze it to death. Shackles
and Little Nell felt the thrill of the orders.
" Come ahead, men ! Keep right ahead, men !
Come on !" The volunteer cavalry regiment,
with all the willingness in the world, went ahead
into the angle of V-shaped Spanish formation.

It seemed that every leaf had turned into a
soda-bottle and was popping its cork. Some of
the explosions seemed to be against the men's
very faces, others against the backs of their necks.
" Now, men ! Keep goin' ahead. Keep on goin'. "
The forward troops were already engaged. They,
at least, had something at which to shoot. " Now,
captain, if you're ready." " Stop that swear-
ing there." " Got a match ? " " Steady, now,
men."

A gate appeared in a barbed-wire fence. Within
were billowy fields of long grass, dotted with
palms and luxuriant mango trees. It was Elysian
—a place for lovers, fair as Eden in its radiance
of sun, under its blue sky. One might have expected to see white-robed figures walking slowly
in the shadows. A dead man, with a bloody face,
lay twisted in a curious contortion at the waist.

Someone was shot in the leg, his pins knocked cleanly from under him.

" Keep goin', men." The air roared, and the ground fled reelingly under their feet. Light, shadow, trees, grass. Bullets spat from every side. Once they were in a thicket, and the men, blanched and bewildered, turned one way, and then another, not knowing which way to turn. " Keep goin', men." Soon they were in the sun-light again. They could see the long scant line, which was being drained man by man—one might say drop by drop. The musketry rolled forth in great full measure from the magazine carbines. " Keep goin', men." " Christ, I'm shot!" " They're flankin' us, sir." " We're bein' fired into by our own crowd, sir." " Keep goin', men." A low ridge before them was a bottling establish-ment blowing up in detail. From the right—it seemed at that time to be the far right—they could hear steady, crashing volleys—the United States regulars in action.

Then suddenly—to use a phrase of the street—the whole bottom of the thing fell out. It was suddenly and mysteriously ended. The Spaniards had run away, and some of the regulars were chas-ing them. It was a victory.

When the wounded men dropped in the tall

grass they quite disappeared, as if they had sunk in water. Little Nell and Shackles were walking along through the fields, disputing.

"Well, damn it, man!" cried Shackles, "we *must* get a list of the killed and wounded."

"That is not nearly so important," quoth little Nell, academically, "as to get the first account to New York of the first action of the army in Cuba."

They came upon Tailor, lying with a bared torso and a small red hole through his left lung. He was calm, but evidently out of temper. "Good God, Tailor!" they cried, dropping to their knees like two pagans; "are you hurt, old boy?"

"Hurt?" he said gently. "No, 'tis not so deep as a well nor so wide as a church-door, but 'tis enough, d' you see? You understand, do you? Idiots!"

Then he became very official. "Shackles, feel and see what's under my leg. It's a small stone, or a burr, or something. Don't be clumsy now! Be careful! Be careful!" Then he said, angrily, "Oh, you didn't find it at all. Damn it!"

In reality there was nothing there, and so Shackles could not have removed it. "Sorry, old boy," he said, meekly.

"Well, you may observe that I can't stay here more than a year," said Tailor, with some oratory,

" and the hospital people have their own work in hand. It behoves you, Nell, to fly to Siboney, arrest a despatch boat, get a cot and some other things, and some minions to carry me. If I get once down to the base I'm all right, but if I stay here I'm dead. Meantime Shackles can stay here and try to look as if he liked it."

There was no disobeying the man. Lying there with a little red hole in his left lung, he dominated them through his helplessness, and through their fear that if they angered him he would move and —bleed.

" Well? " said Little Nell.

" Yes," said Shackles, nodding.

Little Nell departed.

"That blanket you lent me," Tailor called after him, " is back there somewhere with Point."

Little Nell noted that many of the men who were wandering among the wounded seemed so spent with the toil and excitement of their first action that they could hardly drag one leg after the other. He found himself suddenly in the same condition. His face, his neck, even his mouth, felt dry as sun-baked bricks, and his legs were foreign to him. But he swung desperately into his five-mile task. On the way he passed many things : bleeding men carried by comrades ;

others making their way grimly, with encrimsoned arms; then the little settlement of the hospital squad; men on the ground everywhere, many in the path; one young captain dying, with great gasps, his body pale blue, and glistening, like the inside of a rabbit's skin. But the voice of the Cuban wood-dove, soft, mellow, sweet, singing only of love, was no longer heard from the wealth of foliage.

Presently the hurrying correspondent met another regiment coming to assist—a line of a thousand men in single file through the jungle. "Well, how is it going, old man?" "How is it coming on?" "Are we doin' 'em?" Then, after an interval, came other regiments, moving out. He had to take to the bush to let these long lines pass him, and he was delayed, and had to flounder amid brambles. But at last, like a successful pilgrim, he arrived at the brow of the great hill overlooking Siboney. His practised eye scanned the fine broad brow of the sea with its clustering ships, but he saw thereon no *Eclipse* despatch boats. He zigzagged heavily down the hill, and arrived finally amid the dust and outcries of the base. He seemed to ask a thousand men if they had seen an *Eclipse* boat on the water, or an *Eclipse* correspondent on the shore. They all answered, " No."

He was like a poverty-stricken and unknown suppliant at a foreign Court. Even his plea got only ill-hearings. He had expected the news of the serious wounding of Tailor to appal the other correspondents, but they took it quite calmly. It was as if their sense of an impending great battle between two large armies had quite got them out of focus for these minor tragedies. Tailor was hurt—yes? They looked at Little Nell, dazed. How curious that Tailor should be almost the first —how *very* curious—yes. But, as far as arousing them to any enthusiasm of active pity, it seemed impossible. He was lying up there in the grass, was he? Too bad, too bad, too bad!

Little Nell went alone and lay down in the sand with his back against a rock. Tailor was prostrate up there in the grass. Never mind. Nothing was to be done. The whole situation was too colossal. Then into his zone came Walkley the invincible.

"Walkley!" yelled Little Nell. Walkley came quickly, and Little Nell lay weakly against his rock and talked. In thirty seconds Walkley understood everything, had hurled a drink of whisky into Little Nell, had admonished him to lie quiet, and had gone to organise and manipulate. When he returned he was a trifle dubious

and backward. Behind him was a singular squad
of volunteers from the *Adolphus*, carrying among
them a wire-woven bed.

"Look here, Nell!" said Walkley, in bashful
accents; "I've collected a battalion here which
is willing to go bring Tailor; but—they say—you
—can't you show them where he is?"

"Yes," said Little Nell, arising.

.   .   .   .   .   .

When the party arrived at Siboney, and de-
posited Tailor in the best place, Walkley had
found a house and stocked it with canned soups.
Therein Shackles and Little Nell revelled for a
time, and then rolled on the floor in their blankets.
Little Nell tossed a great deal. "Oh, I'm so tired.
Good God, I'm tired. I'm—tired."

In the morning a voice aroused them. It was
a swollen, important, circus voice saying, "Where
is Mr. Nell? I wish to see him immediately."

"Here I am, Rogers," cried Little Nell.

"Oh, Nell," said Rogers, "here's a despatch to
me which I thought you had better read."

Little Nell took the despatch. It was: "Tell
Nell can't understand his inaction; tell him come
home first steamer from Port Antonio, Jamaica."

THE REVENGE OF THE ADOLPHUS

I

"Stand by."

Shackles had come down from the bridge of the *Adolphus* and flung this command at three fellow-correspondents who in the galley were busy with pencils trying to write something exciting and interesting from four days quiet cruising. They looked up casually. "What for? They did not intend to arouse for nothing. Ever since Shackles had heard the men of the navy directing each other to stand by for this thing and that thing, he had used the two words as his pet phrase and was continually telling his friends to stand by. Sometimes its portentous and emphatic reiteration became highly exasperating and men were apt to retort sharply. "Well, I *am* standing by, ain't I?" On this occasion they detected that he was serious. "Well, what for?" they repeated. In his answer Shackles was reproachful as well as impressive. "Stand by? Stand by for a Spanish gunboat. A Spanish gunboat in chase! Stand by for *two* Spanish gunboats—*both* of them in chase!"

The others looked at him for a brief space and were almost certain that they saw truth written upon his countenance. Whereupon they tumbled out of the galley and galloped up to the bridge. The cook with a mere inkling of tragedy was now out on deck bawling, " What's the matter? What's the matter? What's the matter? " Aft, the grimy head of a stoker was thrust suddenly up through the deck, so to speak. The eyes flashed in a quick look astern and then the head vanished. The correspondents were scrambling on the bridge. "Where's my glasses, damn it? Here—let me take a look. Are they Spaniards, Captain? Are you sure? "

The skipper of the *Adolphus* was at the wheel. The pilot-house was so arranged that he could not see astern without hanging forth from one of the side windows, but apparently he had made early investigation. He did not reply at once. At sea, he never replied at once to questions. At the very first, Shackles had discovered the merits of this deliberate manner and had taken delight in it. He invariably detailed his talk with the captain to the other correspondents. "Look here. I've just been to see the skipper. I said ' I

would like to put into Cape Haytien.' Then he
took a little think. Finally he said: 'All right.'
Then I said: 'I suppose we'll need to take on
more coal there?' He took another little think.
I said: 'Ever ran into that port before?' He
took another little think. Finally he said: 'Yes.'
I said 'Have a cigar?' He took another little
think. See? There's where I fooled 'im——"

While the correspondents spun the hurried
questions at him, the captain of the *Adolphus*
stood with his brown hands on the wheel and his
cold glance aligned straight over the bow of his
ship.

"Are they Spanish gunboats, Captain? Are
they, Captain?"

After a profound pause, he said: "Yes." The
four correspondents hastily and in perfect time
presented their backs to him and fastened their
gaze on the pursuing foe. They saw a dull grey
curve of sea going to the feet of the high green
and blue coast-line of north-eastern Cuba, and on
this sea were two miniature ships with clouds of
iron-coloured smoke pouring from their funnels.

One of the correspondents strolled elaborately
to the pilot-house. "Aw—Captain," he drawled,
"do you think they can catch us?"

The captain's glance was still aligned over the

bow of his ship. Ultimately he answered : " I don't know."

From the top of the little *Adolphus'* stack, thick dark smoke swept level for a few yards and then went rolling to leaward in great hot obscuring clouds. From time to time the grimy head was thrust through the deck, the eyes took the quick look astern and then the head vanished. The cook was trying to get somebody to listen to him. " Well, you know, damn it all, it won't be no fun to be ketched by them Spaniards. Be-Gawd, it won't. Look here, what do you think they'll do to us, hey ? Say, I don't like this, you know. I'm damned if I do." The sea, cut by the hurried bow of the *Adolphus*, flung its waters astern in the formation of a wide angle and the lines of the angle ruffled and hissed as they fled, while the thumping screw tormented the water at the stern. The frame of the steamer underwent regular convulsions as in the strenuous sobbing of a child.

The mate was standing near the pilot-house. Without looking at him, the captain spoke his name. " Ed ! "

" Yes, sir," cried the mate with alacrity.

The captain reflected for a moment. Then he said : " Are they gainin' on us ? "

The mate took another anxious survey of the race. " No—o—yes, I think they are—a little."

After a pause the captain said : " Tell the chief to shake her up more."

The mate, glad of an occupation in these tense minutes, flew down to the engine-room door. "Skipper says shake 'er up more!" he bawled. The head of the chief engineer appeared, a grizzly head now wet with oil and sweat. " What ? " he shouted angrily. It was as if he had been propelling the ship with his own arms. Now he was told that his best was not good enough. " What ? shake 'er up more ? Why she can't carry another pound, I tell you ! Not another ounce ! We——" Suddenly he ran forward and climbed to the bridge. " Captain," he cried in the loud harsh voice of one who lived usually amid the thunder of machinery, " she can't do it, sir ! Be-Gawd, she can't ! She's turning over now faster than she ever did in her life and we'll all blow to hell——"

The low-toned, impassive voice of the captain suddenly checked the chief's clamour. " I'll blow her up," he said, " but I won't git ketched if I kin help it." Even then the listening correspondents found a second in which to marvel that the captain had actually explained his point of view to another human being.

The engineer stood blank. Then suddenly he cried : " All right, sir ! " He threw a hurried look of despair at the correspondents, the deck of the *Adolphus*, the pursuing enemy, Cuba, the sky and the sea; he vanished in the direction of his post.

A correspondent was suddenly regifted with the power of prolonged speech. " Well, you see, the game is up, damn it. See ? We can't get out of it. The skipper will blow up the whole bunch before he'll let his ship be taken, and the Spaniards are gaining. Well, that's what comes from going to war in an eight-knot tub." He bitterly accused himself, the others, and the dark, sightless, indifferent world.

This certainty of coming evil affected each one differently. One was made garrulous; one kept absent-mindedly snapping his fingers and gazing at the sea; another stepped nervously to and fro, looking everywhere as if for employment for his mind. As for Shackles he was silent and smiling, but it was a new smile that caused the lines about his mouth to betray quivering weakness. And each man looked at the others to discover their degree of fear and did his best to conceal his own, holding his crackling nerves with all his strength.

As the *Adolphus* rushed on, the sun suddenly

emerged from behind grey clouds and its rays
dealt titanic blows so that in a few minutes the
sea was a glowing blue plain with the golden shine
dancing at the tips of the waves. The coast of
Cuba glowed with light. The pursuers displayed
detail after detail in the new atmosphere. The
voice of the cook was heard in high vexation.
"Am I to git dinner as usual? How do I know?
Nobody tells me what to do? Am I to git
dinner as usual?"

The mate answered ferociously. "Of course
you are! What do you s'pose? Ain't you the
cook, you damn fool?"

The cook retorted in a mutinous scream.
"Well, how would I know? If this ship is goin'
to blow up——"

II

The captain called from the pilot-house. "Mr.
Shackles! Oh, Mr. Shackles!" The correspond-
ent moved hastily to a window. "What is it,
Captain?" The skipper of the *Adolphus* raised
a battered finger and pointed over the bows.
"See 'er?" he asked, laconic but quietly jubilant.
Another steamer was smoking at full speed over
8

the sun-lit seas. A great billow of pure white was on her bows. "Great Scott!" cried Shackles. "Another Spaniard?"

"No," said the captain, "that there is a United States cruiser!"

"What?" Shackles was dumfounded into muscular paralysis. "No! Are you *sure?*"

The captain nodded. "Sure, take the glass. See her ensign? Two funnels, two masts with fighting tops. She ought to be the *Chancellorville.*"

Shackles choked. "Well, I'm blowed!"

"Ed!" said the captain.

"Yessir!"

"Tell the chief there is no hurry."

Shackles suddenly bethought him of his companions. He dashed to them and was full of quick scorn of their gloomy faces. "Hi, brace up there! Are you blind? Can't you see her?"

"See what?"

"Why, the *Chancellorville,* you blind mice!" roared Shackles. "See 'er? See 'er? See 'er?"

The others sprang, saw, and collapsed. Shackles was a madman for the purpose of distributing the news. "Cook!" he shrieked. "Don't you see 'er, cook? Good Gawd, man, don't you see 'er?" He ran to the lower deck and howled his

information everywhere. Suddenly the whole
ship smiled. Men clapped each other on the
shoulder and joyously shouted. The captain
thrust his head from the pilot-house to look back
at the Spanish ships. Then he looked at the
American cruiser. "Now, we'll see," he said
grimly and vindictively to the mate. "Guess
somebody else will do some running," the mate
chuckled.

The two gunboats were still headed hard for
the *Adolphus* and she kept on her way. The
American cruiser was coming swiftly. "It's the
Chancellorville !" cried Shackles. "I know her!
We'll see a fight at sea, my boys! A fight at
sea!" The enthusiastic correspondents pranced
in Indian revels.

The *Chancellorville*—2000 tons—18.6 knots—
10 five-inch guns—came on tempestuously, sheer-
ing the water high with her sharp bow. From
her funnels the smoke raced away in driven sheets.
She loomed with extraordinary rapidity like a
ship bulging and growing out of the sea. She
swept by the *Adolphus* so close that one could
have thrown a walnut on board. She was a glistening grey apparition with a blood-red water-
line, with brown gun-muzzles and white-clothed
motionless jack-tars; and in her rush she was

silent, deadly silent.   Probably there entered the
mind of every man on board the *Adolphus* a feeling of almost idolatry for this living thing, stern
but, to their thought, incomparably beautiful.
They would have cheered but that each man
seemed to feel that a cheer would be too puny a
tribute.

It was at first as if she did not see the *Adolphus*.
She was going to pass without heeding this little
vagabond of the high-seas.   But suddenly a megaphone gaped over the rail of her bridge and a
voice was heard measuredly, calmly intoning.
" Hello—there! Keep—well—to—the—north'ard
—and—out of my—way—and I'll—go—in—and
—see—what—those—people—want——"   Then
nothing was heard but the swirl of water.   In a
moment the *Adolphus* was looking at a high grey
stern.   On the quarter-deck, sailors were poised
about the breach of the after-pivot-gun.

The correspondents were revelling.   " Captain," yelled Shackles, " we can't miss this! We
must see it ! "   But the skipper had already flung
over the wheel.   " Sure," he answered almost at
once.   " We can't miss it."

The cook was arrogantly, grossly triumphant.
His voice rang along the deck.   " There, now !
How will the Spinachers like that ? Now, it's

our turn! We've been doin' the runnin' away but now we'll do the chasin'!" Apparently feeling some twinge of nerves from the former strain, he suddenly demanded: "Say, who's got any whisky? I'm near dead for a drink."

When the *Adolphus* came about, she laid her course for a position to the northward of a coming battle, but the situation suddenly became complicated. When the Spanish ships discovered the identity of the ship that was steaming toward them, they did not hesitate over their plan of action. With one accord they turned and ran for port. Laughter arose from the *Adolphus*. The captain broke his orders, and, instead of keeping to the northward, he headed in the wake of the impetuous *Chancellorville*. The correspondents crowded on the bow.

The Spaniards when their broadsides became visible were seen to be ships of no importance, mere little gunboats for work in the shallows back of the reefs, and it was certainly discreet to refuse encounter with the five-inch guns of the *Chancellorville*. But the joyful *Adolphus* took no account of this discretion. The pursuit of the Spaniards had been so ferocious that the quick change to heels-overhead flight filled that corner of the mind which is devoted to the spirit of revenge. It was this that moved Shackles to yell taunts futilely at the far-away ships. " Well, how do you like it, eh? How do you like it?" The *Adolphus* was drinking compensation for her previous agony.

The mountains of the shore now shadowed high into the sky and the square white houses of a town could be seen near a vague cleft which seemed to mark the entrance to a port. The gunboats were now near to it.

Suddenly white smoke streamed from the bow of the *Chancellorville* and developed swiftly into a great bulb which drifted in fragments down the wind. Presently the deep-throated boom of the gun came to the ears on board the *Adolphus*. The shot kicked up a high jet of water into the air astern of the last gunboat. The black smoke from the funnels of the cruiser made her look like a collier on fire, and in her desperation she tried many more long shots, but presently the *Adolphus*, murmuring disappointment, saw the *Chancellorville* sheer from the chase.

In time they came up with her and she was an indignant ship. Gloom and wrath was on the forecastle and wrath and gloom was on the quarter-deck. A sad voice from the bridge said: " Just missed 'em." Shackles gained permission to board the cruiser, and in the cabin, he talked to Lieutenant-Commander Surrey, tall, bald-headed and angry. "Shoals," said the captain of the *Chancellorville.* "I can't go any nearer and those gunboats could steam along a stone sidewalk if only it was wet." Then his bright eyes became brighter. "I tell you what! The *Chicken,* the *Holy Moses* and the *Mongolian* are on station off Nuevitas. If you will do me a favour—why, to-morrow I will give those people a game!"

III.

The *Chancellorville* lay all night watching off the port of the two gunboats and, soon after daylight, the lookout descried three smokes to the westward and they were later made out to be the *Chicken,* the *Holy Moses* and the *Adolphus,* the latter tagging hurriedly after the United States vessels.

The *Chicken* had been a harbour tug but she was now the *U. S. S. Chicken,* by your leave. She carried a six-pounder forward and a six-pounder aft and her main point was her conspicuous vulnerability. The *Holy Moses* had been the private yacht of a Philadelphia millionaire. She carried six six-pounders and her main point was the chaste beauty of the officer's quarters.

On the bridge of the *Chancellorville*, Lieutenant-Commander Surrey surveyed his squadron with considerable satisfaction. Presently he signalled to the lieutenant who commanded the *Holy Moses* and to the boatswain who commanded the *Chicken* to come aboard the flag-ship. This was all very well for the captain of the yacht, but it was not so easy for the captain of the tug-boat who had two heavy lifeboats swung fifteen feet above the water. He had been accustomed to talking with senior officers from his own pilot house through the intercession of the blessed megaphone. However he got a lifeboat overside and was pulled to the *Chancellorville* by three men—which cut his crew almost into halves.

In the cabin of the *Chancellorville*, Surrey disclosed to his two captains his desires concerning the Spanish gunboats and they were glad for being ordered down from the Nuevitas station where life was very dull. He also announced that there was a shore battery containing, he believed, four field guns—three-point-twos. His draught— he spoke of it as *his* draught—would enable him to go in close enough to engage the battery at moderate range, but he pointed out that the main

parts of the attempt to destroy the Spanish gunboats must be left to the *Holy Moses* and the
Chicken. His business, he thought, could only
be to keep the air so singing about the ears of the
battery that the men at the guns would be unable
to take an interest in the dash of the smaller
American craft into the bay.

The officers spoke in their turns. The captain
of the *Chicken* announced that he saw no diffi-
culties. The squadron would follow the senior
officer in line ahead, the *S. O.* would engage the
batteries as soon as possible, she would turn to
starboard when the depth of water forced her to
do so and the *Holy Moses* and the *Chicken* would
run past her into the bay and fight the Spanish
ships wherever they were to be found. The
captain of the *Holy Moses* after some moments
of dignified thought said that he had no sugges-
tions to make that would better this plan.

Surrey pressed an electric bell ; a marine orderly
appeared ; he was sent with a message. The
message brought the navigating officer of the
Chancellorville to the cabin and the four men
nosed over a chart.

In the end Surrey declared that he had made
up his mind and the juniors remained in expect-
ant silence for three minutes while he stared at

the bulkhead. Then he said that the plan of the *Chicken's* captain seemed to him correct in the main. He would make one change. It was that he should first steam in and engage the battery and the other vessels should remain in their present positions until he signalled them to run into the bay. If the squadron steamed ahead in line, the battery could, if it chose, divide its fire between the cruiser and the gunboats constituting the more important attack. He had no doubt, he said, that he could soon silence the battery by tumbling the earth-works on to the guns and driving away the men even if he did not succeed in hitting the pieces. Of course he had no doubt of being able to silence the battery in twenty minutes. Then he would signal for the *Holy Moses* and the *Chicken* to make their rush, and of course he would support them with his fire as much as conditions enabled him. He arose then indicating that the conference was at an end. In the few moments more that all four men remained in the cabin, the talk changed its character completely. It was now unofficial, and . the sharp badinage concealed furtive affections, Academy friendships, the feelings of old-time ship-mates, hiding everything under a veil of jokes. " Well, good luck to you, old boy ! Don't get that val-

uable packet of yours sunk under you. Think
how it would weaken the navy. Would you mind
buying me three pairs of pajamas in the town
yonder? If your engines get disabled, tote her
under your arm. You can do it. Good-bye, old
man, don't forget to come out all right——"

When the captains of the *Holy Moses* and the
the *Chicken* emerged from the cabin, they strode
the deck with a new step. They were proud
men. The marine on duty above their boats
looked at them curiously and with awe. He detected something which meant action, conflict,
The boats' crews saw it also. As they pulled their
steady stroke, they studied fleetingly the face of
the officer in the stern sheets. In both cases they
perceived a glad man and yet a man filled with a
profound consideration of the future.

IV

A bird-like whistle stirred the decks of the
Chancellorville. It was followed by the hoarse
bellowing of the boatswain's mate. As the cruiser
turned her bow toward the shore, she happened
to steam near the *Adolphus*. The usual calm
voice hailed the despatch boat. "Keep—that—

gauze under-shirt of yours—well—out of the—
line of fire."

" Ay, ay, sir ! "

The cruiser then moved slowly toward the
shore, watched by every eye in the smaller American vessels. She was deliberate and steady, and
this was reasonable even to the impatience of the
other craft because the wooded shore was likely
to suddenly develop new factors. Slowly she
swung to starboard ; smoke belched over her and
the roar of a gun came along the water.

The battery was indicated by a long thin streak
of yellow earth. The first shot went high, plough-
ing the chaparral on the hillside. The *Chancellorville* wore an air for a moment of being deep in
meditation. She flung another shell, which landed
squarely on the earth-work, making a great dun
cloud. Before the smoke had settled, there was
a crimson flash from the battery. To the watchers
at sea, it was smaller than a needle. The shot
made a geyser of crystal water, four hundred yards
from the *Chancellorville.*

The cruiser, having made up her mind, suddenly
went at the battery, hammer and tongs. She
moved to and fro casually, but the thunder of her
guns was gruff and angry. Sometimes she was
quite hidden in her own smoke, but with exceed-

ing regularity the earth of the battery spurted into the air. The Spanish shells, for the most part, went high and wide of the cruiser, jetting the water far away.

Once a Spanish gunner took a festive side-show chance at the waiting group of the three nondescripts. It went like a flash over the *Adolphus*, singing a wistful metallic note. Whereupon the *Adolphus* broke hurriedly for the open sea, and men on the *Holy Moses* and the *Chicken* laughed hoarsely and cruelly. The correspondents had been standing excitedly on top of the pilot-house, but at the passing of the shell, they promptly eliminated themselves by dropping with a thud to the deck below. The cook again was giving tongue. "Oh, say, this won't do! I'm damned if it will! We ain't no armoured cruiser, you know. If one of them shells hits us—well, we finish right there. 'Tain't like as if it was our *business*, foolin' 'round within the range of them guns. There's no sense in it. Them other fellows don't seem to mind it, but it's their *business*. If it's your *business*, you go ahead and do it, but if it ain't, you—look at that, would you!"

The *Chancellorville* had sent up a spread of flags, and the *Holy Moses* and the *Chicken* were steaming in.

V

They, on the *Chancellorville*, sometimes could see into the bay, and they perceived the enemy's gunboats moving out as if to give battle. Surrey feared that this impulse would not endure or that it was some mere pretence for the edification of the town's people and the garrison, so he hastily signalled the *Holy Moses* and the *Chicken* to go in. Thankful for small favours, they came on like charging bantams. The battery had ceased firing. As the two auxiliaries passed under the stern of the cruiser, the megaphone hailed them. "You —will—see—the—en—em—y—soon —as—you— round—the—point. A—fine—chance. Good— luck."

As a matter of fact, the Spanish gunboats had not been informed of the presence of the *Holy Moses* and the *Chicken* off the bar, and they were just blustering down the bay over the protective shoals to make it appear that they scorned the *Chancellorville*. But suddenly, from around the point, there burst into view a steam yacht, closely followed by a harbour tug. The gunboats took one swift look at this horrible sight and fled screaming.

Lieutenant Reigate, commanding the *Holy Moses*, had under his feet a craft that was capable of some speed, although before a solemn tribunal, one would have to admit that she conscientiously belied almost everything that the contractors had said of her, originally. Boatswain Pent, commanding the *Chicken*, was in possession of an utterly different kind. The *Holy Moses* was an antelope ; the *Chicken* was a man who could carry a piano on his back. In this race Pent had the mortification of seeing his vessel outstripped badly.

The entrance of the two American craft had had a curious effect upon the shores of the bay. Apparently everyone had slept in the assurance that the *Chancellorville* could not cross the bar, and that the *Chancellorville* was the only hostile ship. Consequently, the appearance of the *Holy Moses* and the *Chicken*, created a curious and complete emotion. Reigate, on the bridge of the *Holy Moses*, laughed when he heard the bugles shrilling and saw through his glasses the wee figures of men running hither and thither on the shore. It was the panic of the china when the bull entered the shop. The whole bay was bright with sun. Every detail of the shore was plain. From a brown hut abeam of the *Holy Moses*, some little men ran out waving their arms and turning their tiny faces to look at the enemy. Directly ahead, some four miles, appeared the scattered white houses of a town with a wharf, and some schooners in front of it. The gunboats were making for the town. There was a stone fort on the hill overshadowing, but Reigate conjectured that there was no artillery in it.

There was a sense of something intimate and impudent in the minds of the Americans. It was like climbing over a wall and fighting a man in his own garden. It was not that they could be in any wise shaken in their resolve ; it was simply that the overwhelmingly Spanish aspect of things made them feel like gruff intruders. Like many of the emotions of war-time, this emotion had nothing at all to do with war.

Reigate's only commissioned subordinate called up from the bow gun. " May I open fire, sir ? I think I can fetch that last one."

"Yes." Immediately the six-pounder crashed, and in the air was the spinning-wire noise of the flying shot. It struck so close to the last gunboat that it appeared that the spray went aboard. The swift-handed men at the gun spoke of it. " Gave 'm a bath that time anyhow. First one they've ever had. Dry 'em off this time, Jim." The young ensign said : " Steady." And so the *Holy Moses*

raced in, firing, until the whole town, fort, water-
front, and shipping were as plain as if they had been
done on paper by a mechanical draftsman. The
gunboats were trying to hide in the bosom of the
town. One was frantically tying up to the wharf
and the other was anchoring within a hundred
yards of the shore. The Spanish infantry, of
course, had dug trenches along the beach, and suddenly the air over the *Holy Moses* sung with bullets. The shore-line thrummed with musketry.
Also some antique shells screamed.

VI

The *Chicken* was doing her best. Pent's post-
ure at the wheel seemed to indicate that her best
was about thirty-four knots. In his eagerness he
was braced as if he alone was taking in a 10,000
ton battleship through Hell Gate.

But the *Chicken* was not too far in the rear and
Pent could see clearly that he was to have no
minor part to play. Some of the antique shells
had struck the *Holy Moses* and he could see the
escaped steam shooting up from her. She lay
close inshore and was lashing out with four six-
pounders as if this was the last opportunity she

9

would have to fire them. She had made the
Spanish gunboats very sick. A solitary gun on
the one moored to the wharf was from time to
time firing wildly ; otherwise the gunboats were
silent. But the beach in front of the town was a
line of fire. The *Chicken* headed for the *Holy
Moses* and, as soon as possible, the six-pounder
in her bow began to crack at the gunboat moored
to the wharf.

In the meantime, the *Chancellorville* prowled
off the bar, listening to the firing, anxious, acutely
anxious, and feeling her impotency in every inch
of her smart steel frame. And in the meantime,
the *Adolphus* squatted on the waves and brazenly
waited for news. One could thoughtfully count
the seconds and reckon that, in this second and
that second, a man had died—if one chose. But
no one did it. Undoubtedly, the spirit was that
the flag should come away with honour, honour
complete, perfect, leaving no loose unfinished end
over which the Spaniards could erect a monument
of satisfaction, glorification. The distant guns
boomed to the ears of the silent blue-jackets at
their stations on the cruiser.

The *Chicken* steamed up to the *Holy Moses*
and took into her nostrils the odour of steam, gun-
powder and burnt things. Rifle bullets simply

steamed over them both. In the merest flash of time, Pent took into his remembrance the body of a dead quartermaster on the bridge of his consort. The two megaphones uplifted together, but Pent's eager voice cried out first.

"Are you injured, sir?"

"No, not completely. My engines can get me out after—after we have sunk those gunboats." The voice had been utterly conventional but it changed to sharpness. "Go in and sink that gunboat at anchor."

As the *Chicken* rounded the *Holy Moses* and started inshore, a man called to him from the depths of finished disgust. "They're takin' to their boats, sir." Pent looked and saw the men of the anchored gunboat lower their boats and pull like mad for shore.

The *Chicken*, assisted by the *Holy Moses*, began a methodical killing of the anchored gunboat. The Spanish infantry on shore fired frenziedly at the Chicken. Pent, giving the wheel to a waiting sailor, stepped out to a point where he could see the men at the guns. One bullet spanged past him and into the pilot-house. He ducked his head into the window. "That hit you, Murry?" he inquired with interest.

"No, sir," cheerfully responded the man at the wheel.

Pent became very busy superintending the fire of his absurd battery. The anchored gunboat simply would not sink. It evinced that unnatural stubbornness which is sometimes displayed by inanimate objects. The gunboat at the wharf had sunk as if she had been scuttled but this riddled thing at anchor would not even take fire. Pent began to grow flurried—privately. He could not stay there for ever. Why didn't the damned gunboat admit its destruction. Why——

He was at the forward gun when one of his engine room force came to him and, after saluting, said serenely : " The men at the after-gun are all down, sir."

It was one of those curious lifts which an enlisted man, without in any way knowing it, can give his officer. The impudent tranquillity of the man at once set Pent to rights and the stoker departed admiring the extraordinary coolness of his captain.

The next few moments contained little but heat, an odour, applied mechanics and an expectation of death. Pent developed a fervid and amazed appreciation of the men, his men, men he knew very well, but strange men. What explained them? He was doing his best because he was captain of the *Chicken* and he lived or died by the *Chicken*.

But what could move these men to watch his eye in bright anticipation of his orders and then obey them with enthusiastic rapidity? What caused them to speak of the action as some kind of a joke—particularly when they knew he could overhear them? What manner of men? And he anointed them secretly with his fullest affection.

Perhaps Pent did not think all this during the battle. Perhaps he thought it so soon after the battle that his full mind became confused as to the time. At any rate, it stands as an expression of his feeling.

The enemy had gotten a field-gun down to the shore and with it they began to throw three-inch shells at the *Chicken*. In this war it was usual that the down-trodden Spaniards in their ignorance should use smokeless powder while the Americans, by the power of the consistent everlasting three-ply, wire-woven, double back-action imbecility of a hay-seed government, used powder which on sea and on land cried their position to heaven, and, accordingly, good men got killed without reason. At first, Pent could not locate the field-gun at all, but as soon as he found it, he ran aft with one man and brought the after six-pounder again into action. He paid little heed to the old gun crew. One was lying on his face apparently dead; another was prone with a wound in the chest, while the third sat with his back to the deck-house holding a smitten arm. This last one called out huskily, " Give 'm hell, sir."

The minutes of the battle were either days, years, or they were flashes of a second. Once Pent looking up was astonished to see three shell holes in the *Chicken's* funnel—made surreptitiously, so to speak. . . . "If we don't silence that field-gun, she'll sink us, boys." . . . The eyes of the man sitting with his back against the deck-house were looking from out his ghastly face at the new gun-crew. He spoke with the supreme laziness of a wounded man. " Give 'm hell." . . . Pent felt a sudden twist of his shoulder. He was wounded—slightly. . . . The anchored gunboat was in flames.

———

VII

PENT took his little blood-stained tow-boat out to the *Holy Moses*. The yacht was already under way for the bay entrance. As they were passing out of range the Spaniards heroically redoubled their fire—which is their custom. Pent, moving busily about the decks, stopped suddenly at the door of the engine-room. His face was set and

his eyes were steely.   He spoke to one of the en-
gineers.   "During the action I saw you firing at
the enemy with a rifle.   I told you once to stop,
and then I saw you at it again.   Pegging away
with a rifle is no part of your business.   I want
you to understand that you are in trouble."   The
humbled man did not raise his eyes from the deck.
Presently the *Holy Moses* displayed an anxiety for
the *Chicken's* health.

"One killed and four wounded, sir."

"Have you enough men left to work your ship?"

After deliberation, Pent answered : "No, sir."

"Shall I send you assistance?"

"No, sir.   I can get to sea all right."

As they neared the point they were edified by
the sudden appearance of a serio-comic ally.   The
Chancellorville at last had been unable to stand
the strain, and had sent in her launch with an
ensign, five seamen and a number of marksmen
marines.   She swept hot-foot around the point,
bent on terrible slaughter; the one-pounder of
her bow presented a formidable appearance.   The
Holy Moses and the *Chicken* laughed until they
brought indignation to the brow of the young
ensign.   But he forgot it when with some of his
men he boarded the *Chicken* to do what was possible for the wounded.   The nearest surgeon was

aboard the *Chancellorville*. There was absolute
silence on board the cruiser as the *Holy Moses*
steamed up to report. The blue-jackets listened
with all their ears. The commander of the yacht
spoke slowly into his megaphone : " We have—
destroyed—the two—gun-boats—sir." There was
a burst of confused cheering on the forecastle of
the *Chancellorville*, but an officer's cry quelled it.

"Very—good. Will—you—come aboard ? "

Two correspondents were already on the deck
of the cruiser. Before the last of the wounded
were hoisted aboard the cruiser the *Adolphus* was
on her way to Key West. When she arrived at
that port of desolation Shackles fled to file the
telegrams and the other correspondents fled to
the hotel for clothes, good clothes, clean clothes ;
and food, good food, much food ; and drink, much
drink, any kind of drink.

Days afterward, when the officers of the noble
squadron received the newspapers containing an
account of their performance, they looked at each
other somewhat dejectedly : " Heroic assault—
grand daring of Boatswain Pent—superb accuracy
of the *Holy Moses'* fire—gallant tars of the *Chicken*
—their names should be remembered as long as
America stands—terrible losses of the enemy——"

When the Secretary of the Navy ultimately

read the report of Commander Surrey, S. O. P.,
he had to prick himself with a dagger in order to
remember that anything at all out of the ordinary
had occurred.

THE SERGEANT'S PRIVATE MAD HOUSE

THE moonlight was almost steady blue flame and all this radiance was lavished out upon a still lifeless wilderness of stunted trees and cactus plants. The shadows lay upon the ground, pools of black and sharply outlined, resembling substances, fabrics, and not shadows at all. From afar came the sound of the sea coughing among the hollows in the coral rock.

The land was very empty; one could easily imagine that Cuba was a simple vast solitude; one could wonder at the moon taking all the trouble of this splendid illumination. There was no wind ; nothing seemed to live.

But in a particular large group of shadows lay an outpost of some forty United States marines. If it had been possible to approach them from any direction without encountering one of their sentries, one could have gone stumbling among sleeping men and men who sat waiting, their blankets tented over their heads ; one would have been in among them before one's mind could have

decided whether they were men or devils. If a
marine moved, he took the care and the time of
one who walks across a death-chamber. The lieutenant in command reached for his watch and the
nickel chain gave forth the faintest tinkling sound.
He could see the glistening five or six pairs of
eyes that slowly turned to regard him. His sergeant lay near him and he bent his face down to
whisper. "Who's on post behind the big cactus
plant?"

"Dryden," rejoined the sergeant just over his
breath.

After a pause the lieutenant murmured : "He's
got too many nerves. I shouldn't have put him
there." The sergeant asked if he should crawl
down and look into affairs at Dryden's post. The
young officer nodded assent and the sergeant,
softly cocking his rifle, went away on his hands and
knees. The lieutenant with his back to a dwarf
tree, sat watching the sergeant's progress for the
few moments that he could see him moving from
one shadow to another. Afterward, the officer
waited to hear Dryden's quick but low-voiced
challenge, but time passed and no sound came from
the direction of the post behind the cactus bush.

The sergeant, as he came nearer and nearer to
this cactus bush—a number of peculiarly dignified

columns throwing shadows of inky darkness—
had slowed his pace, for he did not wish to trifle
with the feelings of the sentry, and he was expecting the stern hail and was ready with the immediate answer which turns away wrath. He was not
made anxious by the fact that he could not yet
see Dryden, for he knew that the man would be
hidden in a way practised by sentry marines since
the time when two men had been killed by a disease of excessive confidence on picket. Indeed,
as the sergeant went still nearer, he became more
and more angry. Dryden was evidently a most
proper sentry.

Finally he arrived at a point where he could see
Dryden seated in the shadow, staring into the
bushes ahead of him, his rifle ready on his knee.
The sergeant in his rage longed for the peaceful
precincts of the Washington Marine Barracks
where there would have been no situation to prevent the most complete non-commissioned oratory.
He felt indecent in his capacity of a man able to
creep up to the back of a G Company member on
guard duty. Never mind; in the morning back
at camp——

But, suddenly, he felt afraid. There was something wrong with Dryden. He remembered old
tales of comrades creeping out to find a picket

seated against a tree perhaps, upright enough but
stone dead. The sergeant paused and gave the
inscrutable back of the sentry a long stare. Dubious he again moved forward. At three paces,
he hissed like a little snake. Dryden did not
show a sign of hearing. At last, the sergeant was
in a position from which he was able to reach out
and touch Dryden on the arm. Whereupon was
turned to him the face of a man livid with mad
fright. The sergeant grabbed him by the wrist
and with discreet fury shook him. " Here! Pull
yourself together! "

Dryden paid no heed but turned his wild face
from the newcomer to the ground in front.
Don't you see 'em, sergeant? Don't you see 'em? "

" Where? " whispered the sergeant.

" Ahead, and a little on the right flank. A
reg'lar skirmish line. Don't you see 'em? "

" Naw," whispered the sergeant. Dryden began to shake. He began moving one hand from
his head to his knee and from his knee to his
head rapidly, in a way that is without explanation.
" I don't dare fire," he wept. " If I do they'll see
me, and oh, how they'll pepper me! "

The sergeant lying on his belly, understood one
thing. Dryden had gone mad. Dryden was the
March Hare. The old man gulped down his up-

roarious emotions as well as he was able and used
the most simple device. "Go," he said, "and
tell the lieutenant while I cover your post for
you."

"No! They'd see me! They'd see me! And
then they'd pepper me! O, how they'd pepper
me!"

The sergeant was face to face with the biggest
situation of his life. In the first place he knew
that at night a large or small force of Spanish
guerillas was never more than easy rifle range
from any marine outpost, both sides maintaining
a secrecy as absolute as possible in regard to their
real position and strength. Everything was on
a watch-spring foundation. A loud word might
be paid for by a night-attack which would involve
five hundred men who needed their earned sleep,
not to speak of some of them who would need
their lives. The slip of a foot and the rolling of
a pint of gravel might go from consequence to
consequence until various crews went to general
quarters on their ships in the harbour, their batteries booming as the swift search-light flashes
tore through the foliage. Men would get killed
—notably the sergeant and Dryden—and outposts would be cut off and the whole night would
be one pitiless turmoil. And so Sergeant George

H. Peasley began to run his private madhouse behind the cactus-bush.

"Dryden," said the sergeant, "you do as I tell you and go tell the lieutenant."

"I don't dare move," shivered the man. "They'll see me if I move. They'll see me. They're almost up now. Let's hide——"

"Well, then you stay here a moment and I'll go and——"

Dryden turned upon him a look so tigerish that the old man felt his hair move. "Don't you stir," he hissed. "You want to give me away. You want them to see me. Don't you stir." The sergeant decided not to stir.

He became aware of the slow wheeling of eternity, its majestic incomprehensibility of movement. Seconds, minutes, were quaint little things, tangible as toys, and there were billions of them, all alike. "Dryden," he whispered at the end of a century in which, curiously, he had never joined the marine corps at all but had taken to another walk of life and prospered greatly in it. "Dryden, this is all foolishness." He thought of the expedient of smashing the man over the head with his rifle, but Dryden was so supernaturally alert that there surely would issue some small scuffle and there could be not even the fraction of a scuffle. The sergeant relapsed into the contemplation of another century.

His patient had one fine virtue. He was in such terror of the phantom skirmish line that his voice never went above a whisper, whereas his delusion might have expressed itself in hyena yells and shots from his rifle. The sergeant, shuddering, had visions of how it might have been—the mad private leaping into the air and howling and shooting at his friends and making them the centre of the enemy's eager attention. This, to his mind, would have been conventional conduct for a maniac. The trembling victim of an idea was somewhat puzzling. The sergeant decided that from time to time he would reason with his patient. "Look here, Dryden, you don't see any real Spaniards. You've been drinking or—something. Now——"

But Dryden only glared him into silence. Dryden was inspired with such a profound contempt of him that it was become hatred. "Don't you stir!" And it was clear that if the sergeant did stir, the mad private would introduce calamity. "Now," said Peasley to himself, "if those guerillas *should* take a crack at us to-night, they'd find a lunatic asylum right in the front and it would be astonishing."

The silence of the night was broken by the quick low voice of a sentry to the left some distance. The breathless stillness brought an effect to the words as if they had been spoken in one's ear.

"*Halt—who's there—halt or I'll fire !*" Bang!

At the moment of sudden attack particularly at night, it is improbable that a man registers much detail of either thought or action. He may afterward say : " I was here." He may say : " I was there." " I did this." " I did that." But there remains a great incoherency because of the tumultuous thought which seethes through the head. " Is this defeat ? " At night in a wilderness and against skilful foes half-seen, one does not trouble to ask if it is also Death. Defeat is Death, then, save for the miraculous. But the exaggerating magnifying first thought subsides in the ordered mind of the soldier and he knows, soon, what he is doing and how much of it. The sergeant's immediate impulse had been to squeeze close to the ground and listen—listen—above all else, listen. But the next moment he grabbed his private asylum by the scruff of its neck, jerked it to its feet and started to retreat upon the main outpost.

To the left, rifle-flashes were bursting from the shadows. To the rear, the lieutenant was giving

10

some hoarse order or admonition. Through the
air swept some Spanish bullets, very high, as if
they had been fired at a man in a tree. The private asylum came on so hastily that the sergeant
found he could remove his grip, and soon they
were in the midst of the men of the outpost.
Here there was no occasion for enlightening the
lieutenant. In the first place such surprises required statement, question and answer. It is impossible to get a grossly original and fantastic
idea through a man's head in less than one
minute of rapid talk, and the sergeant knew
the lieutenant could not spare the minute. He
himself had no minutes to devote to anything but
the business of the outpost. And the madman
disappeared from his pen and he forgot about
him.

It was a long night and the little fight was as
long as the night. It was a heart-breaking work.
The forty marines lay in an irregular oval. From
all sides, the Mauser bullets sang low and hard.
Their occupation was to prevent a rush, and to
this end they potted carefully at the flash of a
Mauser—save when they got excited for a moment,
in which case their magazines rattled like a great
Waterbury watch. Then they settled again to a
systematic potting.

The enemy were not of the regular Spanish forces. They were of a corps of guerillas, native-born Cubans, who preferred the flag of Spain. They were all men who knew the craft of the woods and were all recruited from the district. They fought more like red Indians than any people but the red Indians themselves. Each seemed to possess an individuality, a fighting individuality, which is only found in the highest order of irregular soldiers. Personally they were as distinct as possible, but through equality of knowledge and experience, they arrived at concert of action. So long as they operated in the wilderness, they were formidable troops. It mattered little whether it was daylight or dark; they were mainly invisible. They had schooled from the Cubans insurgent to Spain. As the Cubans fought the Spanish troops, so would these particular Spanish troops fight the Americans. It was wisdom.

The marines thoroughly understood the game. They must lie close and fight until daylight when the guerillas promptly would go away. They had withstood other nights of this kind, and now their principal emotion was probably a sort of frantic annoyance.

Back at the main camp, whenever the roaring volleys lulled, the men in the trenches could hear

their comrades of the outpost, and the guerillas
pattering away interminably. The moonlight
faded and left an equal darkness upon the wilderness. A man could barely see the comrade at his
side. Sometimes guerillas crept so close that
the flame from their rifles seemed to scorch the
faces of the marines, and the reports sounded as
if from two or three inches of their very noses.
If a pause came, one could hear the guerillas gabbling to each other in a kind of drunken delirium.
The lieutenant was praying that the ammunition
would last. Everybody was praying for daybreak.

A black hour came finally, when the men were
not fit to have their troubles increased. The
enemy made a wild attack on one portion of the
oval, which was held by about fifteen men. The
remainder of the force was busy enough, and the
fifteen were naturally left to their devices. Amid
the whirl of it, a loud voice suddenly broke out in
song :

> "When shepherds guard their flocks by night,
>   All seated on the ground,
> An angel of the Lord came down
> And glory shone around."

" Who the hell is that ? " demanded the lieutenant from a throat full of smoke. There was
almost a full stop of the firing. The Americans

were somewhat puzzled. Practical ones muttered
that the fool should have a bayonet-hilt shoved
down his throat. Others felt a thrill at the strange-
ness of the thing. Perhaps it was a sign!

> "The minstrel boy to the war has gone,
> In the ranks of death you'll find him,
> His father's sword he has girded on
> And his wild harp slung behind him."

This croak was as lugubrious as a coffin. "Who
is it? Who is it?" snapped the lieutenant.
"Stop him, somebody."

"It's Dryden, sir," said old Sergeant Peasley, as
he felt around in the darkness for his madhouse.
"I can't find him—yet."

> "Please, O, please, O, do not let me fall;
> You're—gurgh-ugh——"

The sergeant had pounced upon him.

This singing had had an effect upon the Spaniards. At first they had fired frenziedly at the
voice, but they soon ceased, perhaps from sheer
amazement. Both sides took a spell of meditation.

The sergeant was having some difficulty with
his charge. "Here, you, grab 'im. Take 'im by
the throat. Be quiet, you devil."

One of the fifteen men, who had been hard-
pressed, called out, "We've only got about one
clip a-piece, Lieutenant. If they come again——"

The lieutenant crawled to and fro among his men, taking clips of cartridges from those who had many. He came upon the sergeant and his madhouse. He felt Dryden's belt and found it simply stuffed with ammunition. He examined Dryden's rifle and found in it a full clip. The madhouse had not fired a shot. The lieutenant distributed these valuable prizes among the fifteen men. As the men gratefully took them, one said : " If they had come again hard enough, they would have had us, sir,—maybe."

But the Spaniards did not come again. At the first indication of daybreak, they fired their customary good-bye volley. The marines lay tight while the slow dawn crept over the land. Finally the lieutenant arose among them, and he was a bewildered man, but very angry. " Now where is that idiot, Sergeant ? "

" Here he is, sir," said the old man cheerfully. He was seated on the ground beside the recumbent Dryden who, with an innocent smile on his face, was sound asleep.

" Wake him up," said the lieutenant briefly.

The sergeant shook the sleeper. " Here, Minstrel Boy, turn out. The lieutenant wants you."

Dryden climbed to his feet and saluted the officer with a dazed and childish air. " Yes, sir."

The lieutenant was obviously having difficulty in governing his feelings, but he managed to say with calmness, "You seem to be fond of singing, Dryden? Sergeant, see if he has any whisky on him."

"Sir?" said the madhouse stupefied. "Singing—fond of singing?"

Here the sergeant interposed gently, and he and the lieutenant held palaver apart from the others. The marines, hitching more comfortably their almost empty belts, spoke with grins of the madhouse. "Well, the Minstrel Boy made 'em clear out. They couldn't stand it. But—I wouldn't want to be in his boots. He'll see fireworks when the old man interviews him on the uses of grand opera in modern warfare. How do you think he managed to smuggle a bottle along without us finding it out?"

When the weary outpost was relieved and marched back to camp, the men could not rest until they had told a tale of the voice in the wilderness. In the meantime the sergeant took Dryden aboard a ship, and to those who took charge of the man, he defined him as "the most useful —— —— crazy man in the service of the United States."

VIRTUE IN WAR

I

GATES had left the regular army in 1890, those parts of him which had not been frozen having been well fried. He took with him nothing but an oaken constitution and a knowledge of the plains and the best wishes of his fellow-officers. The Standard Oil Company differs from the United States Government in that it understands the value of the loyal and intelligent services of good men and is almost certain to reward them at the expense of incapable men. This curious practice emanates from no beneficent emotion of the Standard Oil Company, on whose feelings you could not make a scar with a hammer and chisel. It is simply that the Standard Oil Company knows more than the United States Government and makes use of virtue whenever virtue is to its advantage. In 1890 Gates really felt in his bones that, if he lived a rigorously correct life and several score of his class-mates and intimate friends died off, he would get command of a troop of horse by the time he was unfitted by age to be an active cavalry leader. He left the service of the United States and entered the service of the Standard Oil Company. In the course of time he knew that, if he lived a rigorously correct life, his position and income would develop strictly in parallel with the worth of his wisdom and experience, and he would not have to walk on the corpses of his friends.

But he was not happier. Part of his heart was in a barracks, and it was not enough to discourse of the old regiment over the port and cigars to ears which were polite enough to betray a languid ignorance. Finally came the year 1898, and Gates dropped the Standard Oil Company as if it were hot. He hit the steel trail to Washington and there fought the first serious action of the war. Like most Americans, he had a native State, and one morning he found himself major in a volunteer infantry regiment whose voice had a peculiar sharp twang to it which he could remember from childhood. The colonel welcomed the West Pointer with loud cries of joy; the lieutenant-colonel looked at him with the pebbly eye of distrust; and the senior major, having had up to this time the best battalion in the regiment, strongly disapproved of him. There were only

two majors, so the lieutenant-colonel commanded
the first battalion, which gave him an occupation.
Lieutenant-colonels under the new rules do not
always have occupations. Gates got the third
battalion—four companies commanded by intelligent officers who could gauge the opinions of
their men at two thousand yards and govern
themselves accordingly. The battalion was immensely interested in the new major. It thought
it ought to develop views about him. It thought
it was its blankety-blank business to find out immediately if it liked him personally. In the company streets the talk was nothing else. Among
the non-commissioned officers there were eleven
old soldiers of the regular army, and they knew—
and cared—that Gates had held commission in the
" Sixteenth Cavalry "—as *Harper's Weekly* says.
Over this fact they rejoiced and were glad, and
they stood by to jump lively when he took command. He would know his work and he would
know *their* work, and then in battle there would
be killed only what men were absolutely necessary and the sick list would be comparatively free
of fools.

The commander of the second battalion had
been called by an Atlanta paper, " Major Rickets
C. Carmony, the commander of the second battal-

ion of the 307th ———, is when at home one of the
biggest wholesale hardware dealers in his State.
Last evening he had ice-cream, at his own expense, served out at the regular mess of the battalion, and after dinner the men gathered about
his tent where three hearty cheers for the popular
major were given." Carmony had bought twelve
copies of this newspaper and mailed them home
to his friends.

In Gates's battalion there were more kicks than
ice-cream, and there was no ice-cream at all. Indignation ran high at the rapid manner in which
he proceeded to make soldiers of them. Some of
his officers hinted finally that the men wouldn't
stand it. They were saying that they had enlisted to fight for their country—yes, but they
weren't going to be bullied day in and day out
by a perfect stranger. They were patriots, they
were, and just as good men as ever stepped—just
as good as Gates or anybody like him. But, grad-
ually, despite itself, the battalion progressed. The
men were not altogether conscious of it. They
evolved rather blindly. Presently there were
fights with Carmony's crowd as to which was the
better battalion at drills, and at last there was no
argument. It was generally admitted that Gates
commanded the crack battalion. The men,

believing that the beginning and the end of all
soldiering was in these drills of precision, were
somewhat reconciled to their major when they
began to understand more of what he was trying
to do for them, but they were still fiery untamed
patriots of lofty pride and they resented his manner toward them. It was abrupt and sharp.

The time came when everybody knew that the
Fifth Army Corps was the corps designated for
the first active service in Cuba. The officers and
men of the 307th observed with despair that their
regiment was not in the Fifth Army Corps. The
colonel was a strategist. He understood everything in a flash. Without a moment's hesitation
he obtained leave and mounted the night express
for Washington. There he drove Senators and
Congressmen in span, tandem and four-in-hand.
With the telegraph he stirred so deeply the gov-
ernor, the people and the newspapers of his State
that whenever on a quiet night the President put
his head out of the White House he could hear the
distant vast commonwealth humming with indignation. And as it is well known that the Chief
Executive listens to the voice of the people, the
307th was transferred to the Fifth Army Corps.
It was sent at once to Tampa, where it was bri-
gaded with two dusty regiments of regulars, who

looked at it calmly and said nothing. The brigade commander happened to be no less a person
than Gates's old colonel in the " Sixteenth Cavalry "—as *Harper's Weekly* says—and Gates was
cheered. The old man's rather solemn look
brightened when he saw Gates in the 307th.
There was a great deal of battering and pounding
and banging for the 307th at Tampa, but the men
stood it more in wonder than in anger. The two
regular regiments carried them along when they
could, and when they couldn't waited impatiently
for them to come up. Undoubtedly the regulars
wished the volunteers were in garrison at Sitka,
but they said practically nothing. They minded
their own regiments. The colonel was an invaluable man in a telegraph office. When came the
scramble for transports the colonel retired to a
telegraph office and talked so ably to Washington
that the authorities pushed a number of corps
aside and made way for the 307th, as if on it depended everything. The regiment got one of the
best transports, and after a series of delays and
some starts, and an equal number of returns, they
finally sailed for Cuba.

II

Now Gates had a singular adventure on the second morning after his arrival at Atlanta to take his post as a major in the 307th.

He was in his tent, writing, when suddenly the flap was flung away and a tall young private stepped inside.

" Well, Maje," said the newcomer, genially, " how goes it ? "

The major's head flashed up, but he spoke without heat.

" Come to attention and salute."

" Huh ! " said the private.

" Come to attention and salute."

The private looked at him in resentful amazement, and then inquired :

" Ye ain't mad, are ye? Ain't nothin' to get huffy about, is there ? "

" I—— Come to attention and salute."

" Well," drawled the private, as he stared, " seein' as ye are so darn perticular, I don't care if I do—if it'll make yer meals set on yer stomick any better."

Drawing a long breath and grinning ironically, he lazily pulled his heels together and saluted with a flourish.

"There," he said, with a return to his earlier
genial manner. "How's that suit ye, Maje?"

There was a silence which to an impartial ob-
server would have seemed pregnant with dynamite
and bloody death. Then the major cleared his
throat and coldly said :

"And now, what is your business?"

"Who—me?" asked the private. "Oh, I just
sorter dropped in." With a deeper meaning he
added : "Sorter dropped in in a friendly way,
thinkin' ye was mebbe a different kind of a feller
from what ye be."

The inference was clearly marked.

It was now Gates's turn to stare, and stare he
unfeignedly did.

"Go back to your quarters," he said at length.

The volunteer became very angry.

"Oh, ye needn't be so up-in-th'-air, need ye?
Don't know's I'm dead anxious to inflict my com-
pany on yer since I've had a good look at ye.
There may be men in this here battalion what's
had just as much edjewcation as you have, and
I'm damned if they ain't got better *manners*.
Good-mornin'," he said, with dignity ; and, pass-
ing out of the tent, he flung the flap back in place
with an air of slamming it as if it had been a door.
He made his way back to his company street,

striding high.   He was furious.   He met a large
crowd of his comrades.

"What's the matter, Lige?" asked one, who
noted his temper.

"Oh, nothin'," answered Lige, with terrible
feeling.   "Nothin'.   I jest been lookin' over the
new major—that's all."

"What's he like?" asked another.

"Like?" cried Lige.   "He's like nothin'.   He
ain't out'n the same kittle as us.   No.   Gawd
made him all by himself—sep'rate.   He's a speshul
produc', he is, an' he won't have no truck with
jest common—*men*, like you be."

He made a venomous gesture which included
them all.

"Did he set on ye?" asked a soldier.

"Set on me?   No," replied Lige, with contempt.
"I set on *him*.   I sized 'im up in a minute.   'Oh,
I don't know,' I says, as I was comin' out; 'guess
you ain't the only man in the world,' I says."

For a time Lige Wigram was quite a hero.   He
endlessly repeated the tale of his adventure, and
men admired him for so soon taking the conceit
out of the new officer.   Lige was proud to think
of himself as a plain and simple patriot who had
refused to endure any high-soaring nonsense.

But he came to believe that he had not dis-

turbed the singular composure of the major, and
this concreted his hatred. He hated Gates, not
as a soldier sometimes hates an officer, a hatred
half of fear. Lige hated as man to man. And
he was enraged to see that so far from gaining
any hatred in return, he seemed incapable of making Gates have any thought of him save as a unit
in a body of three hundred men. Lige might just
as well have gone and grimaced at the obelisk in
Central Park.

When the battalion became the best in the regi-
ment he had no part in the pride of the companies.
He was sorry when men began to speak well of
Gates. He was really a very consistent hater.

III

The transport occupied by the 307th was commanded by some sort of a Scandinavian, who was
afraid of the shadows of his own topmasts. He
would have run his steamer away from a floating
Gainsborough hat, and, in fact, he ran her away
from less on some occasions. The officers, wish-
ing to arrive with the other transports, sometimes
remonstrated, and to them he talked of his owners.
Every officer in the convoying warships loathed
11

him, for in case any hostile vessel should appear
they did not see how they were going to protect
this rabbit, who would probably manage during a
fight to be in about a hundred places on the broad,
broad sea, and all of them offensive to the navy's
plan. When he was not talking of his owners he
was remarking to the officers of the regiment
that a steamer really was not like a valise, and
that he was unable to take his ship under his arm
and climb trees with it. He further said that
"them naval fellows" were not near so smart as
they thought they were.

From an indigo sea arose the lonely shore of
Cuba. Ultimately, the fleet was near Santiago,
and most of the transports were bidden to wait a
minute while the leaders found out their minds.
The skipper, to whom the 307th were prisoners,
waited for thirty hours half way between Jamaica
and Cuba. He explained that the Spanish fleet
might emerge from Santiago Harbour at any time,
and he did not propose to be caught. His
owners—— Whereupon the colonel arose as one
having nine hundred men at his back, and he
passed up to the bridge and he spake with the
captain. He explained indirectly that each in-
dividual of his nine hundred men had decided to
be the first American soldier to land for this cam-

paign, and that in order to accomplish the marvel
it was necessary for the transport to be nearer
than forty-five miles from the Cuban coast. If
the skipper would only land the regiment the
colonel would consent to his then taking his interesting old ship and going to h—— with it.
And the skipper spake with the colonel. He
pointed out that as far as he officially was concerned, the United States Government did not
exist. He was responsible solely to his owners.
The colonel pondered these sayings. He perceived that the skipper meant that he was running
his ship as he deemed best, in consideration of
the capital invested by his owners, and that he
was not at all concerned with the feelings of a
certain American military expedition to Cuba.
He was a free son of the sea—he was a sovereign
citizen of the republic of the waves. He was like
Lige.

However, the skipper ultimately incurred the
danger of taking his ship under the terrible guns
of the *New York, Iowa, Oregon, Massachusetts,
Indiana, Brooklyn, Texas* and a score of cruisers
and gunboats. It was a brave act for the captain
of a United States transport, and he was visibly
nervous until he could again get to sea, where he
offered praises that the accursed 307th was no

longer sitting on his head. For almost a week
he rambled at his cheerful will over the adjacent
high seas, having in his hold a great quantity of
military stores as successfully secreted as if they
had been buried in a copper box in the corner-
stone of a new public building in Boston. He
had had his master's certificate for twenty-one
years, and those people couldn't tell a marlin-spike
from the starboard side of the ship.

The 307th was landed in Cuba, but to their
disgust they found that about ten thousand
regulars were ahead of them. They got immediate orders to move out from the base on the
road to Santiago. Gates was interested to note
that the only delay was caused by the fact that
many men of the other battalions strayed off
sight-seeing. In time the long regiment wound
slowly among hills that shut them from sight of
the sea.

For the men to admire, there were palm-trees,
little brown huts, passive, uninterested Cuban
soldiers much worn from carrying American rations inside and outside. The weather was not
oppressively warm, and the journey was said to
be only about seven miles. There were no rumours save that there had been one short fight and
the army had advanced to within sight of San-

tiago. Having a peculiar faculty for the derision
of the romantic, the 307th began to laugh. Actually there was not *anything* in the world which
turned out to be as books describe it. Here they
had landed from the transport expecting to be at
once flung into line of battle and sent on some
kind of furious charge, and now they were trudging along a quiet trail lined with somnolent trees
and grass. The whole business so far struck them
as being a highly tedious burlesque.

After a time they came to where the camps of
regular regiments marked the sides of the road—
little villages of tents no higher than a man's
waist. The colonel found his brigade commander
and the 307th was sent off into a field of long
grass, where the men grew suddenly solemn with
the importance of getting their supper.

In the early evening some regulars told one of
Gates's companies that at daybreak this division
would move to an attack upon something.

" How d' you know? " said the company,
deeply awed.

" Heard it."

" Well, what are we to attack? "

" Dunno."

The 307th was not at all afraid, but each man began to imagine the morrow. The regulars seemed

to have as much interest in the morrow as they did in the last Christmas. It was none of their affair, apparently.

"Look here," said Lige Wigram, to a man in the 17th Regular Infantry, "whereabouts are we goin' ter-morrow an' who do we run up against— do ye know?"

The 17th soldier replied, truculently: "If I ketch th' —— —— —— what stole my terbaccer, I'll whirl in an' break every —— —— bone in his body."

Gates's friends in the regular regiments asked him numerous questions as to the reliability of his organisation. Would the 307th stand the racket? They were certainly not contemptuous; they simply did not seem to consider it important whether the 307th would or whether it would not.

"Well," said Gates, "they won't run the length of a tent-peg if they can gain any idea of what they're fighting; they won't bunch if they've about six acres of open ground to move in ; they won't get rattled at all if they see you fellows taking it easy, and they'll fight like the devil as long as they thoroughly, completely, absolutely, satisfactorily, exhaustively understand what the business is. They're lawyers. All excepting my battalion."

IV

Lige awakened into a world obscured by blue fog. Somebody was gently shaking him. " Git up; we're going to move." The regiment was buckling up itself. From the trail came the loud creak of a light battery moving ahead. The tones of all men were low ; the faces of the officers were composed, serious. The regiment found itself moving along behind the battery before it had time to ask itself more than a hundred questions. The trail wound through a dense tall jungle, dark, heavy with dew.

The battle broke with a snap—far ahead. Presently Lige heard from the air above him a faint low note as if somebody were blowing softly in the mouth of a bottle. It was a stray bullet which had wandered a mile to tell him that war was before him. He nearly broke his neck looking upward. " Did ye hear that?" But the men were fretting to get out of this gloomy jungle. They wanted to see something. The faint ruprup-rrrrup-rup on in the front told them that the fight had begun ; death was abroad, and so the mystery of this wilderness excited them. This wilderness was portentously still and dark.

They passed the battery aligned on a hill above the trail, and they had not gone far when the gruff guns began to roar and they could hear the rocket-like swish of the flying shells. Presently everybody must have called out for the assistance of the 307th. Aides and couriers came flying back to them.

" Is this the 307th? Hurry up your men, please, Colonel. You're needed more every minute."

Oh, they were, were they? Then the regulars were not going to do *all* the fighting? The old 307th was bitterly proud or proudly bitter. They left their blanket rolls under the guard of God and pushed on, which is one of the reasons why the Cubans of that part of the country were, later, so well equipped. There began to appear fields, hot, golden-green in the sun. On some palm-dotted knolls before them they could see little lines of black dots—the American advance. A few men fell, struck down by other men who, perhaps half a mile away, were aiming at somebody else. The loss was wholly in Carmony's battalion, which immediately bunched and backed away, coming with a shock against Gates's advance company. This shock sent a tremor through all of Gates's battalion until men in the very last files cried out nervously, " Well, what in hell is up

now?" There came an order to deploy and ad.
vance. An occasional hoarse yell from the regulars could be heard. The deploying made Gates's
heart bleed for the colonel. The old man stood
there directing the movement, straight, fearless,
sombrely defiant of—everything. Carmony's four
companies were like four herds. And all the time
the bullets from no living man knows where kept
pecking at them and pecking at them. Gates,
the excellent Gates, the highly educated and
strictly military Gates, grew rankly insubordinate.
He knew that the regiment was suffering from
nothing but the deadly range and oversweep of
the modern rifle, of which many proud and confident nations know nothing save that they have
killed savages with it, which is the least of all in-
formations.

Gates rushed upon Carmony.

" —— —— it, man, if you can't get your people
to deploy, for —— sake give me a chance! I'm
stuck in the woods!"

Carmony gave nothing, but Gates took all he
could get and his battalion deployed and advanced
like men. The old colonel almost burst into
tears, and he cast one quick glance of gratitude at
Gates, which the younger officer wore on his heart
like a secret decoration.

There was a wild scramble up hill, down dale, through thorny thickets. Death smote them with a kind of slow rhythm, leisurely taking a man now here, now there, but the cat-spit sound of the bullets was always. A large number of the men of Carmony's battalion came on with Gates. They were willing to do anything, anything. They had no real fault, unless it was that early conclusion that any brave high-minded youth was necessarily a good soldier immediately, from the beginning. In them had been born a swift feeling that the unpopular Gates knew everything, and they followed the trained soldier.

If they followed him, he certainly took them into it. As they swung heavily up one steep hill, like so many wind-blown horses, they came suddenly out into the real advance. Little blue groups of men were making frantic rushes forward and then flopping down on their bellies to fire volleys while other groups made rushes. Ahead they could see a heavy house-like fort which was inadequate to explain from whence came the myriad bullets. The remainder of the scene was landscape. Pale men, yellow men, blue men came out of this landscape quiet and sad-eyed with wounds. Often they were grimly facetious. There is nothing in the American regulars so amazing as his conduct when he is wounded—his apologetic limp, his deprecatory arm-sling, his embarrassed and ashamed shot-hole through the lungs. The men of the 307th looked at calm creatures who had divers punctures and they were made better. These men told them that it was only necessary to keep a-going. They of the 307th lay on their bellies, red, sweating and panting, and heeded the voice of the elder brother.

Gates walked back of his line, very white of face, but hard and stern past anything his men knew of him. After they had violently adjured him to lie down and he had given weak backs a cold, stiff touch, the 307th charged by rushes. The hatless colonel made frenzied speech, but the man of the time was Gates. The men seemed to feel that this was his business. Some of the regular officers said afterward that the advance of the 307th was very respectable indeed. They were rather surprised, they said. At least five of the crack regiments of the regular army were in this division, and the 307th could win no more than a feeling of kindly appreciation.

Yes, it was very good, very good indeed, but did you notice what was being done at the same moment by the 12th, the 17th, the 7th, the 8th, the 25th, the——

Gates felt that his charge was being a success. He was carrying out a successful function. Two captains fell bang on the grass and a lieutenant slumped quietly down with a death wound. Many men sprawled suddenly. Gates was keeping his men almost even with the regulars, who were charging on his flanks. Suddenly he thought that he must have come close to the fort and that a Spaniard had tumbled a great stone block down upon his leg. Twelve hands reached out to help him, but he cried:

"No—d—— your souls—go on—go on!"

He closed his eyes for a moment, and it really was only for a moment. When he opened them he found himself alone with Lige Wigram, who lay on the ground near him.

"Maje," said Lige, "yer a good man. I've been a-follerin' ye all day an' I want to say yer a good man."

The major turned a coldly scornful eye upon the private.

"Where are you wounded? Can you walk? Well, if you can, go to the rear and leave me alone. I'm bleeding to death, and you bother me."

Lige, despite the pain in his wounded shoulder, grew indignant.

" Well," he mumbled, " you and me have been on th' outs fer a long time, an' I only wanted to tell ye that what I seen of ye t'day has made me feel mighty different."

" Go to the rear—if you can walk," said the major.

" Now, Maje, look here. A little thing like that——"

" Go to the rear."

Lige gulped with sobs.

" Maje, I know I didn't understand ye at first, but ruther'n let a little thing like that come between us, I'd—I'd——"

" Go to the rear."

In this reiteration Lige discovered a resemblance to that first old offensive phrase, " Come to attention and salute." He pondered over the resemblance and he saw that nothing had changed. The man bleeding to death was the same man to whom he had once paid a friendly visit with unfriendly results. He thought now that he perceived a certain hopeless gulf, a gulf which is real or unreal, according to circumstances. Sometimes all men are equal; occasionally they are not. If Gates had ever criticised Lige's manipulation of a hay fork on the farm at home, Lige would have furiously disdained his hate or blame.

He saw now that he must not openly approve the major's conduct in war. The major's pride was in his business, and his, Lige's congratulations, were beyond all enduring.

The place where they were lying suddenly fell under a new heavy rain of bullets. They sputtered about the men, making the noise of large grasshoppers.

"Major!" cried Lige. "Major Gates! It won't do for ye to be left here, sir. Ye'll be killed."

"But you can't help it, lad. You take care of yourself."

"I'm damned if I do," said the private, vehemently. "If I can't git *you* out, I'll stay and wait."

The officer gazed at his man with that same icy, contemptuous gaze.

"I'm—I'm a dead man anyhow. You go to the rear, do you hear?"

"No."

The dying major drew his revolver, cocked it and aimed it unsteadily at Lige's head.

"Will you obey orders?"

"No."

"One?"

"No."

" Two ? "

" No."

Gates weakly dropped his revolver.

" Go to the devil, then.   You're no soldier, but
——" He tried to add something, " But——"
He heaved a long moan.   " But—you— —you—
oh, I'm so-o-o tired."

———

V

After the battle, three correspondents happened
to meet on the trail. They were hot, dusty,
weary, hungry and thirsty, and they repaired to
the shade of a mango tree and sprawled luxu-
riously. Among them they mustered twoscore
friends who on that day had gone to the far shore
of the hereafter, but their senses were no longer
resonant. Shackles was babbling plaintively about
mint-juleps, and the others were bidding him to
have done.

" By-the-way," said one, at last, " it's too bad
about poor old Gates of the 307th. He bled to
death. His men were crazy. They were blub-
bering and cursing around there like wild people.
It seems that when they got back there to look

for him they found him just about gone, and another wounded man was trying to stop the flow
with his hat! His hat, mind you. Poor old
Gatesie!"

" Oh, no, Shackles!" said the third man of the
party. " Oh, no, you're wrong. The best mint-
juleps in the world are made right in New York,
Philadelphia or Boston. That Kentucky idea is
only a tradition."

A wounded man approached them. He had
been shot through the shoulder and his shirt had
been diagonally cut away, leaving much bare skin.
Over the bullet's point of entry there was a kind
of a white spider, shaped from pieces of adhesive
plaster. Over the point of departure there was a
bloody bulb of cotton strapped to the flesh by
other pieces of adhesive plaster. His eyes were
dreamy, wistful, sad. " Say, gents, have any of
ye got a bottle?" he asked.

A correspondent raised himself suddenly and
looked with bright eyes at the soldier.

"Well, you have got a nerve," he said grinning. " Have we got a bottle, eh! Who in
h——— do you think we are? If we had a bottle of
good licker, do you suppose we could let the
whole army drink out of it? You have too much
faith in the generosity of men, my friend !"

The soldier stared, ox-like, and finally said, "Huh?"

"I say," continued the correspondent, somewhat more loudly, "that if we had had a bottle we would have probably finished it ourselves by this time."

"But," said the other, dazed, "I *meant* an empty bottle. I didn't mean no *full* bottle."

The correspondent was humorously irascible.

"An empty bottle! You must be crazy! Who ever heard of a man looking for an empty bottle? It isn't sense! I've seen a million men looking for full bottles, but you're the first man I ever saw who insisted on the bottle's being empty. What in the world do you want it for?"

"Well, ye see, mister," explained Lige, slowly, "our major he was killed this mornin' an' we're jes' goin' to bury him, an' I thought I'd jest take a look 'round an' see if I couldn't borry an empty bottle, an' then I'd take an' write his name an' reg'ment on a paper an' put it in th' bottle an' bury it with him, so's when they come fer to dig him up sometime an' take him home, there sure wouldn't be no mistake."

"Oh!"

12

MARINES SIGNALLING UNDER FIRE
AT GUANTANAMO

THEY were four Guantanamo marines, officially known for the time as signalmen, and it was their duty to lie in the trenches of Camp McCalla, that faced the water, and, by day, signal the *Marblehead* with a flag and, by night, signal the *Marblehead* with lanterns. It was my good fortune—at that time I considered it my bad fortune, indeed —to be with them on two of the nights when a wild storm of fighting was pealing about the hill ; and, of all the actions of the war, none were so hard on the nerves, none strained courage so near the panic point, as those swift nights in Camp McCalla. With a thousand rifles rattling ; with the field-guns booming in your ears ; with the diabolic Colt automatics clacking ; with the roar of the *Marblehead* coming from the bay, and, last, with Mauser bullets sneering always in the air a few inches over one's head, and with this enduring from dusk to dawn, it is extremely doubtful it any one who was there will be able to forget it easily. The noise ; the impenetrable darkness ;

the knowledge from the sound of the bullets that the enemy was on three sides of the camp ; the infrequent bloody stumbling and death of some man with whom, perhaps, one had messed two hours previous; the weariness of the body, and the more terrible weariness of the mind, at the endlessness of the thing, made it wonderful that at least some of the men did not come out of it with their nerves hopelessly in shreds.

But, as this interesting ceremony proceeded in the darkness, it was necessary for the signal squad to coolly take and send messages. Captain Mc-Calla always participated in the defence of the camp by raking the woods on two of its sides with the guns of the *Marblehead*. Moreover, he was the senior officer present, and he wanted to know what was happening. All night long the crews of the ships in the bay would stare sleeplessly into the blackness toward the roaring hill.

The signal squad had an old cracker-box placed on top of the trench. When not signalling they hid the lanterns in this box ; but as soon as an order to send a message was received, it became necessary for one of the men to stand up and expose the lights. And then—oh, my eye—how the guerillas hidden in the gulf of night would turn loose at those yellow gleams !

Signalling in this way is done by letting one lantern remain stationary—on top of the cracker-box, in this case—and moving the other over to the left and right and so on in the regular gestures of the wig-wagging code. It is a very simple system of night communication, but one can see that it presents rare possibilities when used in front of an enemy who, a few hundred yards away, is overjoyed at sighting so definite a mark.

How, in the name of wonders, those four men at Camp McCalla were not riddled from head to foot and sent home more as repositories of Spanish ammunition than as marines is beyond all comprehension. To make a confession—when one of these men stood up to wave his lantern, I, lying in the trench, invariably rolled a little to the right or left, in order that, when he was shot, he would not fall on me. But the squad came off scathless, despite the best efforts of the most formidable corps in the Spanish army—the Escuadra de Guantanamo. That it was the most formidable corps in the Spanish army of occupation has been told me by many Spanish officers and also by General Menocal and other insurgent officers. General Menocal was Garcia's chief-of-staff when the latter was operating busily in Santiago province. The regiment was composed solely of *prac-*

ticos, or guides, who knew every shrub and tree on the ground over which they moved.

Whenever the adjutant, Lieutenant Draper, came plunging along through the darkness with an order—such as: "Ask the *Marblehead* to please shell the woods to the left"— my heart would come into my mouth, for I knew then that one of my pals was going to stand up behind the lanterns and have all Spain shoot at him.

The answer was always upon the instant:

"Yes, sir." Then the bullets began to snap, snap, snap, at his head while all the woods began to crackle like burning straw. I could lie near and watch the face of the signalman, illumed as it was by the yellow shine of lantern light, and the absence of excitement, fright, or any emotion at all on his countenance, was something to astonish all theories out of one's mind. The face was in every instance merely that of a man intent upon his business, the business of wig-wagging into the gulf of night where a light on the *Marblehead* was seen to move slowly.

These times on the hill resembled, in some days, those terrible scenes on the stage—scenes of intense gloom, blinding lightning, with a cloaked devil or assassin or other appropriate character muttering deeply amid the awful roll of the thunder-drums. It was theatric beyond words : one felt like a leaf in this booming chaos, this prolonged tragedy of the night. Amid it all one could see from time to time the yellow light on the face of a preoccupied signalman.

Possibly no man who was there ever before understood the true eloquence of the breaking of the day. We would lie staring into the east, fairly ravenous for the dawn. Utterly worn to rags, with our nerves standing on end like so many bristles, we lay and watched the east—the unspeakably obdurate and slow east. It was a wonder that the eyes of some of us did not turn to glass balls from the fixity of our gaze.

Then there would come into the sky a patch of faint blue light. It was like a piece of moonshine. Some would say it was the beginning of daybreak ; others would declare it was nothing of the kind. Men would get very disgusted with each other in these low-toned arguments held in the trenches. For my part, this development in the eastern sky destroyed many of my ideas and theories concerning the dawning of the day ; but then I had never before had occasion to give it such solemn attention.

This patch widened and whitened in about tne

speed of a man's accomplishment if he should be
in the way of painting Madison Square Garden
with a camel's hair brush. The guerillas always set
out to whoop it up about this time, because they
knew the occasion was approaching when it would
be expedient for them to elope. I, at least, always grew furious with this wretched sunrise. I
thought I could have walked around the world
in the time required for the old thing to get up
above the horizon.

One midnight, when an important message was
to be sent to the *Marblehead*, Colonel Huntington came himself to the signal place with Adju-
dant Draper and Captain McCauley, the quartermaster. When the man stood up to signal, the
colonel stood beside him. At sight of the lights,
the Spaniards performed as usual. They drove
enough bullets into that immediate vicinity to kill
all the marines in the corps.

Lieutenant Draper was agitated for his chief.
"Colonel, won't you step down, sir?"

"Why, I guess not," said the grey old veteran
in his slow, sad, always-gentle way. "I am in no
more danger than the man."

"But, sir——" began the adjutant.

"Oh, it's all right, Draper."

So the colonel and the private stood side to side

and took the heavy fire without either moving a muscle.

Day was always obliged to come at last, punctuated by a final exchange of scattering shots. And the light shone on the marines, the dumb guns, the flag. Grimy yellow face looked into grimy yellow face, and grinned with weary satisfaction. Coffee!

Usually it was impossible for many of the men to sleep at once. It always took me, for instance, some hours to get my nerves combed down. But then it was great joy to lie in the trench with the four signalmen, and understand thoroughly that that night was fully over at last, and that, although the future might have in store other bad nights, that one could never escape from the prison-house which we call the past.

At the wild little fight at Cusco there were some splendid exhibitions of wig-wagging under fire. Action began when an advanced detachment of marines under Lieutenant Lucas with the Cuban guides had reached the summit of a ridge overlooking a small valley where there was a house, a well, and a thicket of some kind of shrub with great broad, oily leaves. This thicket, which was perhaps an acre in extent, contained the guerillas. The valley was open to the sea. The distance from the top of the ridge to the thicket was barely two hundred yards.

The *Dolphin* had sailed up the coast in line with the marine advance, ready with her guns to assist in any action. Captain Elliott, who commanded the two hundred marines in this fight, suddenly called out for a signalman. He wanted a man to tell the *Dolphin* to open fire on the house and the thicket. It was a blazing, bitter hot day on top of the ridge with its shrivelled chaparral and its straight, tall cactus plants. The sky was bare and blue, and hurt like brass. In two minutes the prostrate marines were red and sweating like so many hull-buried stokers in the tropics.

Captain Elliott called out :

" Where's a signalman ? Who's a signalman here ? "

A red-headed " mick "—I think his name was Clancy—at any rate, it will do to call him Clancy —twisted his head from where he lay on his stomach pumping his Lee, and, saluting, said that he was a signalman.

There was no regulation flag with the expedition, so Clancy was obliged to tie his blue polka-dot neckerchief on the end of his rifle. It did not

make a very good flag. At first Clancy moved a
ways down the safe side of the ridge and wig-
wagged there very busily. But what with the flag
being so poor for the purpose, and the background
of ridge being so dark, those on the *Dolphin* did
not see it. So Clancy had to return to the top of
the ridge and outline himself and his flag against
the sky.

The usual thing happened. As soon as the
Spaniards caught sight of this silhouette, they let
go like mad at it. To make things more comfortable for Clancy, the situation demanded that he
face the sea and turn his back to the Spanish
bullets. This was a hard game, mark you—to
stand with the small of your back to volley firing.
Clancy thought so. Everybody thought so. We
all cleared out of his neighbourhood. If he wanted
sole possession of any particular spot on that hill,
he could have it for all we would interfere with
him.

It cannot be denied that Clancy was in a hurry.
I watched him. He was so occupied with the
bullets that snarled close to his ears that he was
obliged to repeat the letters of his message softly
to himself. It seemed an intolerable time before
the *Dolphin* answered the little signal. Meanwhile, we gazed at him, marvelling every second

that he had not yet pitched headlong. He swore
at times.

Finally the *Dolphin* replied to his frantic ges-
ticulation, and he delivered his message. As his
part of the transaction was quite finished—whoop!
—he dropped like a brick into the firing line and
began to shoot ; began to get " hunky " with all
those people who had been plugging at him.
The blue polka-dot neckerchief still fluttered from
the barrel of his rifle. I am quite certain that he
let it remain there until the end of the fight.

The shells of the *Dolphin* began to plough up the
thicket, kicking the bushes, stones, and soil into
the air as if somebody was blasting there.

Meanwhile, this force of two hundred marines
and fifty Cubans and the force of—probably—six
companies of Spanish guerillas were making such
an awful din that the distant Camp McCalla was
all alive with excitement. Colonel Huntington
sent out strong parties to critical points on the
road to facilitate, if necessary, a safe retreat, and
also sent forty men under Lieutenant Magill to
come up on the left flank of the two companies
in action under Captain Elliott. Lieutenant Magill
and his men had crowned a hill which covered entirely the flank of the fighting companies, but
when the *Dolphin* opened fire, it happened that

Magill was in the line of the shots. It became necessary to stop the *Dolphin* at once. Captain Elliott was not near Clancy at this time, and he called hurriedly for another signalman.

Sergeant Quick arose, and announced that he was a signalman. He produced from somewhere a blue polka-dot neckerchief as large as a quilt. He tied it on a long, crooked stick. Then he went to the top of the ridge, and turning his back to the Spanish fire, began to signal to the *Dolphin*. Again we gave a man sole possession of a particular part of the ridge. We didn't want it. He could have it and welcome. If the young sergeant had had the smallpox, the cholera, and the yellow fever, we could not have slid out with more celerity.

As men have said often, it seemed as if there was in this war a God of Battles who held His mighty hand before the Americans. As I looked at Sergeant Quick wig-wagging there against the sky, I would not have given a tin tobacco-tag for his life. Escape for him seemed impossible. It seemed absurd to hope that he would not be hit ; I only hoped that he would be hit just a little, little, in the arm, the shoulder, or the leg.

I watched his face, and it was as grave and serene as that of a man writing in his own library.

He was the very embodiment of tranquillity in occupation. He stood there amid the animal-like babble of the Cubans, the crack of rifles, and the whistling snarl of the bullets, and wig-wagged whatever he had to wig-wag without heeding anything but his business. There was not a single trace of nervousness or haste.

To say the least, a fight at close range is absorbing as a spectacle. No man wants to take his eyes from it until that time comes when he makes up his mind to run away. To deliberately stand up and turn your back to a battle is in itself hard work. To deliberately stand up and turn your back to a battle and hear immediate evidences of the boundless enthusiasm with which a large company of the enemy shoot at you from an adjacent thicket is, to my mind at least, a very great feat. One need not dwell upon the detail of keeping the mind carefully upon a slow spelling of an important code message.

I saw Quick betray only one sign of emotion. As he swung his clumsy flag to and fro, an end of it once caught on a cactus pillar, and he looked sharply over his shoulder to see what had it. He gave the flag an impatient jerk. He looked annoyed.

THIS MAJESTIC LIE

In the twilight, a great crowd was streaming
up the Prado in Havana. The people had been
down to the shore to laugh and twiddle their
fingers at the American blockading fleet—mere
colourless shapes on the edge of the sea. Gor-
geous challenges had been issued to the far-away
ships by little children and women while the men
laughed. Havana was happy, for it was known
that the illustrious sailor Don Patricio de Montojo
had with his fleet met the decaying ships of one
Dewey and smitten them into stuffing for a baby's
pillow. Of course the American sailors were
drunk at the time, but the American sailors were
always drunk. Newsboys galloped among the
crowd crying *La Lucha* and *La Marina*. The
papers said : " This is as we foretold. How could
it be otherwise when the cowardly Yankees met
our brave sailors?" But the tongues of the exu-
berant people ran more at large. One man said in
a loud voice : " How unfortunate it is that we still
have to buy meat in Havana when so much pork
is floating in Manila Bay!" Amid the conse-

quent laughter, another man retorted : "Oh,
never mind ! That pork in Manila is rotten. It
always was rotten." Still another man said :
" But, little friend, it would make good manure
for our fields if only we had it." And still another man said : " Ah, wait until our soldiers get
with the wives of the Americans and there will be
many little Yankees to serve hot on our tables.
The men of the *Maine* simply made our appetites
good. Never mind the pork in Manila. There
will be plenty." Women laughed ; children
laughed because their mothers laughed ; everybody laughed. And—a word with you—these
people were cackling and chuckling and insulting
their own dead, their own dead men of Spain, for
if the poor green corpses floated then in Manila
Bay they were not American corpses.

The newsboys came charging with an extra.
The inhabitants of Philadelphia had fled to the
forests because of a Spanish bombardment and
also Boston was besieged by the Apaches who
had totally invested the town. The Apache
artillery had proven singularly effective and an
American garrison had been unable to face it. In
Chicago millionaires were giving away their
palaces for two or three loaves of bread. These
despatches were from Madrid and every word was

truth, but they added little to the enthusiasm because the crowd—God help mankind—was greatly
occupied with visions of Yankee pork floating in
Manila Bay. This will be thought to be embit-
tered writing. Very well; the writer admits its
untruthfulness in one particular. It is untruthful
in that it fails to reproduce one-hundredth part
of the grossness and indecency of popular expression in Havana up to the time when the people
knew they were beaten.

There were no lights on the Prado or in other
streets because of a military order. In the slow-
moving crowd, there was a young man and an old
woman. Suddenly the young man laughed a
strange metallic laugh and spoke in English, not
cautiously. " That's damned hard to listen to."

The woman spoke quickly. " Hush, you little
idiot. Do you want to be walkin' across that
grass-plot in Cabanas with your arms tied behind
you?" Then she murmured sadly : " Johnnie, I
wonder if that's true—what they say about
Manila?"

" I don't know," said Johnnie, " but I think
they're lying."

As they crossed the Plaza, they could see that
the Café Tacon was crowded with Spanish officers
in blue and white pajama uniforms. Wine and

brandy was being wildly consumed in honour of the victory at Manila. "Let's hear what they say," said Johnnie to his companion, and they moved across the street and in under the *portales*. The owner of the Café Tacon was standing on a table making a speech amid cheers. He was advocating the crucifixion of such Americans as fell into Spanish hands and—it was all very sweet and white and tender, but above all, it was chivalrous, because it is well known that the Spaniards are a chivalrous people. It has been remarked both by the English newspapers and by the bulls that are bred for the red death. And secretly the corpses in Manila Bay mocked this jubilee ; the mocking, mocking corpses in Manila Bay.

To be blunt, Johnnie was an American spy. Once he had been the manager of a sugar plantation in Pinar del Rio, and during the insurrection it had been his distinguished function to pay tribute of money, food and forage alike to Spanish columns and insurgent bands. He was performing this straddle with benefit to his crops and with mildew to his conscience when Spain and the United States agreed to skirmish, both in the name of honour. It then became a military necessity that he should change his base. Whatever of the province that was still alive was sorry

13

to see him go for he had been a very dexterous man and food and wine had been in his house even when a man with a mango could gain the envy of an entire Spanish battalion. Without doubt he had been a mere trimmer, but it was because of his crop and he always wrote the word thus: C R O P. In those days a man of peace and commerce was in a position parallel to the watchmaker who essayed a task in the midst of a drunken brawl with oaths, bottles and bullets flying about his intent bowed head. So many of them—or all of them—were trimmers, and to any armed force they fervently said: " God assist you." And behold, the trimmers dwelt safely in a tumultuous land and without effort save that their little machines for trimming ran night and day. So many a plantation became covered with a maze of lies as if thick-webbing spiders had run from stalk to stalk in the cane. So sometimes a planter incurred an equal hatred from both sides and when in trouble there was no camp to which he could flee save, straight in air, the camp of the heavenly host.

If Johnnie had not had a crop, he would have been plainly on the side of the insurgents, but his crop staked him down to the soil at a point where the Spaniards could always be sure of finding him

—him or his crop—it is the same thing. But
when war came between Spain and the United
States he could no longer be the cleverest trimmer
in Pinar del Rio. And he retreated upon Key
West losing much of his baggage train, not because of panic but because of wisdom. In Key
West, he was no longer the manager of a big
Cuban plantation ; he was a little tan-faced refugee
without much money. Mainly he listened ; there
was nought else to do. In the first place he was
a young man of extremely slow speech and in the
Key West Hotel tongues ran like pin-wheels. If
he had projected his methodic way of thought
and speech upon this hurricane, he would have
been as effective as the man who tries to smoke
against the gale. This truth did not impress him.
Really, he was impressed with the fact that although he knew much of Cuba, he could not talk
so rapidly and wisely of it as many war-correspondents who had not yet seen the island. Usually
he brooded in silence over a bottle of beer and the
loss of his crop. He received no sympathy, although there was a plentitude of tender souls.
War's first step is to make expectation so high
that all present things are fogged and darkened
in a tense wonder of the future. None cared
about the collapse of Johnnie's plantation when

all were thinking of the probable collapse of cities and fleets.

In the meantime, battle-ships, monitors, cruisers, gunboats and torpedo craft arrived, departed, arrived, departed. Rumours sang about the ears of warships hurriedly coaling. Rumours sang about the ears of warships leisurely coming to anchor. This happened and that happened and if the news arrived at Key West as a mouse, it was often enough cabled north as an elephant. The correspondents at Key West were perfectly capable of adjusting their perspective, but many of the editors in the United States were like deaf men at whom one has to roar. A few quiet words of information was not enough for them; one had to bawl into their ears a whirlwind tale of heroism, blood, death, victory—or defeat—at any rate, a tragedy. The papers should have sent playwrights to the first part of the war. Play-wrights are allowed to lower the curtain from time to time and say to the crowd: "Mark, ye, now! Three or four months are supposed to elapse. But the poor devils at Key West were obliged to keep the curtain up all the time. "This isn't a continuous performance." "Yes, it is; it's *got* to be a continuous performance. The welfare of the paper demands it. The people want news." Very well:

continuous performance. It is strange how men
of sense can go aslant at the bidding of other men
of sense and combine to contribute to a general
mess of exaggeration and bombast. But we did;
and in the midst of the furor I remember the still
figure of Johnnie, the planter, the ex-trimmer.
He looked dazed.

This was in May.

We all liked him. From time to time some of
us heard in his words the vibrant of a thoughtful
experience. But it could not be well heard; it
was only like the sound of a bell from under the
floor. We were too busy with our own clatter.
He was taciturn and competent while we solved
the war in a babble of tongues. Soon we went
about our peaceful paths saying ironically one to
another: "War is hell." Meanwhile, managing
editors fought us tooth and nail and we all were
sent boxes of medals inscribed : " Incompetency."
We became furious with ourselves. Why couldn't
we send hair-raising despatches ? Why couldn't
we inflame the wires? All this we did. If a
first-class armoured cruiser which had once been
a tow-boat fired a six-pounder shot from her forward thirteen-inch gun turret, the world heard of
it, you bet. We were not idle men. We had
come to report the war and we did it. Our good

names and our salaries depended upon it and we
were urged by our managing-editors to remember
that the American people were a collection of
super-nervous idiots who would immediately have
convulsions if we did not throw them some news
—any news. It was not true, at all. The American people were anxious for things decisive to
happen; they were not anxious to be lulled to
satisfaction with a drug. But we lulled them.
We told them this and we told them that, and I
warrant you our screaming sounded like the noise
of a lot of sea-birds settling for the night among
the black crags.

In the meantime, Johnnie stared and meditated.
In his unhurried, unstartled manner he was singularly like another man who was flying the
pennant as commander-in-chief of the North
Atlantic Squadron. Johnnie was a refugee; the
admiral was an admiral. And yet they were much
akin, these two. Their brother was the Strategy
Board—the only capable political institution of
the war. At Key West the naval officers spoke
of their business and were devoted to it and were
bound to succeed in it, but when the flag-ship was
in port the only two people who were independent
and sane were the admiral and Johnnie. The rest
of us were lulling the public with drugs.

There was much discussion of the new batteries
at Havana. Johnnie was a typical American. In
Europe a typical American is a man with a hard
eye, chin-whiskers and a habit of speaking through
his nose. Johnnie was a young man of great
energy, ready to accomplish a colossal thing for
the basic reason that he was ignorant of its mag-
nitude. In fact he attacked all obstacles in life in
a spirit of contempt, seeing them smaller than
they were until he had actually surmounted them
—when he was likely to be immensely pleased
with himself. Somewhere in him there was a
sentimental tenderness, but it was like a light seen
afar at night ; it came, went, appeared again in a
new place, flickered, flared, went out, left you in
a void and angry. And if his sentimental tenderness was a light, the darkness in which it puzzled
you was his irony of soul. This irony was directed first at himself ; then at you ; then at the
nation and the flag ; then at God. It was a midnight in which you searched for the little elusive,
ashamed spark of tender sentiment. Sometimes,
you thought this was all pretext, the manner and
the way of fear of the wit of others; sometimes
you thought he was a hardened savage ; usually
you did not think but waited in the cheerful certainty that in time the little flare of light would
appear in the gloom.

Johnnie decided that he would go and spy upon the fortifications of Havana. If any one wished to know of those batteries it was the admiral of the squadron, but the admiral of the squadron knew much. I feel sure that he knew the size and position of every gun. To be sure, new guns might be mounted at any time, but they would not be big guns, and doubtless he lacked in his cabin less information than would be worth a man's life. Still, Johnnie decided to be a spy. He would go and look. We of the newspapers pinned him fast to the tail of our kite and he was taken to see the admiral. I judge that the admiral did not display much interest in the plan. But at any rate it seems that he touched Johnnie smartly enough with a brush to make him, officially, a spy. Then Johnnie bowed and left the cabin. There was no other machinery. If Johnnie was to end his life and leave a little book about it, no one cared—least of all, Johnnie and the admiral. When he came aboard the tug, he displayed his usual stalwart and rather selfish zest for fried eggs. It was all some kind of an ordinary matter. It was done every day. It was the business of packing pork, sewing shoes, binding hay. It was commonplace. No one could adjust it, get it in proportion, until—afterwards. On a dark night, they heaved him into a small boat and rowed him to the beach.

And one day he appeared at the door of a little lodging-house in Havana kept by Martha Clancy, born in Ireland, bred in New York, fifteen years married to a Spanish captain, and now a widow, keeping Cuban lodgers who had no money with which to pay her. She opened the door only a little way and looked down over her spectacles at him.

"Good-mornin', Martha," he said.

She looked a moment in silence. Then she made an indescribable gesture of weariness. "Come in," she said. He stepped inside. "And in God's name couldn't you keep your neck out of this rope? And so you had to come here, did you—to Havana? Upon my soul, Johnnie, my son, you are the biggest fool on two legs."

He moved past her into the court-yard and took his old chair at the table—between the winding stairway and the door—near the orange tree. "Why am I?" he demanded stoutly. She made no reply until she had taken seat in her rocking-chair and puffed several times upon a cigarette. Then through the smoke she said meditatively: "Everybody knows yc are a damned little mambi." Sometimes she spoke with an Irish accent.

He laughed. I'm no more of a mambi than *you* are, anyhow."

"I'm no mambi. But your name is poison to half the Spaniards in Havana. That you know. And if you were once safe in Cayo Hueso, 'tis nobody but a born fool who would come blunderin' into Havana again. Have ye had your dinner?"

"What have you got?" he asked before committing himself.

She arose and spoke without confidence as she moved toward the cupboard. "There's some codfish salad."

"*What?*" said he.

"Codfish salad."

"*Codfish what?*"

"Codfish salad. Ain't it good enough for ye? Maybe this is Delmonico's—no? Maybe ye never heard that the Yankees have us blockaded, hey? Maybe ye think food can be picked in the streets here now, hey? I'll tell ye one thing, my son, if you stay here long you'll see the want of it and so you had best not throw. it over your shoulder."

The spy settled determinedly in his chair and delivered himself his final decision. "That may all be true, but I'm *damned* if I eat codfish salad."

Old Martha was a picture of quaint despair.
" You'll not? "

" No! "

" Then," she sighed piously, "may the Lord
have mercy on ye, Johnnie, for you'll never do
here. 'Tis not the time for you. You're due
after the blockade. Will you do me the favour of
translating why you won't eat codfish salad, you
skinny little insurrecto? "

" Cod-fish salad! " he said with a deep sneer.
" Who ever heard of it! "

Outside, on the jumbled pavement of the street,
an occasional two-wheel cart passed with deafen-
ing thunder, making one think of the overturning
of houses. Down from the pale sky over the
patio came a heavy odour of Havana itself, a
smell of old straw. The wild cries of vendors
could be heard at intervals.

" You'll not? "

" No."

" And why not? "

" Cod-fish salad? Not by a blame sight! "

" Well—all right then. You are more of a pig-
headed young imbecile than even I thought from
seeing you come into Havana here where half the
town knows you and the poorest Spaniard would
give a gold piece to see you go into Cabanas and

forget to come out. Did I tell you, my son Alfred is sick? Yes, poor little fellow, he lies up in the room you used to have. The fever. And did you see Woodham in Key West? Heaven save us, what quick time he made in getting out. I hear Figtree and Button are working in the cable office over there—no? And when is the war going to end? Are the Yankees going to try to take Havana? It will be a hard job, Johnnie? The Spaniards say it is impossible. Everybody is laughing at the Yankees. I hate to go into the street and hear them. Is General Lee going to lead the army? What's become of Springer? I see you've got a new pair of shoes."

In the evening there was a sudden loud knock at the outer door. Martha looked at Johnnie and Johnnie looked at Martha. He was still sitting in the patio, smoking. She took the lamp and set it on a table in the little parlour. This parlour connected the street-door with the patio, and so Johnnie would be protected from the sight of the people who knocked by the broad illuminated tract. Martha moved in pensive fashion upon the latch. "Who's there?" she asked casually.

"The police." There it was, an old melodramatic incident from the stage, from the romances. One could scarce believe it. It had all the dig-

nity of a classic resurrection. "The police!"
One sneers at its probability; it is too venerable.
But so it happened.

"Who?" said Martha.

"The police!"

"What do you want here?"

"Open the door and we'll tell you."

Martha drew back the ordinary huge bolts of a
Havana house and opened the door a trifle. "Tell
me what you want and begone quickly," she said,
"for my little boy is ill of the fever——"

She could see four or five dim figures, and now
one of these suddenly placed a foot well within
the door so that she might not close it. "We
have come for Johnnie. We must search your
house."

"Johnnie? Johnnie? Who is Johnnie?" said
Martha in her best manner.

The police inspector grinned with the light upon
his face. "Don't you know Señor Johnnie from
Pinar del Rio?" he asked.

"Before the war—yes. But now—where is he
—he must be in Key West?"

"He is in your house."

"He? In my house? Do me the favour to
think that I have some intelligence. Would I be
likely to be harbouring a Yankee in these times?

You must think I have no more head than an
Orden Publico. And I'll not have you search my
house, for there is no one here save my son—who
is maybe dying of the fever—and the doctor. The
doctor is with him because now is the crisis, and
any one little thing may kill or cure my boy, and
you will do me the favour to consider what may
happen if I allow five or six heavy-footed police-
men to go tramping all over my house. You may
think——"

"Stop it," said the chief police officer at last.
He was laughing and weary and angry.

Martha checked her flow of Spanish. "There!"
she thought, "I've done my best. He ought to
fall in with it." But as the police entered she
began on them again. "You will search the house
whether I like it or no. Very well; but if anything happens to my boy? It is a nice way of
conduct, anyhow—coming into the house of a
widow at night and talking much about this Yankee
and——"

"For God's sake, señora, hold your tongue.
We——"

"Oh, yes, the señora can for God's sake very
well hold her tongue, but that wouldn't assist you
men into the street where you belong. Take
care: if my sick boy suffers from this prowling!

No, you'll find nothing in that wardrobe. And do you think he would be under the table? Don't overturn all that linen. Look you, when you go upstairs, tread lightly."

Leaving a man on guard at the street door and another in the patio, the chief policeman and the remainder of his men ascended to the gallery from which opened three sleeping-rooms. They were followed by Martha abjuring them to make no noise. The first room was empty; the second room was empty; as they approached the door of the third room, Martha whispered supplications. "Now, in the name of God, don't disturb my boy." The inspector motioned his men to pause and then he pushed open the door. Only one weak candle was burning in the room and its yellow light fell upon the bed whereon was stretched the figure of a little curly-headed boy in a white nightey. He was asleep, but his face was pink with fever and his lips were murmuring some half-coherent childish nonsense. At the head of the bed stood the motionless figure of a man. His back was to the door, but upon hearing a noise he held a solemn hand. There was an odour of medicine. Out on the balcony, Martha apparently was weeping.

The inspector hesitated for a moment; then he

noiselessly entered the room and with his yellow
cane prodded under the bed, in the cupboard and
behind the window-curtains. Nothing came of it.
He shrugged his shoulders and went out to the
balcony. He was smiling sheepishly. Evidently
he knew that he had been beaten. " Very good,
Señora," he said. " You are clever ; some day I
shall be clever, too. He shook his finger at her.
He was threatening her but he affected to be
playful. " Then—beware ! Beware ! "

Martha replied blandly, " My late husband, El
Capitan Señor Don Patricio de Castellon y Valla-
dolid was a cavalier of Spain and if he was alive
to-night he would now be cutting the ears from
the heads of you and your miserable men who
smell frightfully of cognac."

" Por Dios ! " muttered the inspector as followed
by his band he made his way down the spiral
staircase. " It is a tongue ! One vast tongue ! "
At the street-door they made ironical bows ; they
departed ; they were angry men.

Johnnie came down when he heard Martha
bolting the door behind the police. She brought
back the lamp to the table in the patio and stood
beside it, thinking. Johnnie dropped into his old
chair. The expression on the spy's face was curious ; it pictured glee, anxiety, self-complacency ;

above all it pictured self-complacency. Martha said nothing; she was still by the lamp, musing.

The long silence was suddenly broken by a tremendous guffaw from Johnnie. "Did you ever see sich a lot of fools!" He leaned his head far back and roared victorious merriment.

Martha was almost dancing in her apprehension. "Hush! Be quiet, you little demon! Hush! Do me the favour to allow them to get to the corner before you bellow like a walrus. Be quiet."

The spy ceased his laughter and spoke in indignation. "Why?" he demanded. "Ain't I got a right to laugh?"

"Not with a noise like a cow fallin' into a cucumber-frame," she answered sharply. "Do me the favour——" Then she seemed overwhelmed with a sense of the general hopelessness of Johnnie's character. She began to wag her head. "Oh, but you are the boy for gettin' yourself into the tiger's cage without even so much as the thought of a pocket-knife in your thick head. You would be a genius of the first water if you only had a little sense. And now you're here, what are you going to do?"

He grinned at her. "I'm goin' to hold an inspection of the land and sea defences of the city of Havana."

14

Martha's spectacles dropped low on her nose and, looking over the rims of them in grave meditation, she said : " If you can't put up with codfish salad you had better make short work of your inspection of the land and sea defences of the city of Havana. You are likely to starve in the meantime. A man who is particular about his food has come to the wrong town if he is in Havana now."

" No, but——" asked Johnnie seriously. " Haven't you any bread ? "

" *Bread !* "

" Well, coffee then? Coffee alone will do."

" *Coffee !* "

Johnnie arose deliberately and took his hat. Martha eyed him. " And where do you think you are goin' ? " she asked cuttingly.

Still deliberate, Johnnie moved in the direction of the street-door. " I'm goin' where I can get something to eat."

Martha sank into a chair with a moan which was a finished opinion—almost a definition—of Johnnie's behaviour in life. " And where will you go ? " she asked faintly.

" Oh, I don't know," he rejoined. " Some café. Guess I'll go to the Café Aguacate. They feed you well there. I remember——"

" *You* remember? *They* remember! They know you as well as if you were the sign over the door."

" Oh, they won't give me away," said Johnnie with stalwart confidence.

" Gi-give you away? Give you a-way?" stammered Martha.

The spy made no answer but went to the door, unbarred it and passed into the street. Martha caught her breath and ran after him and came face to face with him as he turned to shut the door. " Johnnie, if ye come back, bring a loaf of bread. I'm dyin' for one good honest bite in a slice of bread."

She heard his peculiar derisive laugh as she bolted the door. She returned to her chair in the patio. " Well, there," she said with affection, admiration and contempt. " There he goes! The most hard-headed little ignoramus in twenty nations! What does he care? Nothin'! And why is it? Pure bred-in-the-bone ignorance. Just because he can't stand codfish salad he goes out to a café! A café where they know him as if they had made him! . . . Well . . . . I won't see him again, probably. . . . But if he comes back, I hope he brings some bread. I'm near dead for it."

II

Johnnie strolled carelessly through dark narrow streets. Near every corner were two Orden Publicos—a kind of soldier-police—quiet in the shadow of some doorway, their Remingtons ready, their eyes shining. Johnnie walked past as if he owned them, and their eyes followed him with a sort of a lazy mechanical suspicion which was militant in none of its moods.

Johnnie was suffering from a desire to be splendidly imprudent. He wanted to make the situation gasp and thrill and tremble. From time to time he tried to conceive the idea of his being caught, but to save his eyes he could not imagine it. Such an event was impossible to his peculiar breed of fatalism which could not have conceded death until he had mouldered seven years.

He arrived at the Café Aguacate and found it much changed. The thick wooden shutters were up to keep light from shining into the street. Inside, there were only a few Spanish officers. Johnnie walked to the private rooms at the rear. He found an empty one and pressed the electric button. When he had passed through the main

part of the café no one had noted him. The first
to recognise him was the waiter who answered
the bell. This worthy man turned to stone
before the presence of Johnnie.

" Buenos noche, Francisco," said the spy,
enjoying himself. " I have hunger. Bring me
bread, butter, eggs and coffee." There was a
silence; the waiter did not move; Johnnie smiled
casually at him.

The man's throat moved; then like one suddenly re-endowed with life, he bolted from the
room. After a long time, he returned with the
proprietor of the place. In the wicked eye of the
latter there gleamed the light of a plan. He did
not respond to Johnnie's genial greeting, but at
once proceeded to develop his position. " Johnnie," he said, " bread is very dear in Havana. It
is very dear."

" Is it?" said Johnnie looking keenly at the
speaker. He understood at once that here was
some sort of an attack upon him.

" Yes," answered the proprietor of the Café
Aguacate slowly and softly. " It is very dear. I
think to-night one small bit of bread will cost you
one centene—in advance." A centene approxi-
mates five dollars in gold."

The spy's face did not change. He appeared

to reflect. "And how much for the butter?" he asked at last.

The proprietor gestured. "There is no butter. Do you think we can have everything with those Yankee pigs sitting out there on their ships?"

"And how much for the coffee?" asked Johnnie musingly.

Again the two men surveyed each other during a period of silence. Then the proprietor said gently, "I think your coffee will cost you about two centenes."

"And the eggs?"

"Eggs are very dear. I think eggs would cost you about three centenes for each one."

The new looked at the old; the North Atlantic looked at the Mediterranean; the wooden nutmeg looked at the olive. Johnnie slowly took six centenes from his pocket and laid them on the table. "That's for bread, coffee, and *one* egg. I don't think I could eat more than one egg to-night. I'm not so hungry as I was."

The proprietor held a perpendicular finger and tapped the table with it. "Oh, señor," he said politely, "I think you would like two eggs."

Johnnie saw the finger. He understood it. "Ye-e-es," he drawled. "I would like two eggs." He placed three more centenes on the table.

" And a little thing for the waiter ? I am sure his services will be excellent, invaluable."

" Ye-e-es, for the waiter." Another centene was laid on the table.

The proprietor bowed and preceded the waiter out of the room. There was a mirror on the wall and, springing to his feet, the spy thrust his face close to the honest glass. " Well, I'm damned ! " he ejaculated. " Is this me or is this the Honourable D. Hayseed Whiskers of Kansas ? Who am I, anyhow ? Five dollars in gold ! . . . Say, these people are clever. They know their business, they do. Bread, coffee and two eggs and not even sure of getting it ! Fifty dol— . . . Never mind ; wait until the war is over. Fifty dollars gold ! " He sat for a long time ; nothing happened. " Eh," he said at last, " that's the game." As the front door of the café closed upon him, he heard the proprietor and one of the waiters burst into derisive laughter.

Martha was waiting for him. " And here ye are, safe back," she said with delight as she let him enter. " And did ye bring the bread ? Did ye bring the bread ? "

But she saw that he was raging like a lunatic. His face was red and swollen with temper ; his eyes shot forth gleams. Presently he stood

before her in the patio where the light fell on him.
"Don't speak to me," he choked out waving his
arms. "Don't speak to me! *Damn* your bread!
I went to the Café Aguacate! Oh, yes, I went
there! Of course, I did! And do you know
what they did to me? No! Oh, they didn't do
anything to me at all! Not a thing! Fifty dollars! Ten gold pieces!"

"May the saints guard us," cried Martha. "And
what was that for?"

"Because they wanted them more than I did,"
snarled Johnnie. "Don't you see the game. I
go into the Café Aguacate. The owner of the
place says to himself, 'Hello! Here's that
Yankee what they call Johnnie. He's got no
right here in Havana. Guess I'll peach on him
to the police. They'll put him in Cabanas as a
spy.' Then he does a little more thinking, and
finally he says, 'No; I guess I won't peach on
him just this minute. First, I'll take a small
flyer myself.' So in he comes and looks me right
in the eye and says, 'Excuse me but it will be a
centene for the bread, a centene for the coffee,
and eggs are at three centenes each. Besides
there will be a small matter of another gold-piece
for the waiter.' I think this over. I think it over
hard. . . . He's clever anyhow. . . . When this

cruel war is over, I'll be after him. . . . I'm a nice secret agent of the United States government, I am. I come here to be too clever for all the Spanish police, and the first thing I do is get buncoed by a rotten, little thimble-rigger in a café. Oh, yes, I'm all right."

"May the saints guard us!" cried Martha again. "I'm old enough to be your mother, or maybe, your grandmother, and I've seen a lot; but it's many a year since I laid eyes on such a ign'rant and wrong-headed little, red Indian as ye are! Why didn't ye take my advice and stay here in the house with decency and comfort. But he must be all for doing everything high and mighty. The Café Aguacate, if ye please. No plain food for his highness. He turns up his nose at cod-fish sal——"

"Thunder and lightnin', are you going to ram that thing down my throat every two minutes, are you?" And in truth she could see that one more reference to that illustrious viand would break the back of Johnnie's gentle disposition as one breaks a twig on the knee. She shifted with Celtic ease. "Did ye bring the bread?" she asked.

He gazed at her for a moment and suddenly laughed. "I forgot to mention," he informed

her impressively, "that they did not take the
trouble to give me either the bread, the coffee or
the eggs."

"The powers!" cried Martha.

"But it's all right. I stopped at a shop."
From his pockets, he brought a small loaf, some
kind of German sausage and a flask of Jamaica
rum. "About all I could get. And they didn't
want to sell them either. They expect presently
they can exchange a box of sardines for a grand
piano."

"'We are not blockaded by the Yankee warships; we are blockaded by our grocers,'" said
Martha, quoting the epidemic Havana saying.
But she did not delay long from the little loaf.
She cut a slice from it and sat eagerly munching.
Johnnie seemed more interested in the Jamaica
rum. He looked up from his second glass, however, because he heard a peculiar sound. The old
woman was weeping. "Hey, what's this?" he
demanded in distress, but with the manner of a
man who thinks gruffness is the only thing that
will make people feel better and cease. "What's
this anyhow? What are you cryin' for?"

"It's the bread," sobbed Martha. "It's the—
the br-e-a-ddd."

"Huh? What's the matter with it?"

" It's so good, so g-good." The rain of tears
did not prevent her from continuing her unusual
report. " Oh, it's so good! This is the first in
weeks. I didn't know bread could be so l-like
heaven."

" Here," said Johnnie seriously. " Take a little
mouthful of this rum. It will do you good."

" No; I only want the bub-bub-bread."

" Well, take the bread, too. . . . There you
are. Now you feel better. . . . By Jove, when
I think of that Café Aguacate man! Fifty dollars
gold! And then not to get anything either. Say,
after the war, I'm going there, and I'm just going
to raze that place to the ground. You see! I'll
make him think he can charge ME fifteen dollars
for an egg. . . . And then not give me the egg."

III

Johnnie's subsequent activity in Havana could
truthfully be related in part to a certain temporary price of eggs. It is interesting to note how
close that famous event got to his eye so that,
according to the law of perspective, it was as big
as the Capitol of Washington, where centres the
spirit of his nation. Around him, he felt a similar

and ferocious expression of life which informed him too plainly that if he was caught, he was doomed. Neither the garrison nor the citizens of Havana would tolerate any nonsense in regard to him if he was caught. He would have the steel screw against his neck in short order. And what was the main thing to bear him up against the desire to run away before his work was done? A certain temporary price of eggs! It not only hid the Capitol at Washington; it obscured the dangers in Havana.

Something was learned of the Santa Clara battery, because one morning an old lady in black accompanied by a young man—evidently her son —visited a house which was to rent on the height, in rear of the battery. The portero was too lazy and sleepy to show them over the premises, but he granted them permission to investigate for themselves. They spent most of their time on the flat parapeted roof of the house. At length they came down and said that the place did not suit them. The portero went to sleep again.

Johnnie was never discouraged by the thought that his operations would be of small benefit to the admiral commanding the fleet in adjacent waters, and to the general commanding the army which was not going to attack Havana from the

land side. At that time it was all the world's
opinion that the army from Tampa would presently appear on the Cuban beach at some con-
venient point to the east or west of Havana. It
turned out, of course, that the condition of the
defences of Havana was of not the slightest military importance to the United States since the
city was never attacked either by land or sea.
But Johnnie could not foresee this. He continued
to take his fancy risk, continued his majestic lie,
with satisfaction, sometimes with delight, and
with pride. And in the psychologic distance was
old Martha dancing with fear and shouting:
" Oh, Johnnie, me son, what a born fool ye are ! "

Sometimes she would address him thus : " And
when ye learn all this, how are ye goin' to get out
with it ? " She was contemptuous.

He would reply, as serious as a Cossack in his
fatalism. " Oh, I'll get out some way."

His manœuvres in the vicinity of Regla and
Guanabacoa were of a brilliant character. He
haunted the sunny long grass in the manner of a
jack-rabbit. Sometimes he slept under a palm,
dreaming of the American advance fighting its
way along the military road to the foot of Spanish
defences. Even when awake, he often dreamed
it and thought of the all-day crash and hot roar

of an assault. Without consulting Washington, he had decided that Havana should be attacked from the south-east. An advance from the west could be contested right up to the bar of the Hotel Inglaterra, but when the first ridge in the south-east would be taken, the whole city with most of its defences would lie under the American siege guns. And the approach to this position was as reasonable as is any approach toward the muzzles of magazine rifles. Johnnie viewed the grassy fields always as a prospective battle-ground, and one can see him lying there, filling the landscape with visions of slow-crawling black infantry columns, galloping batteries of artillery, streaks of faint blue smoke marking the modern firing lines, clouds of dust, a vision of ten thousand tragedies. And his ears heard the noises.

But he was no idle shepherd boy with a head haunted by sombre and glorious fancies. On the contrary, he was much occupied with practical matters. Some months after the close of the war, he asked me: " Were you ever fired at from very near?" I explained some experiences which I had stupidly esteemed as having been rather near. " But did you ever have 'm fire a volley on you from close—very close—say, thirty feet?"

Highly scandalised I answered, " No; in that

case, I would not be the crowning feature of the
Smithsonian Institute."

"Well," he said, "it's a funny effect. You feel
as every hair on your head had been snatched out
by the roots." Questioned further he said, "I
walked right up on a Spanish outpost at daybreak once, and about twenty men let go at me.
Thought I was a Cuban army, I suppose."

"What did you do?"

"I run."

"Did they hit you, at all?"

"Naw."

It had been arranged that some light ship of
the squadron should rendezvous with him at a
certain lonely spot on the coast on a certain day
and hour and pick him up. He was to wave
something white. His shirt was not white, but he
waved it whenever he could see the signal-tops
of a war-ship. It was a very tattered banner.
After a ten-mile scramble through almost pathless
thickets, he had very little on him which respectable men would call a shirt, and the less one says
about his trousers the better. This naked savage,
then, walked all day up and down a small bit of
beach waving a brown rag. At night, he slept in
the sand. At full daybreak he began to wave
his rag; at noon he was waving his rag; at night-

fall he donned his rag and strove to think of it as a shirt. Thus passed two days, and nothing had happened. Then he retraced a twenty-five mile way to the house of old Martha. At first she took him to be one of Havana's terrible beggars and cried, "And do you come here for alms? Look out, that I do not beg of you." The one unchanged thing was his laugh of pure mockery. When she heard it, she dragged him through the door. He paid no heed to her ejaculations but went straight to where he had hidden some gold. As he was untying a bit of string from the neck of a small bag, he said, "How is little Alfred?" "Recovered, thank Heaven." He handed Martha a piece of gold. "Take this and buy what you can on the corner. I'm hungry." Martha departed with expedition. Upon her return, she was beaming. She had foraged a thin chicken, a bunch of radishes and two bottles of wine. Johnnie had finished the radishes and one bottle of wine when the chicken was still a long way from the table. He called stoutly for more, and so Martha passed again into the street with another gold piece. She bought more radishes, more wine and some cheese. They had a grand feast, with Johnnie audibly wondering until a late hour why he had waved his rag in vain.

There was no end to his suspense, no end to his work. He knew everything. He was an animate guide-book. After he knew a thing once, he verified it in several different ways in order to make sure. He fitted himself for a useful career, like a young man in a college—with the difference that the shadow of the garote fell ever upon his way, and that he was occasionally shot at, and that he could not get enough to eat, and that his existence was apparently forgotten, and that he contracted the fever. But——

One cannot think of the terms in which to describe a futility so vast, so colossal. He had builded a little boat, and the sea had receded and left him and his boat a thousand miles inland on the top of a mountain. The war-fate had left Havana out of its plan and thus isolated Johnnie and his several pounds of useful information. The war-fate left Havana to become the somewhat indignant victim of a peaceful occupation at the close of the conflict, and Johnnie's data were worth as much as a carpenter's lien on the north pole. He had suffered and laboured for about as complete a bit of absolute nothing as one could invent. If the company which owned the sugar plantation had not generously continued his salary during the war, he would not have been able to pay his ex-

penses on the amount allowed him by the government, which, by the way, was a more complete
bit of absolute nothing than one could possibly
invent.

IV

I met Johnnie in Havana in October, 1898. If
I remember rightly the U. S. S. *Resolute* and the
U. S. S. *Scorpion* were in the harbour, but beyond
these two terrible engines of destruction there were
not as yet any of the more stern signs of the
American success. Many Americans were to be
seen in the streets of Havana where they were not
in any way molested. Among them was Johnnie
in white duck and a straw hat, cool, complacent
and with eyes rather more steady than ever. I
addressed him upon the subject of his supreme
failure, but I could not perturb his philosophy. In
reply he simply asked me to dinner. " Come to
the Café Aguacate at 7:30 to-night," he said. " I
haven't been there in a long time. We shall see
if they cook as well as ever." I turned up
promptly and found Johnnie in a private room
smoking a cigar in the presence of a waiter who
was blue in the gills. " I've ordered the dinner,"

he said cheerfully. " Now I want to see if you won't be surprised how well they can do here in Havana." I was surprised. I was dumfounded. Rarely in the history of the world have two rational men sat down to such a dinner. It must have taxed the ability and endurance of the entire working force of the establishment to provide it. The variety of dishes was of course related to the markets of Havana, but the abundance and general profligacy was related only to Johnnie's imagination. Neither of us had an appetite. Our fancies fled in confusion before this puzzling luxury. I looked at Johnnie as if he were a native of Thibet. I had thought him to be a most simple man, and here I found him revelling in food like a fat, old senator of Rome's decadence. And if the dinner itself put me to open-eyed amazement, the names of the wines finished everything. Apparently Johnny had had but one standard, and that was the cost. If a wine had been very expensive, he had ordered it. I began to think him probably a maniac. At any rate, I was sure that we were both fools. Seeing my fixed stare, he spoke with affected languor : " I wish peacocks' brains and melted pearls were to be had here in Havana. We'd have 'em." Then he grinned. As a mere skirmisher I said, " In New York, we think we

dine well; but really this, you know—well—
Havana——"

Johnnie waved his hand pompously. " Oh, I
know."

Directly after coffee, Johnnie excused himself
for a moment and left the room. When he returned he said briskly, " Well, are you ready to
go?" As soon as we were in a cab and safely out
of hearing of the Café Aguacate, Johnnie lay back
and laughed long and joyously.

But I was very serious. " Look here, Johnnie,"
I said to him solemnly, " when you invite me to
dine with you, don't you ever do *that* again. And
I'll tell you one thing—when you dine with me
you will probably get the ordinary table d'hôte."
I was an older man.

" Oh, that's all right," he cried. And then he
too grew serious. " Well, as far as I am concerned
—as far as I am concerned," he said, " the war is
now over."

WAR MEMORIES

"BUT to get the real thing!" cried Vernall, the war-correspondent. "It seems impossible! It is because war is neither magnificent nor squalid; it is simply life, and an expression of life can always evade us. We can never tell life, one to another, although sometimes we think we can."

When I climbed aboard the despatch-boat at Key West, the mate told me irritably that as soon as we crossed the bar, we would find ourselves monkey-climbing over heavy seas. It wasn't my fault, but he seemed to insinuate that it was all a result of my incapacity. There were four correspondents in the party. The leader of us came aboard with a huge bunch of bananas, which he hung like a chandelier in the centre of the tiny cabin. We made acquaintance over, around, and under this bunch of bananas, which really occupied the cabin as a soldier occupies a sentry box. But the bunch did not become really aggressive until we were well at sea. Then it began to spar.

With the first roll of the ship, it launched its honest pounds at McCurdy and knocked him wildly through the door to the deck-rail, where he hung cursing hysterically. Without a moment's pause, it made for me. I flung myself head-first into my bunk and watched the demon sweep Brownlow into a corner and wedge his knee behind a sea-chest. Kary gave a shrill cry and fled. The bunch of bananas swung to and fro, silent, determined, ferocious, looking for more men. It had cleared a space for itself. My comrades looked in at the door, calling upon me to grab the thing and hold it. I pointed out to them the security and comfort of my position. They were angry. Finally the mate came and lashed the thing so that it could not prowl about the cabin and assault innocent war-correspondents. You see? War! A bunch of bananas rampant because the ship rolled.

In that early period of the war we were forced to continue our dreams. And we were all dreamers, envisioning the seas with death grapples, ship and ship. Even the navy grew cynical. Officers on the bridge lifted their megaphones and told you in resigned voices that they were out of ice, onions, and eggs. At other times, they would shoot quite casually at us with six-pounders. This

industry usually progressed in the night, but it
sometimes happened in the day. There was never
any resentment on our side, although at moments
there was some nervousness. They were impressively quick with their lanyards; our means of
replying to signals were correspondingly slow.
They gave you opportunity to say, " Heaven guard
me!" Then they shot. But we recognised the
propriety of it. Everything was correct save the
war, which lagged and lagged and lagged. It did
not play; it was not a gory giant; it was a bunch
of bananas swung in the middle of the cabin.

Once we had the honour of being rammed at
midnight by the U. S. S. *Machias.* In fact the exceeding industry of the naval commanders of the
Cuban blockading fleet caused a certain liveliness
to at times penetrate our mediocre existence.
We were all greatly entertained over an immediate
prospect of being either killed by rapid fire guns,
cut in half by the ram or merely drowned, but
even our great longing for diversion could not
cause us to ever again go near the *Machias* on a
dark night. We had sailed from Key West on a
mission that had nothing to do with the coast of
Cuba, and steaming due east and some thirty-
five miles from the Cuban land, we did not think
we were liable to an affair with any of the fierce

American cruisers. Suddenly a familiar signal of red and white lights flashed like a brooch of jewels on the pall that covered the sea. It was far away and tiny, but we knew all about it. It was the electric question of an American war-ship and it demanded a swift answer in kind. The man behind the gun! What about the man in front of the gun? The war-ship signals vanished and the sea presented nothing but a smoky black stretch lit with the hissing white tops of the flying waves. A thin line of flame swept from a gun.

Thereafter followed one of those silences which had become so peculiarly instructive to the blockade-runner. Somewhere in the darkness we knew that a slate-coloured cruiser, red below the water-line and with a gold scroll on her bows, was flying over the waves toward us, while upon the dark decks the men stood at general quarters in silence about the long thin guns, and it was the law of life and death that we should make true answer in about the twelfth part of a second. Now I shall with regret disclose a certain dreadful secret of the despatch-boat service. Our signals, far from being electric, were two lanterns which we kept in a tub and covered with a tarpaulin. The tub was placed just forward of the pilot-house, and when we were accosted at night it was everybody's duty to scramble wildly for the tub and grab out the lanterns and wave them. It amounted to a slowness of speech. I remember a story of an army sentry who upon hearing a noise in his front one dark night called his usual sharp query. " Halt—who's there? Halt or I'll fire!" And getting no immediate response he fired even as he had said, killing a man with a hair-lip who unfortunately could not arrange his vocal machinery to reply in season. We were something like a boat with a hair-lip. And sometimes it was very trying to the nerves. . . . The pause was long. Then a voice spoke from the sea through a megaphone. It was faint but clear. "What ship is that?" No one hesitated over his answer in cases of this kind. Everybody was desirous of imparting fullest information. There was another pause. Then out of the darkness flew an American cruiser, silent as death, handled as ferociously as if the devil commanded her. Again the little voice hailed from the bridge. "What ship is that?" Evidently the reply to the first hail had been misunderstood or not heard. This time the voice rang with menace, menace of immediate and certain destruction, and the last word was intoned savagely and **strangely across the windy darkness as if the** officer would explain that the cruiser was after either fools or the common enemy. The yells in return did not stop her. She was hurling herself forward to ram us amidships, and the people on the little *Three Friends* looked at a tall swooping bow, and it was keener than any knife that has ever been made. As the cruiser lunged every man imagined the gallant and famous but frail *Three Friends* cut into two parts as neatly as if she had been cheese. But there was a sheer and a hard sheer to starboard, and down upon our quarter swung a monstrous thing larger than any ship in the world—the U. S. S. *Machias.* She had a freeboard of about three hundred feet and the top of her funnel was out of sight in the clouds like an Alp. I shouldn't wonder that at the top of that funnel there was a region of perpetual snow. And at a range which swiftly narrowed to nothing every gun in her port-battery swung deliberately into aim. It was closer, more deliciously intimate than a duel across a handkerchief. We all had an opportunity of looking miles down the muzzles of this festive artillery before came the collision. Then the *Machias* reeled her steel shoulder against the wooden side of the *Three Friends* and up went a roar as if a vast shingle roof had fallen. The poor little tug dipped as if she meant to pass under the war-ship, staggered and finally righted, trembling from head to foot. The cries of the splintered timbers ceased. The men on the tug gazed at each other with white faces shining faintly in the darkness. The *Machias* backed away even as the *Three Friends* drew slowly ahead, and again we were alone with the piping of the wind and the slash of the gale-driven water. Later, from some hidden part of the sea, the bullish eye of a search-light looked at us and the widening white rays bathed us in the glare. There was another hail. "Hello there, *Three Friends!*" "Ay, ay, sir!" "Are you injured?" Our first mate had taken a lantern and was studying the side of the tug, and we held our breath for his answer. I was sure that he was going to say that we were sinking. Surely there could be no other ending to this terrific bloodthirsty assault. But the first mate said, "No, sir." Instantly the glare of the search-light was gone; the *Machias* was gone; the incident was closed.

I was dining once on board the flag-ship, the *New York*, armoured cruiser. It was the junior officers' mess, and when the coffee came, a young ensign went to the piano and began to bang out a popular tune. It was a cheerful scene, and it resembled only a cheerful scene. Suddenly we heard the whistle of the bos'n's mate, and directly above us, it seemed, a voice, hoarse as that of a sea-lion, bellowed a command: "Man the port battery." In a moment the table was vacant; the popular tune ceased in a jangle. On the quar ter-deck assembled a group of officers—spectators. The quiet evening sea, lit with faint red lights, went peacefully to the feet of a verdant shore. One could hear the far-away measured tumbling of surf upon a reef. Only this sound pulsed in the air. The great grey cruiser was as still as the earth, the sea, and the sky. Then they let off a four-inch.gun directly under my feet. I thought it turned me a back-somersault. That was the effect upon my mind. But it appears I did not move. The shell went carousing off to the Cuban shore, and from the vegetation there spirted a cloud of dust. Some of the officers on the quarter-deck laughed. Through their glasses they had seen a Spanish column of cavalry much agitated by the appearance of this shell among them. As far as I was concerned, there was nothing but the spirt of dust from the side of a long-suffering island. When I returned to my coffee I found that most of the young officers had also returned. Japanese boys were bringing liquors.

The piano's clattering of the popular air was often interrupted by the boom of a four-inch gun. A bunch of bananas!

One day, our despatch-boat found the shores of Guantanamo Bay flowing past on either side. It was at nightfall and on the eastward point a small village was burning, and it happened that a fiery light was thrown upon some palm-trees so that it made them into enormous crimson feathers. The water was the colour of blue steel; the Cuban woods were sombre; high shivered the gory feathers. The last boatloads of the marine battalion were pulling for the beach. The marine officers gave me generous hospitality to the camp on the hill. That night there was an alarm and amid a stern calling of orders and a rushing of men, I wandered in search of some other man who had no occupation. It turned out to be the young assistant surgeon, Gibbs. We foregathered in the centre of a square of six companies of marines. There was no firing. We thought it rather comic. The next night there was an alarm; there was some firing; we lay on our bellies; it was no longer comic. On the third night the alarm came early; I went in search of Gibbs, but I soon gave over an active search for the more congenial occupation of lying flat and feeling the

hot hiss of the bullets trying to cut my hair. For
the moment I was no longer a cynic. I was a
child who, in a fit of ignorance, had jumped into
the vat of war. I heard somebody dying near
me. He was dying hard. Hard. It took him a
long time to die. He breathed as all noble machinery breathes when it is making its gallant
strife against breaking, breaking. But he was
going to break. He was going to break. It
seemed to me, this breathing, the noise of a heroic
pump which strives to subdue a mud which comes
upon it in tons. The darkness was impenetrable.
The man was lying in some depression within
seven feet of me. Every wave, vibration, of his
anguish beat upon my senses. He was long past
groaning. There was only the bitter strife for air
which pulsed out into the night in a clear penetrating whistle with intervals of terrible silence in
which I held my own breath in the common un-
conscious aspiration to help. I thought this man
would never die. I wanted him to die. Ultimately he died. At the moment the adjutant
came bustling along erect amid the spitting bullets. I knew him by his voice. " Where's the
doctor? There's some wounded men over there.
Where's the doctor?" A man answered briskly :
" Just died this minute, sir." It was as if he had

said : " Just gone around the corner this minute, sir." Despite the horror of this night's business, the man's mind was somehow influenced by the coincidence of the adjutant's calling aloud for the doctor within a few seconds of the doctor's death. It—what shall I say? It interested him, this coincidence.

The day broke by inches, with an obvious and maddening reluctance. From some unfathomable source I procured an opinion that my friend was not dead at all—the wild and quivering darkness had caused me to misinterpret a few shouted words. At length the land brightened in a violent atmosphere, the perfect dawning of a tropic day, and in this light I saw a clump of men near me. At first I thought they were all dead. Then I thought they were all asleep. The truth was that a group of wan-faced, exhausted men had gone to sleep about Gibbs' body so closely and in such abandoned attitudes that one's eye could not pick the living from the dead until one saw that a certain head had beneath it a great dark pool.

In the afternoon a lot of men went bathing, and in the midst of this festivity firing was resumed. It was funny to see the men come scampering out of the water, grab at their rifles and go into action attired in nought but their cartridge-belts. The

attack of the Spaniards had interrupted in some
degree the services over the graves of Gibbs and
some others. I remember Paine came ashore
with a bottle of whisky which I took from him
violently. My faithful shooting boots began to
hurt me, and I went to the beach and poulticed
my feet in wet clay, sitting on the little rickety
pier near where the corrugated iron cable-station
showed how the shells slivered through it. Some
marines, desirous of mementoes, were poking
with sticks in the smoking ruins of the hamlet.
Down in the shallow water crabs were meander-
ing among the weeds, and little fishes moved
slowly in schools.

The next day we went shooting. It was exactly
like quail shooting. I'll tell you. These guerillas who so cursed our lives had a well some five
miles away, and it was the only water supply
within about twelve miles of the marine camp. It
was decided that it would be correct to go forth
and destroy the well. Captain Elliott, of C company, was to take his men with Captain Spicer's
company, D, out to the well, beat the enemy
away and destroy everything. He was to start
at the next daybreak. He asked me if I cared to
go, and, of course, I accepted with glee ; but all
that night I was afraid. Bitterly afraid. The

moon was very bright, shedding a magnificent radiance upon the trenches. I watched the men of C and D companies lying so tranquilly—some snoring, confound them—whereas I was certain that I could never sleep with the.weight of a coming battle upon my mind, a battle in which the poor life of a war-correspondent might easily be taken by a careless enemy. But if I was frightened I was also very cold. It was a chill night and I wanted a heavy top-coat almost as much as I wanted a certificate of immunity from rifle bullets. These two feelings were of equal importance to my mind. They were twins. Elliott came and flung a tent-fly over Lieutenant Bannon and me as we lay on the ground back of the men. Then I was no longer cold, but I was still afraid, for tent-flies cannot mend a fear. In the morning I wished for some mild attack of disease, something that would incapacitate me for the business of going out gratuitously to be bombarded. But I was in an awkwardly healthy state, and so I must needs smile and look pleased with my prospects. We were to be guided by fifty Cubans, and I gave up all dreams of a postponement when I saw them shambling off in single file through the cactus. We followed presently. " Where you people goin' to?" " Don't know,

16

Jim." "Well, good luck to you, boys." This
was the world's lazy inquiry and conventional
God-speed. Then the mysterious wilderness
swallowed us.

The men were silent because they were ordered
to be silent, but whatever faces I could observe
were marked with a look of serious meditation.
As they trudged slowly in single file they were
reflecting upon—what? I don't know. But at
length we came to ground more open. The sea
appeared on our right, and we saw the gunboat
Dolphin steaming along in a line parallel to ours.
I was as glad to see her as if she had called out
my name. The trail wound about the bases of
some high bare spurs. If the Spaniards had occupied them I don't see how we could have gone
further. But upon them were only the dove-
voiced guerilla scouts calling back into the hills
the news of our approach. The effect of sound is
of course relative. I am sure I have never heard
such a horrible sound as the beautiful cooing of
the wood-dove when I was certain that it came
from the yellow throat of a guerilla. Elliott sent
Lieutenant Lucas with his platoon to ascend the
hills and cover our advance by the trail. We
halted and watched them climb, a long black
streak of men in the vivid sunshine of the hill-

side. We did not know how tall were these hills until we saw Lucas and his men on top, and they were no larger than specks. We marched on until, at last, we heard—it seemed in the sky— the sputter of firing. This devil's dance was begun. The proper strategic movement to cover the crisis seemed to me to be to run away home and swear I had never started on this expedition. But Elliott yelled : " Now, men ; straight up this hill." The men charged up against the cactus, and, because I cared for the opinion of others, I found myself tagging along close at Elliott's heels. I don't know how I got up that hill, but I think it was because I was afraid to be left behind. The immediate rear did not look safe. The crowd of strong young marines afforded the only spectacle of provisional security. So I tagged along at Elliott's heels. The hill was as steep as a Swiss roof. From it sprang out great pillars of cactus, and the human instinct was to assist one's self in the ascent by grasping cactus with one's hands. I remember the watch I had to keep upon this human instinct even when the sound of the bullets was attracting my nervous attention. However, the attractive thing to my sense at the time was the fact that every man of the marines was also climbing away like mad. It was one thing for

Elliott, Spicer, Neville, Shaw and Bannon ; it was another thing for me ; but—what in the devil was it to the men ? Not the same thing surely. It was perfectly easy for any marine to get overcome by the burning heat and, lying down, bequeath the work and the danger to his comrades. The fine thing about " the men " is that you can't explain them. I mean when you take them collectively. They do a thing, and afterward you find that they have done it because they have done it. However, when Elliott arrived at the top of the ridge, myself and many other men were with him. But there was no battle scene. Off on another ridge we could see Lucas' men and the Cubans peppering away into a valley. The bullets about our ears were really intended to lodge in them. We went over there.

I walked along the firing line and looked at the men. I kept somewhat on what I shall call the *lee* side of the ridge. Why ? Because I was afraid of being shot. No other reason. Most of the men as they lay flat, shooting, looked contented, almost happy. They were pleased, these men, at the situation. I don't know. I cannot imagine. But they were pleased, at any rate. I wasn't pleased. I was picturing defeat. I was saying to myself :—" Now if the enemy should suddenly do so-and-so, or so-and-so, why—what would become of me?" During these first few moments I did not see the Spanish position because—I was afraid to look at it. Bullets were hissing and spitting over the crest of the ridge in such showers as to make observation to be a task for a brave man. No, now, look here, why the deuce should I have stuck my head up, eh? Why? Well, at any rate, I didn't until it seemed to be a far less thing than most of the men were doing as if they liked it. Then I saw nothing. At least it was only the bottom of a small valley. In this valley there was a thicket—a big thicket—and this thicket seemed to be crowded with a mysterious class of persons who were evidently trying to kill us. Our enemies? Yes—perhaps—I suppose so. Leave that to the people in the streets at home. They know and cry against the public enemy, but when men go into actual battle not one in a thousand concerns himself with an animus against the men who face him. The great desire is to beat them—beat them whoever they are as a matter, first, of personal safety, second, of personal glory. It is always safest to make the other chap quickly run away. And as he runs away, one feels, as one tries to hit him in the back and knock him sprawling, that he must be a very good

and sensible fellow. But these people apparently
did not mean to run away. They clung to their
thicket and, amid the roar of the firing, one could
sometimes hear their wild yells of insult and defiance. They were actually the most obstinate,
headstrong, mulish people that you could ever imagine. The *Dolphin* was throwing shells into their
immediate vicinity and the fire from the marines
and Cubans was very rapid and heavy, but still
those incomprehensible mortals remained in their
thicket. The scene on the top of the ridge was
very wild, but there was only one truly romantic
figure. This was a Cuban officer who held in one
hand a great glittering machete and in the other
a cocked revolver. He posed like a statue of
victory. Afterwards he confessed to me that he
alone had been responsible for the winning of the
fight. But outside of this splendid person it was
simply a picture of men at work, men terribly
hard at work, red-faced, sweating, gasping toilers.
A Cuban negro soldier was shot though the
heart and one man took the body on his back and
another took it by its feet and trundled away toward the rear looking precisely like a wheel-
barrow. A man in C company was shot through
the ankle and he sat behind the line nursing his
wound. Apparently he was pleased with it. It

seemed to suit him. I don't know why. But beside him sat a comrade with a face drawn, solemn and responsible like that of a New England spinster at the bedside of a sick child.

The fight banged away with a roar like a forest fire. Suddenly a marine wriggled out of the firing line and came frantically to me. "Say, young feller, I'll give you five dollars for a drink of whisky." He tried to force into my hand a gold piece. "Go to the devil," said I, deeply scandalised. "Besides, I haven't got any whisky," "No, but look here," he beseeched me. "If I don't get a drink I'll die. And I'll give you five dollars for it. Honest, I will." I finally tried to escape from him by walking away, but he followed at my heels, importuning me with all the exasperating persistence of a professional beggar and trying to force this ghastly gold piece into my hand. I could not shake him off, and amid that clatter of furious fighting I found myself intensely embarrassed, and glancing fearfully this way and that way to make sure that people did not see me, the villain and his gold. In vain I assured him that if I had any whisky I should place it at his disposal. He could not be turned away. I thought of the European expedient in such a crisis—to jump in a cab. But unfortunately—— In the

meantime I had given up my occupation of tagging at Captain Elliott's heels, because his business
required that he should go into places of great
danger. But from time to time I was under his
attention. Once he turned to me and said : " Mr.
Vernall, will you go and satisfy yourself who those
people are ? " Some men had appeared on a hill
about six hundred yards from our left flank.
" Yes, sir," cried I with, I assure you, the finest
alacrity and cheerfulness, and my tone proved to
me that I had inherited histrionic abilities. This
tone was of course a black lie, but I went off
briskly and was as jaunty as a real soldier while
all the time my heart was in my boots and I was
cursing the day that saw me landed on the shores
of the tragic isle. If the men on the distant hill
had been guerillas, my future might have been
seriously jeopardised, but I had not gone far toward
them when I was able to recognise the uniforms
of the marine corps. Whereupon I scampered
back to the firing line and with the same alacrity
and cheerfulness reported my information. I
mention to you that I was afraid, because there
were about me that day many men who did not
seem to be afraid at all, men with quiet, composed
faces who went about this business as if they proceeded from a sense of habit. They were not old

soldiers ; they were mainly recruits, but many of them betrayed all the emotion and merely the emotion that one sees in the face of a man earnestly at work.

I don't know how long the action lasted. I remember deciding in my own mind that the Spaniards stood forty minutes. This was a mere arbitrary decision based on nothing. But at any rate we finally arrived at the satisfactory moment when the enemy began to run away. I shall never forget how my courage increased. And then began the great bird shooting. From the far side of the thicket arose an easy slope covered with plum-coloured bush. The Spaniards broke in coveys of from six to fifteen men—or birds—and swarmed up this slope. The marines on our ridge then had some fine, open field shooting. No charge could be made because the shells from the *Dolphin* were helping the Spaniards to evacuate the thicket, so the marines had to be content with this extraordinary paraphrase of a kind of sport. It was strangely like the original. The shells from the *Dolphin* were the dogs; dogs who went in and stirred out the game. The marines were suddenly gentlemen in leggings, alive with the sharp instinct which marks the hunter. The Spaniards were the birds. Yes, they were the birds, but I doubt if they would sympathise with my metaphors.

We destroyed their camp, and when the tiled roof of a burning house fell with a crash it was so like the crash of a strong volley of musketry that we all turned with a start, fearing that we would have to fight again on that same day. And this struck me at least as being an impossible thing. They gave us water from the *Dolphin* and we filled our canteens. None of the men were particularly jubilant. They did not altogether appreciate their victory. They were occupied in being glad that the fight was over. I discovered to my amazement that we were on the summit of a hill so high that our released eyes seemed to sweep over half the world. The vast stretch of sea shimmering like fragile blue silk in the breeze, lost itself ultimately in an indefinite pink haze, while in the other direction, ridge after ridge, ridge after ridge, rolled brown and arid into the north. The battle had been fought high in the air—where the rain clouds might have been. That is why everybody's face was the colour of beetroot and men lay on the ground and only swore feebly when the cactus spurs sank into them.

Finally we started for camp. Leaving our wounded, our cactus pincushions, and our heat-

prostrated men on board the *Dolphin*. I did not
see that the men were elate or even grinning with
satisfaction. They seemed only anxious to get to
food and rest. And yet it was plain that Elliott
and his men had performed a service that would
prove invaluable to the security and comfort of
the entire battalion. They had driven the guerillas to take a road along which they would have
to proceed for fifteen miles before they could get
as much water as would wet the point of a pin.
And by the destruction of a well at the scene of
the fight, Elliott made an arid zone almost twenty
miles wide between the enemy and the base camp.
In Cuba this is the best of protections. However,
a cup of coffee! Time enough to think of a brilliant success after one had had a cup of coffee.
The long line plodded wearily through the dusky
jungle which was never again to be alive with
ambushes.

It was dark when we stumbled into camp, and
I was sad with an ungovernable sadness, because
I was too tired to remember where I had left my
kit. But some of my colleagues were waiting on
the beach, and they put me on a despatch-boat to
take my news to a Jamaica cable-station. The
appearance of this despatch-boat struck me with
wonder. It was reminiscent of something with

which I had been familiar in early years. I looked
with dull surprise at three men of the engine-room
force, who sat aft on some bags of coal smoking
their pipes and talking as if there had never been
any battles fought anywhere. The sudden clang
of the gong made me start and listen eagerly, as
if I would be asking: "What was that?" The
chunking of the screw affected me also, but I
seemed to relate it to a former and pleasing experience. One of the correspondents on board
immediately began to tell me of the chief engineer,
who, he said, was a comic old character. I was
taken to see this marvel, which presented itself as
a gray-bearded man with an oil can, who had the
cynical, malicious, egotistic eye of proclaimed and
admired ignorance. I looked dazedly at the venerable impostor. What had he to do with battles
—the humming click of the locks, the odour of
burnt cotton, the bullets, the firing? My friend
told the scoundrel that I was just returned from
the afternoon's action. He said: "That so?"
And looked at me with a smile, faintly, faintly
derisive. You see? I had just come out of my
life's most fiery time, and that old devil looked at
me with that smile. What colossal conceit. The
four-times-damned doddering old head-mechanic
of a derelict junk shop. The whole trouble lay in

the fact that I had not shouted out with mingled
awe and joy as he stood there in his wisdom and
experience, with all his ancient saws and home-
made epigrams ready to fire.

My friend took me to the cabin. What a
squalid hole! My heart sank. The reward after
the labour should have been a great airy chamber,
a gigantic four-poster, iced melons, grilled birds,
wine, and the delighted attendance of my friends.
When I had finished my cablegram, I retired to a
little shelf of a berth, which reeked of oil, while
the blankets had soaked recently with sea-water.
The vessel heeled to leaward in spasmodic attempts to hurl me out, and I resisted with the last
of my strength. The infamous pettiness of it all!
I thought the night would never end. "But never
mind," I said to myself at last, "to-morrow in
Fort Antonio I shall have a great bath and fine
raiment, and I shall dine grandly and there will be
lager beer on ice. And there will be attendants
to run when I touch a bell, and I shall catch every
interested romantist in the town, and spin him the
story of the fight at Cusco." We reached Fort
Antonio and I fled from the cable office to the
hotel. I procured the bath and, as I donned whatever fine raiment I had foraged, I called the boy
and pompously told him of a dinner—a real dinner,

with furbelows and complications, and yet with a
basis of sincerity. He looked at me calf-like for
a moment, and then he went away. After a long
interval, the manager himself appeared and asked
me some questions which led me to see that he
thought I had attempted to undermine and dis-
integrate the intellect of the boy, by the elocution
of Arabic incantations. Well, never mind. In
the end, the manager of the hotel elicited from
me that great cry, that cry which during the war,
rang piteously from thousands of throats, that
last grand cry of anguish and despair : " *Well, then,
in the name of God, can I have a cold bottle of
beer ?* "

Well, you see to what war brings men ? War
is death, and a plague of the lack of small things,
and toil. Nor did I catch my sentimentalists and
pour forth my tale to them, and thrill, appal,
and fascinate them. However, they did feel an
interest in me, for I heard a lady at the hotel ask :
" Who *is* that chap in the very dirty jack-boots ? "
So you see, that whereas you can be very much
frightened upon going into action, you can also
be greatly annoyed after you have come out.

Later, I fell into the hands of one of my closest
friends, and he mercilessly outlined a scheme for
landing to the west of Santiago and getting

through the Spanish lines to some place from which
we could view the Spanish squadron lying in the
harbour.   There was rumour that the *Viscaya* had
escaped, he said, and it would be very nice to
make sure of the truth.   So we steamed to a
point opposite a Cuban camp which my friend
knew, and flung two crop-tailed Jamaica polo ponies into the sea.   We followed in a small boat
and were met on the beach by a small Cuban detachment who immediately caught our ponies and
saddled them for us.   I suppose we felt rather
god-like.   We were almost the first Americans
they had seen and they looked at us with eyes of
grateful affection.   I don't suppose many men
have the experience of being looked at with eyes
of grateful affection.   They guide us to a Cuban
camp where, in a little palm-bark hut, a black-
faced lieutenant-colonel was lolling in a hammock.   I couldn't understand what was said, but
at any rate he must have ordered his half-naked
orderly to make coffee, for it was done.   It was a
dark syrup in smoky tin-cups, but it was better
than the cold bottle of beer which I did not drink
in Jamaica.

The Cuban camp was an expeditious affair of
saplings and palm-bark tied with creepers.   It
could be burned to the ground in fifteen minutes

and in ten reduplicated. The soldiers were in appearance an absolutely good-natured set of half-
starved ragamuffins. Their breeches hung in
threads about their black legs and their shirts
were as nothing. They looked like a collection
of real tropic savages at whom some philanthropist
had flung a bundle of rags and some of the rags
had stuck here and there. But their condition
was now a habit. I doubt if they knew they
were half-naked. Anyhow they didn't care. No
more they should ; the weather was warm. This
lieutenant-colonel gave us an escort of five or six
men and we went up into the mountains, lying
flat on our Jamaica ponies while they went like
rats up and down extraordinary trails. In the
evening we reached the camp of a major who
commanded the outposts. It was high, high in
the hills. The stars were as big as cocoanuts.
We lay in borrowed hammocks and watched the
firelight gleam blood-red on the trees. I remember an utterly naked negro squatting, crimson, by
the fire and cleaning an iron-pot. Some voices
were singing an Afric wail of forsaken love and
death. And at dawn we were to try to steal
through the Spanish lines. I was very, very sorry.

In the cold dawn the situation was the same,
but somehow courage seemed to be in the break-

ing day. I went off with the others quite cheerfully. We came to where the pickets stood behind bulwarks of stone in frameworks of saplings.
They were peering across a narrow cloud-steeped
gulch at a dull fire marking a Spanish post.
There was some palaver and then, with fifteen
men, we descended the side of this mountain,
going down into the chill blue-and-grey clouds.
We had left our horses with the Cuban pickets.
We proceeded stealthily, for we were already
within range of the Spanish pickets. At the
bottom of the cañon it was still night. A brook,
a regular salmon-stream, brawled over the rocks.
There were grassy banks and most delightful trees.
The whole valley was a sylvan fragrance. But—
the guide waved his arm and scowled warningly,
and in a moment we were off, threading thickets,
climbing hills, crawling through fields on our
hands and knees, sometimes sweeping like seven-
teen phantoms across a Spanish road. I was in a
dream, but I kept my eye on the guide and halted
to listen when he halted to listen and ambled onward when he ambled onward. Sometimes he
turned and pantomimed as ably and fiercely as a
man being stung by a thousand hornets. Then
we knew that the situation was extremely delicate.
We were now of course well inside the Spanish

18

lines and we ascended a great hill which over-
looked the harbour of Santiago. There, tranquilly
at anchor, lay the *Oquendo*, the *Maria Theresa*,
the *Christobal Colon*, the *Viscaya*, the *Pluton*, the
Furor. The bay was white in the sun and the
great blacked-hull armoured cruisers were impressive in a dignity massive yet graceful. We did
not know that they were all doomed ships, soon
to go out to a swift death. My friend drew maps
and things while I devoted myself to complete
rest, blinking lazily at the Spanish squadron. We
did not know that we were the last Americans to
view them alive and unhurt and at peace. Then
we retraced our way, at the same noiseless canter.
I did not understand my condition until I considered that we were well through the Spanish
lines and practically out of danger. Then I discovered that I was a dead man. The nervous
force having evaporated I was a mere corpse.
My limbs were of dough and my spinal cord
burned within me as if it were red-hot wire. But
just at this time we were discovered by a Spanish
patrol, and I ascertained that I was not dead at all.
We ultimately reached the foot of the mother-
mountain on whose shoulders were the Cuban
pickets, and here I was so sure of safety that I
could not resist the temptation to die again. I

think I passed into eleven distinct stupors during the ascent of that mountain while the escort stood leaning on their Remingtons. We had done twenty-five miles at a sort of a man-gallop, never once using a beaten track, but always going promiscuously through the jungle and over the rocks. And many of the miles stood straight on end so that it was as hard to come down as it was to go up. But during my stupors, the escort *stood*, mind you, and chatted in low voices. For all the signs they showed, we might have been starting. And they had had nothing to eat but mangoes for over eight days. Previous to the eight days they had been living on mangoes and the carcase of a small lean pony. They were, in fact, of the stuff of Fenimore Cooper's Indians, only they made no preposterous orations. At the major's camp, my friend and I agreed that if our worthy escort would send down a representative with us to the coast, we would send back to them whatever we could spare from the stores of our despatch-boat. With one voice the escort answered that they themselves would go the additional four leagues, as in these starving times they did not care to trust a representative, thank you. " They can't do it; they'll peg out; there must be a limit," I said. " No," answered my friend. " They're all right ; they'd run three times around the whole island for a mouthful of beer." So we saddled up and put off with our fifteen Cuban infantrymen wagging along tirelessly behind us. Sometimes, at the foot of a precipitous hill, a man asked permission to cling to my horse's tail, and then the Jamaica pony would snake him to the summit so swiftly that only his toes seemed to touch the rocks. And for this assistance the man was grateful. When we crowned the last great ridge we saw our squadron to the eastward spread in its patient semicircular about the mouth of the harbour. But as we wound towards the beach we saw a more dramatic thing—our own despatch-boat leaving the rendezvous and putting off to sea. Evidently we were late. Behind me were fifteen stomachs, empty. It was a frightful situation. My friend and I charged for the beach and those fifteen fools began to *run*.

It was no use. The despatch-boat went gaily away trailing black smoke behind her. We turned in distress wondering what we could say to that abused escort. If they massacred us, I felt that it would be merely a virtuous reply to fate and they should in no ways be blamed. There are some things which a man's feelings will not allow him to endure after a diet of mangoes

and pony. However, we perceived to our amazement that they were not indignant at all. They
simply smiled and made a gesture which expressed
an habitual pessimism. It was a philosophy
which denied the existence of everything but
mangoes and pony. It was the Americans who
refused to be comforted. I made a deep vow
with myself that I would come as soon as possible
and play a regular Santa Claus to that splendid
escort. But—we put to sea in a dug-out with
two black boys. The escort waved us a hearty
good-bye from the shore and I never saw them
again. I hope they are all on the police-force in
the new Santiago.

In time we were rescued from the dug-out by
our despatch-boat, and we relieved our feelings by
over-rewarding the two black boys. In fact they
reaped a harvest because of our emotion over our
failure to fill the gallant stomachs of the escort.
They were two rascals. We steamed to the flag-
ship and were given permission to board her.
Admiral Sampson is to me the most interesting
personality of the war. I would not know how
to sketch him for you even if I could pretend to
sufficient material. Anyhow, imagine, first of all,
a marble block of impassivity out of which is
carved the figure of an old man. Endow this

with life, and you've just begun. Then you
must discard all your pictures of bluff, red-faced
old gentlemen who roar against the gale, and understand that the quiet old man is a sailor and an
admiral. This will be difficult; if I told you he
was anything else it would be easy. He resembles
other types; it is his distinction not to resemble
the preconceived type of his standing. When first
I met him I was impressed that he was immensely
bored by the war and with the command of the
North Atlantic Squadron. I perceived a manner
where I thought I perceived a mood, a point of
view. Later, he seemed so indifferent to small
things which bore upon large things that I bowed
to his apathy as a thing unprecedented, marvellous. Still I mistook a manner for a mood. Still
I could not understand that this was the way of
the man. I am not to blame, for my communication was slight and depended upon sufferance—
upon, in fact, the traditional courtesy of the navy.
But finally I saw that it was all manner, that hidden in his indifferent, even apathetic, manner, there
was the alert, sure, fine mind of the best sea-cap-
tain that America has produced since—since Far-
ragut? I don't know. I think—since Hull.

Men follow heartily when they are well led.
They balk at trifles when a blockhead cries go on.

For my part, an impressive thing of the war is the absolute devotion to Admiral Sampson's person—no, to his judgment and wisdom—which was paid by his ship-commanders—Evans of the *Iowa*, Taylor of the *Oregon*, Higginson of the *Massachusetts*, Phillips of the *Texas*, and all the other captains—barring one.   Once, afterward, they called upon him to avenge himself upon a rival— they were there and they would have to say—but he said no-o-o, he guessed it—wouldn't do—any —g-o-oo-o-d—to the—service.

Men feared him, but he never made threats ; men tumbled heels over head to obey him, but he never gave a sharp order ; men loved him, but he said no word, kindly or unkindly ; men cheered for him and he said : "Who are they yelling for ?" Men behaved badly to him and he said nothing. Men thought of glory and he considered the management of ships.   All without a sound.   A noiseless campaign—on his part.   No bunting, no arches, no fireworks ; nothing but the perfect management of a big fleet.   That is a record for you.   No trumpets, no cheers of the populace. Just plain, pure, unsauced accomplishment.   But ultimately he will reap his reward in—in what ?   In text-books on sea-campaigns.   No more.   The people choose their own and they choose the kind

they like. Who has a better right ? Anyhow he
is a great man. And when you are once started
you can continue to be a great man without the
help of bouquets and banquets. He don't need
them—bless your heart.

The flag-ship's battle-hatches were down, and
between decks it was insufferable despite the electric fans. I made my way somewhat forwards,
past the smart orderly, past the companion, on to
the den of the junior mess. Even there they
were playing cards in somebody's cabin. " Hello,
old man. Been ashore ? How'd it look ? It's
your deal, Chick." There was nothing but
steamy wet heat and the decent suppression of
the consequent ill-tempers. The junior officers'
quarters were no more comfortable than the admiral's cabin. I had expected it to be so because
of my remembrance of their gay spirits. But
they were not gay. They were sweltering.
Hello, old man, had I been ashore ? I fled to
the deck, where other officers not on duty were
smoking quiet cigars. The hospitality of the
officers of the flag-ship is another charming memory of the war.

I rolled into my berth on the despatch-boat that
night feeling a perfect wonder of the day. Was
the figure that leaned over the card-game on the

flag-ship, the figure with a whisky and soda in its hand and a cigar in its teeth—was it identical with the figure scrambling, afraid of its life, through Cuban jungle? Was it the figure of the situation of the fifteen pathetic hungry men? It was the same and it went to sleep, hard sleep. I don't know where we voyaged. I think it was Jamaica. But, at any rate, upon the morning of our return to the Cuban coast, we found the sea alive with transports—United States transports from Tampa, containing the Fifth Army Corps under Major-General Shafter. The rigging and the decks of these ships were black with men and everybody wanted to land first. I landed, ultimately, and immediately began to look for an acquaintance. The boats were banged by the waves against a little flimsy dock. I fell ashore somehow, but I did not at once find an acquaintance. I talked to a private in the 2d Massachusetts Volunteers who told me that he was going to write war correspondence for a Boston newspaper. This statement did not surprise me.

There was a straggly village, but I followed the troops who at this time seemed to be moving out by companies. I found three other correspondents and it was luncheon time. Somebody had two bottles of Bass, but it was so warm that it

squirted out in foam. There was no firing ; no
noise of any kind. An old shed was full of soldiers loafing pleasantly in the shade. It was a
hot, dusty, sleepy afternoon ; bees hummed. We
saw Major-General Lawton standing with his staff
under a tree. He was smiling as if he would say :
" Well, this will be better than chasing Apaches."
His division had the advance, and so he had the
right to be happy. A tall man with a grey moustache, light but very strong, an ideal cavalryman.
He appealed to one all the more because of the
vague rumours that his superiors—some of them
were going to take mighty good care that he
shouldn't get much to do. It was rather sickening
to hear such talk, but later we knew that most of
it must have been mere lies.

Down by the landing-place a band of correspondents were making a sort of permanent camp.
They worked like Trojans, carrying wall-tents,
cots, and boxes of provisions. They asked me to
join them, but I looked shrewdly at the sweat on
their faces and backed away. The next day the
army left this permanent camp eight miles to the
rear. The day became tedious. I was glad when
evening came. I sat by a camp-fire and listened
to a soldier of the 8th Infantry who told me that
he was the first enlisted man to land. I lay pre-

tending to appreciate him, but in fact I considered him a great shameless liar. Less than a month ago, I learned that every word he said was gospel truth. I was much surprised. We went for breakfast to the camp of the 20th Infantry, where Captain Greene and his subaltern, Exton, gave us tomatoes stewed with hard bread and coffee. Later, I discovered Greene and Exton down at the beach good-naturedly dodging the waves which seemed to be trying to prevent them from washing the breakfast dishes. I felt tremendously ashamed because my cup and my plate were there, you know, and—— Fate provides some men greased opportunities for making dizzy jackasses of themselves and I fell a victim to my flurry on this occasion. I was a blockhead. I walked away blushing. What? The battles? Yes, I saw something of all of them. I made up my mind that the next time I met Greene and Exton I'd say : " Look here ; why didn't you tell me you had to wash your own dishes that morning so that I could have helped? I felt beastly when I saw you scrubbing there. And me walking around idly." But I never saw Captain Greene again. I think he is in the Philippines now fighting the Tagals. The next time I saw Exton—what? Yes, La Guasimas. That was the " rough rider

fight." However, the next time I saw Exton I—
what do you think? I forgot to speak about it.
But if ever I meet Greene or Exton again—even
if it should be twenty years—I am going to say,
first thing : " Why——" What? Yes. Roosevelt's
regiment and the First and Tenth Regular Cavalry. I'll say, first thing : " Say, why didn't you
tell me you had to wash your own dishes, that
morning, so that I could have helped ? " My
stupidity will be on my conscience until I die, if,
before that, I do not meet either Greene or Exton.
Oh, yes, you are howling for blood, but I tell you it
is more emphatic that I lost my tooth-brush. Did
I tell you that ? Well, I lost it, you see, and I
thought of it for ten hours at a stretch. Oh, yes
—he? He was shot through the heart. But,
look here, I contend that the French cable company buncoed us throughout the war. What ?
Him ? My tooth-brush I never found, but he died
of his wound in time. Most of the regular soldiers
carried their tooth-brushes stuck in the bands of
their hats. It made a quaint military decoration.
I have had a line of a thousand men pass me in
the jungle and not a hat lacking the simple
emblem.

The first of July? All right. My Jamaica
polo-pony was not present. He was still in the

hills to the westward of Santiago, but the Cubans
had promised to fetch him to me. But my kit
was easy to carry. It had nothing superfluous in
it but a pair of spurs which made me indignant
every time I looked at them. Oh, but I must tell
you about a man I met directly after the La
Guasimas fight. Edward Marshall, a correspondent whom I had known with a degree of intimacy
for seven years, was terribly hit in that fight and
asked me if I would not go to Siboney—the base
—and convey the news to his colleagues of the
New York Journal and round up some assistance.
I went to Siboney, and there was not a *Journal*
man to be seen, although usually you judged from
appearances that the *Journal* staff was about as
large as the army. Presently I met two correspondents, strangers to me, but I questioned
them, saying that Marshall was badly shot and
wished for such succour as *Journal* men could
bring from their despatch-boat. And one of
these correspondents replied. He is the man I
wanted to describe. I love him as a brother. He
said : "Marshall? Marshall? Why, Marshall
isn't in Cuba at all. He left for New York just before the expedition sailed from Tampa." I said :
"Beg pardon, but I remarked that Marshall was
shot in the fight this morning, and have you seen

any *Journal* people?" After a pause, he said: " I am sure Marshall is not down here at all. He's in New York." I said: " Pardon me, but I remarked that Marshall was shot in the fight this morning, and have you seen any *Journal* people?" He said: " No; now look here, you must have gotten two chaps mixed somehow. Marshall isn't in Cuba at all. How could he be shot?" I said: " Pardon me, but I remarked that Marshall was shot in the fight this morning, and have you seen any *Journal* people?" He said: " But it can't really be Marshall, you know, for the simple reason that he's not down here." I clasped my hands to my temples, gave one piercing cry to heaven and fled from his presence. I couldn't go on with him. He excelled me at all points. I have faced death by bullets, fire, water, and disease, but to die thus—to wilfully batter myself against the ironclad opinion of this mummy—no, no, not that. In the meantime, it was admitted that a correspondent was shot, be his name Marshall, Bismarck, or Louis XIV. Now, supposing the name of this wounded correspondent had been Bishop Potter? Or Jane Austen? Or Bernhardt? Or Henri Georges Stephane Adolphe Opper de Blowitz? What effect—never mind.

We will proceed to July 1st. On that morning

I marched with my kit—having everything essential save a tooth-brush—the entire army put me to shame, since there must have been at least fifteen thousand tooth-brushes in the invading force—I marched with my kit on the road to Santiago. It was a fine morning and everybody—the doomed and the immunes—how could we tell one from the other—everybody was in the highest spirits. We were enveloped in forest, but we could hear, from ahead, everybody peppering away at everybody. It was like the roll of many drums. This was Lawton over at El Caney. I reflected with complacency that Lawton's division did not concern me in a professional way. That was the affair of another man. My business was with Kent's division and Wheeler's division. We came to El Poso—a hill at nice artillery range from the Spanish defences. Here Grimes's battery was shooting a duel with one of the enemy's batteries. Scovel had established a little camp in the rear of the guns and a servant had made coffee. I invited Whigham to have coffee, and the servant added some hard biscuit and tinned tongue. I noted that Whigham was staring fixedly over my shoulder, and that he waved away the tinned tongue with some bitterness. It was a horse, a dead horse. Then a mule, which had been shot through the nose, wandered up and looked at Whigham. We ran away.

On top of the hill one had a fine view of the Spanish lines. We stared across almost a mile of jungle to ash-coloured trenches on the military crest of the ridge. A goodly distance back of this position were white buildings, all flying great red-cross flags. The jungle beneath us rattled with firing and the Spanish trenches crackled out regular volleys, but all this time there was nothing to indicate a tangible enemy. In truth, there was a man in a Panama hat strolling to and fro behind one of the Spanish trenches, gesticulating at times with a walking stick. A man in a Panama hat, walking with a stick! That was the strangest sight of my life—that symbol, that quaint figure of Mars. The battle, the thunderous row, was his possession. He was the master. He mystified us all with his infernal Panama hat and his wretched walking-stick. From near his feet came volleys and from near his side came roaring shells, but he stood there alone, visible, the one tangible thing. He was a Colossus, and he was half as high as a pin, this being. Always somebody would be saying: "Who *can* that fellow be?"

Later, the American guns shelled the trenches

and a blockhouse near them, and Mars had vanished. It could not have been death. One cannot kill Mars. But there was one other figure, which arose to symbolic dignity. The balloon of our signal corps had swung over the tops of the jungle's trees toward the Spanish trenches. Whereat the balloon and the man in the Panama hat and with a walking stick—whereat these two waged tremendous battle.

Suddenly the conflict became a human thing. A little group of blue figures appeared on the green of the terrible hillside. It was some of our infantry. The attaché of a great empire was at my shoulder, and he turned to me and spoke with incredulity and scorn. "Why, they're trying to take the position," he cried, and I admitted meekly that I thought they were. "But they can't do it, you know," he protested vehemently. "It's impossible." And—good fellow that he was—he began to grieve and wail over a useless sacrifice of gallant men. "It's plucky, you know! By Gawd, it's plucky! But *they can't do it!*" He was profoundly moved; his voice was quite broken. "It will simply be a hell of a slaughter with no good coming out of it."

The trail was already crowded with stretcher-bearers and with wounded men who could walk.

18

One had to stem a tide of mute agony. But I
don't know that it was mute agony. I only
know that it was mute. It was something in which
the silence or, more likely, the reticence was an
appalling and inexplicable fact. One's senses
seemed to demand that these men should cry out.
But you could really find wounded men who exhibited all the signs of a pleased and contented
mood. When thinking of it now it seems strange
beyond words. But at the time—I don't know—
it did not attract one's wonder. A man with a
hole in his arm or his shoulder, or even in the leg
below the knee, was often whimsical, comic.
" Well, this ain't exactly what I enlisted for, boys.
If I'd been told about this in Tampa, I'd have resigned from th' army. Oh, yes, you can get the
same thing if you keep on going. But I think
the Spaniards may run out of ammunition in the
course of a week or ten days." Then suddenly
one would be confronted by the awful majesty of
a man shot in the face. Particularly I remember
one. He had a great dragoon moustache, and
the blood streamed down his face to meet this
moustache even as a torrent goes to meet the
jammed log, and then swarmed out to the tips
and fell in big slow drops. He looked steadily
into my eyes; I was ashamed to return his

glance. You understand? It is very curious—
all that.

The two lines of battle were royally whacking
away at each other, and there was no rest or peace
in all that region. The modern bullet is a far-
flying bird. It rakes the air with its hot spitting
song at distances which, as a usual thing, place the
whole landscape in the danger-zone. There was
no direction from which they did not come. A
chart of their courses over one's head would have
resembled a spider's web. My friend Jimmie, the
photographer, mounted to the firing line with me
and we gallivanted as much as we dared. The
"sense of the meeting" was curious. Most of
the men seemed to have no idea of a grand historic performance, but they were grimly satisfied
with themselves. "Well, begawd, we done it."
Then they wanted to know about other parts of
the line. "How are things looking, old man?
Everything all right?" "Yes, everything is all
right if you can hold this ridge." "Aw, hell,"
said the men, "we'll hold the ridge. Don't you
worry about that, son."

It was Jimmie's first action, and, as we cau
tiously were making our way to the right of our
lines, the crash of the Spanish fire became up-
roarious, and the air simply whistled. I heard a

quavering voice near my shoulder, and, turning, I
beheld Jimmie—Jimmie—with a face bloodless,
white as paper. He looked at me with eyes opened
extremely wide. "Say," he said, "this is pretty
hot, ain't it?" I was delighted. I knew exactly
what he meant. He wanted to have the situation
defined. If I had told him that this was the occasion of some mere idle desultory firing and
recommended that he wait until the real battle began, I think he would have gone in a bee-line for
the rear. But I told him the truth. "Yes,
Jimmie," I replied earnestly, "You can take it
from me that this is patent, double-extra-what-
for." And immediately he nodded. "All right."
If this was a big action, then he was willing to pay
in his fright as a rational price for the privilege of
being present. But if this was only a penny af-
fray, he considered the price exorbitant, and he
would go away. He accepted my assurance with
simple faith, and deported himself with kindly
dignity as one moving amid great things. His
face was still as pale as paper, but that counted
for nothing. The main point was his perfect willingness to be frightened for reasons. I wonder
where is Jimmie? I lent him the Jamaica polo-
pony one day and it ran away with him and flung
him off in the middle of a ford. He appeared to

me afterward and made bitter speech concerning this horse which I had assured him was a gentle and pious animal. Then I never saw Jimmie again.

Then came the night of the first of July. A group of correspondents limped back to El Poso. It had been a day so long that the morning seemed as remote as a morning in the previous year. But I have forgotten to tell you about Reuben McNab. Many years ago, I went to school at a place called Claverack, in New York State, where there was a semi-military institution. Contemporaneous with me, as a student, was Reuben McNab, a long, lank boy, freckled, sandy-haired—an extraordinary boy in no way, and yet, I wager, a boy clearly marked in every recollection. Perhaps there is a good deal in that name. Reuben McNab. You can't fling that name carelessly over your shoulder and lose it. It follows you like the haunting memory of a sin. At any rate, Reuben McNab was identified intimately in my thought with the sunny irresponsible days at Claverack, when all the earth was a green field and all the sky was a rainless blue. Then I looked down into a miserable huddle at Bloody Bend, a huddle of hurt men, dying men, dead men. And there I saw Reuben McNab, a corporal in the 71st New York Volunteers, and with a hole through

his lung.   Also, several holes through his clothing.
"Well, they got me," he said in greeting.   Usually they said that.   There were no long speeches.
"Well, they got me."   That was sufficient.   The
duty of the upright, unhurt, man is then difficult.
I doubt if many of us learned how to speak to our
own wounded.   In the first place, one had to play
that the wound was nothing; oh, a mere nothing ; a
casual interference with movement, perhaps, but
nothing more ; oh, really nothing more.   In the
second place, one had to show a comrade's appreciation of this sad plight.   As a result I think
most of us bungled and stammered in the presence
of our wounded friends.   That's curious, eh?
"Well, they got me," said Reuben McNab.   I
had looked upon five hundred wounded men with
stolidity, or with a conscious indifference which
filled me with amazement.   But the apparition of
Reuben McNab, the schoolmate, lying there in
the mud, with a hole through his lung, awed me
into stutterings, set me trembling with a sense of
terrible intimacy with this war which theretofore
I could have believed was a dream—almost.
Twenty shot men rolled their eyes and looked at
me.   Only one man paid no heed.   He was dying;
he had no time.   The bullets hummed low over
them all.   Death, having already struck, still in-

sisted upon raising a venomous crest. " If you're goin' by the hospital, step in and see me," said Reuben McNab. That was all.

At the correspondents' camp, at El Poso, there was hot coffee. It was very good. I have a vague sense of being very selfish over my blanket and rubber coat. I have a vague sense of spasmodic firing during my sleep ; it rained, and then I awoke to hear that steady drumming of an infantry fire —something which was never to cease, it seemed. They were at it again. The trail from El Poso to the positions along San Juan ridge had become an exciting thoroughfare. Shots from large-bore rifles dropped in from almost every side. At this time the safest place was the extreme front. I remember in particular the one outcry I heard. A private in the 71st, without his rifle, had gone to a stream for some water, and was returning, being but a little in rear of me. Suddenly I heard this cry—" Oh, my God, come quick "—and I was conscious then to having heard the hateful zip of a close shot. He lay on the ground, wriggling. He was hit in the hip. Two men came quickly. Presently everybody seemed to be getting knocked down. They went over like men of wet felt, quietly, calmly, with no more complaint than so many automatons. It was only that lad—

" Oh, my God, come quick." Otherwise, men seemed to consider that their hurts were not worthy of particular attention. A number of people got killed very courteously, tacitly absolving the rest of us from any care in the matter. A man fell; he turned blue; his face took on an expression of deep sorrow; and then his immediate friends worried about him, if he had friends. This was July 1. I crave the permission to leap back again to that date.

On the morning of July 2, I sat on San Juan hill and watched Lawton's division come up. I was absolutely sheltered, but still where I could look into the faces of men who were trotting up under fire. There wasn't a high heroic face among them. They were all men intent on business. That was all. It may seem to you that I am trying to make everything a squalor. That would be wrong. I feel that things were often sublime. But they were *differently* sublime. They were not of our shallow and preposterous fictions. They stood out in a simple, majestic commonplace. It was the behaviour of men on the street. It was the behaviour of men. In one way, each man was just pegging along at the heels of the man before him, who was pegging along at the heels of still anot' man, who was pegging along at the heels of still another man who— It was that in the flat and obvious way. In another way it was pageantry, the pageantry of the accomplishment of naked duty. One cannot speak of it—the spectacle of the common man serenely doing his work, his appointed work. It is the one thing in the universe which makes one fling expression to the winds and be satisfied to simply feel. Thus they moved at San Juan—the soldiers of the United States Regular Army. One pays them the tribute of the toast of silence.

Lying near one of the enemy's trenches was a red-headed Spanish corpse. I wonder how many hundreds were cognisant of this red-headed Spanish corpse? It arose to the dignity of a landmark. There were many corpses but only one with a red head. This red-head. He was always there. Each time I approached that part of the field I prayed that I might find that he had been buried. But he was always there—red-headed. His strong simple countenance was a malignant sneer at the system which was forever killing the credulous peasants in a sort of black night of politics, where the peasants merely followed whatever somebody had told them was lofty and good. But, nevertheless, the red-headed

Spaniard was dead. He was irrevocably dead.
And to what purpose? The honour of Spain?
Surely the honour of Spain could have existed
without the violent death of this poor red-headed
peasant? Ah well, he was buried when the
heavy firing ceased and men had time for such
small things as funerals. The trench was turned
over on top of him. It was a fine, honourable,
soldierly fate—to be buried in a trench, the trench
of the fight and the death. Sleep well, red-
headed peasant. You came to another hemis-
phere to fight because—because you were told to,
I suppose. Well, there you are, buried in your
trench on San Juan hill. That is the end of it,
your life has been taken—that is a flat, frank fact.
And foreigners buried you expeditiously while
speaking a strange tongue. Sleep well, red-
headed mystery.

On the day before the destruction of Cervera's
fleet, I steamed past our own squadron, doggedly
lying in its usual semicircle, every nose pointing
at the mouth of the harbour. I went to Jamaica,
and on the placid evening of the next day I was
again steaming past our own squadron, doggedly
lying in its usual semicircle, every nose pointing
at the mouth of the harbour. A megaphone-hail
from the bridge of one of the yacht-gunboats

came casually over the water. " Hello! hear the
news?" "No; what was it?" "The Spanish
fleet came out this morning." " Oh, of course,
it did." " Honest, I mean." " Yes, I know ;
well, where are they now?" " Sunk." Was
there ever such a preposterous statement? I was
humiliated that my friend, the lieutenant on the
yacht-gunboat, should have measured me as one
likely to swallow this bad joke.

But it was all true ; every word. I glanced back
at our squadron, lying in its usual semicircle, every
nose pointing at the mouth of the harbour. It
would have been absurd to think that anything
had happened. The squadron hadn't changed a
button. There it sat without even a smile on the
face of the tiger. And it had eaten four armoured
cruisers and two torpedo-boat-destroyers while
my back was turned for a moment. Courteously,
but clearly, we announced across the waters that
until despatch-boats came to be manned from the
ranks of the celebrated horse-marines, the lieutenant's statement would probably remain unap-
preciated. He made a gesture, abandoning us to
our scepticism. It infuriates an honourable and
serious man to be taken for a liar or a joker at a
time when he is supremely honourable and serious. However, when we went ashore, we found

Siboney ringing with the news. It was true, then ; that mishandled collection of sick ships had come out and taken the deadly thrashing which was rightfully the due of—I don't know— somebody in Spain—or perhaps nobody anywhere. One likes to wallop incapacity, but one has mingled emotions over the incapacity which is not so much personal as it is the development of centuries. This kind of incapacity cannot be centralised. You cannot hit the head which contains it all. This is the idea, I imagine, which moved the officers and men of our fleet. Almost immediately they began to speak of the Spanish Admiral as " poor old boy " with a lucid suggestion in their tones that his fate appealed to them as being undue hard, undue cruel. And yet the Spanish guns hit nothing. If a man shoots, he should hit something occasionally, and men say that from the time the Spanish ships broke clear of the harbour entrance until they were one by one overpowered, they were each a band of flame. Well, one can only mumble out that when a man shoots he should be required to hit something occasionally.

In truth, the greatest fact of the whole campaign on land and sea seems to be the fact that the Spaniards could only hit by chance, by a fluke.

If he had been an able marksman, no man of our two unsupported divisions would have set foot on San Juan hill on July 1. They should have been blown to smithereens. The Spaniards had no immediate lack of ammunition, for they fired enough to kill the population of four big cities. I admit neither Velasquez nor Cervantes into this discussion, although they have appeared by authority as reasons for something which I do not clearly understand. Well, anyhow they couldn't hit anything. Velasquez? Yes. Cervantes? Yes. But the Spanish troops seemed only to try to make a very rapid fire. Thus we lost many men. We lost them because of the simple fury of the fire ; never because the fire was well-directed, intelligent. But the Americans were called upon to be whipped because of Cervantes and Velasquez. It was impossible.

Out on the slopes of San Juan the dog-tents shone white. Some kind of negotiations were going forward, and men sat on their trousers and waited. It was all rather a blur of talks with officers, and a craving for good food and good water. Once Leighton and I decided to ride over to El Caney, into which town the civilian refugees from Santiago were pouring. The road from the beleaguered city to the out-lying village was a

spectacle to make one moan. There were delicate
gentle families on foot, the silly French boots of the
girls twisting and turning in a sort of absolute paper
futility ; there were sons and grandsons carrying
the venerable patriarch in his own armchair ; there
were exhausted mothers with babes who wailed ;
there were young dandies with their toilettes in
decay ; there were puzzled, guideless women who
didn't know what had happened. The first sentence one heard was the murmurous " What a damn
shame." We saw a godless young trooper of the
Second Cavalry sharply halt a waggon. " Hold on
a minute. You must carry this woman. She's
fainted twice already." The virtuous driver of the
U. S. Army waggon mildly answered : " But I'm
full-up now."   " You can make room for her," said
the private of the Second Cavalry. A young, young
man with a straight mouth. It was merely a plain
bit of nothing—at—all but, thank God, thank
God, he seemed to have not the slightest sense of
excellence. He said : " If you've got any man in
there who can walk at all, you put him out and
let this woman get in."   " But," answered the
teamster, " I'm filled up with a lot of cripples and
grandmothers." Thereupon they discussed the
point fairly, and ultimately the woman was lifted
into the waggon.

The vivid thing was the fact that these people did not visibly suffer. Somehow they were numb. There was not a tear. There was rarely a countenance which was not wondrously casual. There was no sign of fatalistic theory. It was simply that what was happening to-day had happened yesterday, as near as one could judge. I could fancy that these people had been thrown out of their homes every day. It was utterly, utterly casual. And they accepted the ministrations of our men in the same fashion. Everything was a matter of course. I had a filled canteen. I was frightfully conscious of this fact because a filled canteen was a pearl of price ; it was a great thing. It was an enormous accident which led one to offer praises that he was luckier than ten thousand better men.

As Leighton and I rode along, we came to a tree under which a refugee family had halted. They were a man, his wife, two handsome daughters and a pimply son. It was plain that they were superior people, because the girls had dressed for the exodus and wore corsets which captivated their forms with a steel-ribbed vehemence only proper for wear on a sun-blistered road to a distant town. They asked us for water. Water was the gold of the moment. Leighton was almost maud-

lin in his generosity. I remember being angry
with him. He lavished upon them his whole
canteen and he received in return not even a
glance of—what? Acknowledgment? No, they
didn't even admit anything. Leighton wasn't a
human being; he was some sort of a mountain
spring. They accepted him on a basis of pure
natural phenomena. His canteen was purely an
occurrence. In the meantime the pimple-faced
approached me. He asked for water and held out
a pint cup. My response was immediate. I
tilted my canteen and poured into his cup almost
a pint of my treasure. He glanced into the cup
and apparently he beheld there some innocent sediment for which he alone or his people were responsible. In the American camps the men were
accustomed to a sediment. Well, he glanced at
my poor cupful and then negligently poured it out
on the ground and held up his cup for more. I
gave him more; I gave him his cup full again, but
there was something within me which made me
swear him out completely. But he didn't understand a word. Afterward I watched if they were
capable of being moved to help on their less able
fellows on this miserable journey. Not they!
Nor yet anybody else. Nobody cared for anybody
save my young friend of the Second Cavalry, who

rode seriously to and fro doing his best for people,
who took him as a result of a strange upheaval.

The fight at El Caney had been furious. General Vera del Rey with somewhat less than 1000
men—the Spanish accounts say 520—had there
made such a stand that only about 80 battered
soldiers ever emerged from it. The attack cost
Lawton about 400 men. The magazine rifle!
But the town was now a vast parrot-cage of chat-
tering refugees. If, on the road, they were silent,
stolid and serene, in the town they found their
tongues and set up such a cackle as one may
seldom hear. Notably the women ; it is they who
invariably confuse the definition of situations, and
one could wonder in amaze if this crowd of irresponsible, gabbling hens had already forgotten
that this town was the deathbed, so to speak,
of scores of gallant men whose blood was not yet
dry ; whose hands, of the hue of pale amber, stuck
from the soil of the hasty burial. On the way to
El Caney I had conjured a picture of the women
of Santiago, proud in their pain, their despair,
dealing glances of defiance, contempt, hatred at
the invader ; fiery ferocious ladies, so true to their
vanquished and to their dead that they spurned
the very existence of the low-bred churls who
lacked both Velasquez and Cervantes. And

19

instead, there was this mere noise, which reminded
one alternately of a tea-party in Ireland, a village
fête in the south of France, and the vacuous
morning screech of a swarm of sea-gulls. " Good.
There is Donna Maria. This will lower her high
head. This will teach her better manners to her
neighbours. She wasn't too grand to send her
rascal of a servant to borrow a trifle of coffee of
me in the morning, and then when I met her on
the calle—por Dios, she was too blind to see me.
But we are all equal here. No? Little Juan has
a sore toe. Yes, Donna Maria ; many thanks,
many thanks. Juan, do me the favour to be quiet
while Donna Maria is asking about your toe. Oh,
Donna Maria, we were always poor, always. But
you. My heart bleeds when I see how hard this
is for you. The old cat! She gives me a head-
shake."

Pushing through the throng in the plaza we
came in sight of the door of the church, and here
was a strange scene. The church had been turned
into a hospital for Spanish wounded who had fallen
into American hands. The interior of the church
was too cave-like in its gloom for the eyes of the
operating surgeons, so they had had the altar table
carried to the doorway, where there was a bright
light. Framed then in the black archway was

the altar table with the figure of a man upon it. He was naked save for a breech-clout and so close, so clear was the ecclesiastic suggestion, that one's mind leaped to a phantasy that this thin, pale figure had just been torn down from a cross. The flash of the impression was like light, and for this instant it illumined all the dark recesses of one's remotest idea of sacrilege, ghastly and wanton. I bring this to you merely as an effect, an effect of mental light and shade, if you like ; something done in thought similar to that which the French impressionists do in colour ; something meaningless and at the same time overwhelming, crushing, monstrous. " Poor devil ; I wonder if he'll pull through," said Leighton. An American surgeon and his assistants were intent over the prone figure. They wore white aprons. Something small and silvery flashed in the surgeon's hand. An assistant held the merciful sponge close to the man's nostrils, but he was writhing and moaning in some horrible dream of this artificial sleep. As the surgeon's instrument played, I fancied that the man dreamed that he was being gored by a bull. In his pleading, delirious babble occurred constantly the name of the Virgin, the Holy Mother. " Good morning," said the surgeon. He changed his knife to his left hand and gave me a wet palm. The tips of his fingers were wrinkled, shrunken, like those of a boy who has been in swimming too long. Now, in front of the door, there were three American sentries, and it was their business to—to do what? To keep this Spanish crowd from swarming over the operating table! It was perforce a public clinic. They would not be denied. The weaker women and the children jostled according to their might in the rear, while the stronger people, gaping in the front rank, cried out impatiently when the pushing disturbed their long stares. One burned with a sudden gift of public oratory. One wanted to say : " Oh, go away, go away, go away. Leave the man decently alone with his pain, you gogglers. This is not the national sport."

But within the church there was an audience of another kind. This was of the other wounded men awaiting their turn. They lay on their brown blankets in rows along the stone floor. Their eyes, too, were fastened upon the operating-table, but—that was different. Meek-eyed little yellow men lying on the floor awaiting their turns.

One afternoon I was seated with a correspondent friend, on the porch of one of the houses at Siboney. A vast man on horseback came riding along at a foot pace. When he perceived my friend, he pulled up sharply. "Whoa! Where's that mule I lent you?" My friend arose and saluted. "I've got him all right, General, thank you," said my friend. The vast man shook his finger. "Don't you lose him now." "No, sir, I won't; thank you, sir." The vast man rode away. "Who the devil is that?" said I. My friend laughed. "That's General Shafter," said he.

I gave five dollars for the Bos'n—small, black, spry imp of Jamaica sin. When I first saw him he was the property of a fireman on the *Criton*. The fireman had found him—a little wharf rat—in Port Antonio. It was not the purchase of a slave; it was that the fireman believed that he had spent about five dollars on a lot of comic supplies for the Bos'n, including a little suit of sailor clothes. The Bos'n was an adroit and fantastic black gamin. His eyes were like white lights, and his teeth were a row of little piano keys; otherwise he was black. He had both been a jockey and a cabin-boy, and he had the manners of a gentleman. After he entered my service I don't think there was ever an occasion upon which he was useful, save when he told me quaint stories of Guatemala, in which country he seemed to have lived some portion of his infantile existence. Usually he ran funny errands like little foot-races, each about fifteen yards in length.

At Siboney he slept under my hammock like a poodle, and I always expected that, through the breaking of a rope, I would some night descend and obliterate him. His incompetence was spectacular. When I wanted him to do a thing, the agony of supervision was worse than the agony of personal performance. It would have been easier to have gotten my own spurs or boots or blanket than to have the bother of this little incapable's service. But the good aspect was the humorous view. He was like a boy, a mouse, a scoundrel, and a devoted servitor. He was immensely popular. His name of Bos'n became a Siboney stockword. Everybody knew it. It was a name like President McKinley, Admiral Sampson, General Shafter. The Bos'n became a figure. One day he approached me with four one-dollar notes in United States currency. He besought me to preserve them for him, and I pompously tucked them away in my riding breeches, with an air which meant that his funds were now as safe as if they were in a national bank. Still, I asked with some surprise, where he had reaped all this money. He frankly admitted at once that it had been given to him by the enthusiastic soldiery as a tribute to his charm of person and manner. This was not astonishing for Siboney, where money was meaningless.

Money was not worth carrying—" packing." However, a soldier came to our house one morning,
and asked, " Got any more tobacco to sell?" As
befitted men in virtuous poverty, we replied with
indignation. "What tobacco ?" "Why, that
tobacco what the little nigger is sellin' round."
I said, " Bos'n!" He said, "Yes, mawstah."
Wounded men on bloody stretchers were being
carried into the hospital next door. "Bos'n,
you've been stealing my tobacco." His defence
was as glorious as the defence of that forlorn
hope in romantic history, which drew itself up
and mutely died. He lied as desperately, as
savagely, as hopelessly as ever man fought.

One day a delegation from the 33d Michigan came
to me and said : "Are you the proprietor of the
Bos'n?" I said : "Yes." And they said : "Well,
would you please be so kind as to be so good as
to give him to us?" A big battle was expected
for the next day. "Why," I answered, "if you
want him you can have him. But he's a thief,
and I won't let him go save on his personal announcement." The big battle occurred the next
day, and the Bos'n did not disappear in it; but he
disappeared in my interest in the battle, even as a
waif might disappear in a fog. My interest in the
battle made the Bos'n dissolve before my eyes.

Poor little rascal! I gave him up with pain. He was such an innocent villain. He knew no more of thievery than the whole of it. Anyhow one was fond of him. He was a natural scoundrel. He was not an educated scoundrel. One cannot bear the educated scoundrel. He was ingenuous, simple, honest, abashed ruffianism.

I hope the 33d Michigan did not arrive home naked. I hope the Bos'n did not succeed in getting everything. If the Bos'n builds a palace in Detroit, I shall know where he got the money. He got it from the 33d Michigan. Poor little man. He was only eleven years old. He vanished. I had thought to preserve him as a relic, even as one preserves forgotten bayonets and fragments of shell. And now as to the pocket of my riding-breeches. It contained four dollars in United States currency. Bos'n! Hey, Bos'n, where are you? The morning was the morning of battle.

I was on San Juan Hill when Lieutenant Hobson and the men of the *Merrimac* were exchanged and brought into the American lines. Many of us knew that the exchange was about to be made, and gathered to see the famous party. Some of our Staff officers rode out with three Spanish officers—prisoners—these latter being blindfolded before they were taken through the American position. The army was majestically minding its business in the long line of trenches when its eye caught sight of this little procession. " What's that ? What they goin' to do ? " " They're goin' to exchange Hobson." Wherefore every man who was foot-free staked out a claim where he could get a good view of the liberated heroes, and two bands prepared to collaborate on " The Star Spangled Banner." There was a very long wait through the sunshiny afternoon. In our impatience, we imagined them—the Americans and Spaniards—dickering away out there under the big tree like so many peddlers. Once the massed bands, misled by a rumour, stiffened themselves into that dramatic and breathless moment when each man is ready to blow. But the rumour was exploded in the nick of time. We made ill jokes, saying one to another that the negotiations had found diplomacy to be a failure, and were playing freeze-out poker for the whole batch of prisoners.

But suddenly the moment came. Along the cut roadway, toward the crowded soldiers, rode three men, and it could be seen that the central one wore the undress uniform of an officer of the United States navy. Most of the soldiers were sprawled out on the grass, bored and wearied in the sunshine. However, they aroused at the old

circus-parade, torch-light procession cry, " Here
they come." Then the men of the regular army
did a thing. They arose *en masse* and came to
" Attention." Then the men of the regular army
did another thing. They slowly lifted every
weather-beaten hat and drooped it until it touched
the knee. Then there was a magnificent silence,
broken only by the measured hoof-beats of the
little company's horses as they rode through the
gap. It was solemn, funereal, this splendid silent
welcome of a brave man by men who stood on a
hill which they had earned out of blood and
death—simply, honestly, with no sense of excellence, earned out of blood and death.

Then suddenly the whole scene went to rubbish. Before he reached the bottom of the hill,
Hobson was bowing to right and left like another
Boulanger, and, above the thunder of the massed
bands, one could hear the venerable outbreak,
" Mr. Hobson, I'd like to shake the hand of the
man who——" But the real welcome was that welcome of silence. However, one could thrill again
when the tail of the procession appeared—an
army waggon containing the blue-jackets of the
Merrimac adventure. I remember grinning heads
stuck out from under the canvas cover of the
waggon. And the army spoke to the navy.

"Well, Jackie, how does it feel?" And the navy up and answered: "Great! Much obliged to you fellers for comin' here." "Say, Jackie, what did they arrest ye for anyhow? Stealin' a dawg?" The navy still grinned. Here was no rubbish. Here was the mere exchange of language between men.

Some of us fell in behind this small but royal procession and followed it to General Shafter's headquarters, some miles on the road to Siboney. I have a vague impression that I watched the meeting between Shafter and Hobson, but the impression ends there. However, I remember hearing a talk between them as to Hobson's men, and then the blue-jackets were called up to hear the congratulatory remarks of the general in command of the Fifth Army Corps. It was a scene in the fine shade of thickly-leaved trees. The general sat in his chair, his belly sticking ridiculously out before him as if he had adopted some form of artificial inflation. He looked like a joss. If the seamen had suddenly begun to burn a few sticks, most of the spectators would have exhibited no surprise. But the words he spoke were proper, clear, quiet, soldierly, the words of one man to others. The Jackies were comic. At the bidding of their officer they aligned themselves before the general, grinned with embarrassment one to the other, made funny attempts to correct the alignment, and—looked sheepish. They looked sheepish. They looked like bad little boys flagrantly caught. They had no sense of excellence. Here was no rubbish.

Very soon after this the end of the campaign came for me. I caught a fever. I am not sure to this day what kind of a fever it was. It was defined variously. I know, at any rate, that I first developed a languorous indifference to everything in the world. Then I developed a tendency to ride a horse even as a man lies on a cot. Then I—I am not sure—I think I grovelled and groaned about Siboney for several days. My colleagues, Scovel and George Rhea, found me and gave me of their best, but I didn't know whether London Bridge was falling down or whether there was a war with Spain. It was all the same. What of it ? Nothing of it. Everything had happened, perhaps. But I cared not a jot. Life, death, dishonour—all were nothing to me. All I cared for was pickles. *Pickles* at any price ! *Pickles ! !*

If I had been the father of a hundred suffering daughters, I should have waved them all aside and remarked that they could be damned for all I cared. It was not a mood. One can defeat a

mood. It was a physical situation. Sometimes
one cannot defeat a physical situation. I heard
the talk of Siboney and sometimes I answered,
but I was as indifferent as the star-fish flung to die
on the sands. The only fact in the universe was
that my veins burned and boiled. Rhea finally
staggered me down to the army-surgeon who
had charge of the proceedings, and the army-
surgeon looked me over with a keen healthy eye.
Then he gave a permit that I should be sent
home. The manipulation from the shore to the
transport was something which was Rhea's affair.
I am not sure whether we went in a boat or a
balloon. I think it was a boat. Rhea pushed me
on board and I swayed meekly and unsteadily
toward the captain of the ship, a corpulent, well-
conditioned, impickled person pacing noisily on
the spar-deck. "Ahem, yes; well; all right.
Have you got your own food? I hope, for
Christ's sake, you don't expect us to feed you, do
you?" Whereupon I went to the rail and
weakly yelled at Rhea, but he was already afar.
The captain was, meantime, remarking in bellows
that, for Christ's sake, I couldn't expect him to
feed me. I didn't expect to be fed. I didn't
care to be fed. I wished for nothing on earth
but some form of painless pause, oblivion. The

insults of this old pie-stuffed scoundrel did not
affect me then ; they affect me now. I would
like to tell him that, although I like collies, fox-
terriers, and even screw-curled poodles, I do not
like him. He was free to call me superfluous
and throw me overboard, but he was not free to
coarsely speak to a somewhat sick man. I—in
fact I hate him—it is all wrong—I lose whatever ethics I possessed—but—I hate him, and I
demand that you should imagine a milch cow
endowed with a knowledge of navigation and in
command of a ship—and perfectly capable of
commanding a ship — oh, well, never mind.

I was crawling along the deck when somebody
pounced violently upon me and thundered :
" Who in hell are you, sir ? "   I said I was a correspondent. He asked me did I know that I had
yellow fever. I said No. He yelled, " Well, by
Gawd, you isolate yourself, sir." I said ; " Where ? "
At this question he almost frothed at the mouth.
I thought he was going to strike me. " Where ? "
he roared.   " How in hell do I know, sir ?   I
know as much about this ship as you do, sir. But
you isolate yourself, sir." My clouded brain tried
to comprehend these orders. This man was a
doctor in the regular army, and it was necessary
to obey him, so I bestirred myself to learn what

he meant by these gorilla outcries. " All right, doctor ; I'll isolate myself, but I wish you'd tell me where to go." And then he passed into such volcanic humour that I clung to the rail and gasped. " Isolate yourself, sir. Isolate yourself. That's all I've got to say, sir. I don't give a God damn where you go, but when you get there, stay there, sir." So I wandered away and ended up on the deck aft, with my head against the flag-staff and my limp body stretched on a little rug. I was not at all sorry for myself. I didn't care a tent-peg. And yet, as I look back upon it now, the situation was fairly exciting—a voyage of four or five days before me—no food—no friends —above all else, no friends—isolated on deck, and rather ill.

When I returned to the United States, I was able to move my feminine friends to tears by an account of this voyage, but, after all, it wasn't so bad. They kept me on my small reservation aft, but plenty of kindness loomed soon enough. At mess-time, they slid me a tin plate of something, usually stewed tomatoes and bread. Men are always good men. And, at any rate, most of the people were in worse condition than I—poor bandaged chaps looking sadly down at the waves. In a way, I knew the kind. First lieutenants at forty years of age, captains at fifty, majors at 102, lieutenant-colonels at 620, full colonels at 1000, and brigadiers at 9,768,295 plus. A man had to live two billion years to gain eminent rank in the regular army at that time. And, of course, they all had trembling wives at remote western posts waiting to hear the worst, the best, or the middle.

In rough weather, the officers made a sort of a common pool of all the sound legs and arms, and by dint of hanging hard to each other they managed to move from their deck chairs to their cabins and from their cabins again to their deck chairs. Thus they lived until the ship reached Hampton Roads. We slowed down opposite the curiously mingled hotels and batteries at Old Point Comfort, and at our mast-head we flew the yellow-flag, the grim ensign of the plague. Then we witnessed something which informed us that with all this ship-load of wounds and fevers and starvations we had forgotten the fourth element of war. We were flying the yellow flag, but a launch came and circled swiftly about us. There was a little woman in the launch, and she kept looking and looking and looking. Our ship was so high that she could see only those who rung at the rail, but she kept looking and looking and looking. It was plain enough—it was all plain enough—but my heart sank with the fear that she was not going to find him. But presently there was a commotion among some black dough-boys of the 24th Infantry, and two of them ran aft to Colonel Liscum, its gallant commander. Their faces were wreathed in darkey grins of delight. " Kunnel, ain't dat Mis' Liscum, Kunnel?" " What?" said the old man. He got up quickly and appeared at the rail, his arm in a sling. He cried, " Alice!" The little woman saw him, and instantly she covered up her face with her hands as if blinded with a flash of white fire. She made no outcry; it was all in this simply swift gesture, but we—we knew them. It told us. It told us the other part. And in a vision we all saw our own harbour-lights. That is to say those of us who had harbour-lights.

I was almost well, and had defeated the yellow-fever charge which had been brought against me, and so I was allowed ashore among the first. And now happened a strange thing. A hard campaign, full of wants and lacks and absences, brings a man speedily back to an appreciation of things long disregarded or forgotten. In camp, somewhere in the woods between Siboney and Santiago, I happened to think of ice-cream-soda. I had done very well without it for many years; in fact I think I loathe it; but I got to dreaming of ice-cream-soda, and I came near dying of longing for it. I couldn't get it out of my mind, try as I would to concentrate my thoughts upon the land crabs and mud with which I was surrounded. It certainly had been an institution of my childhood, but to have a ravenous longing for it in the year 1898 was about as illogical as to have a ravenous longing for kerosene. All I could do was to swear to myself that if I reached the United States again, I would immediately go to the nearest soda-water fountain and make it look like Spanish Fours. In a loud, firm voice, I would say, " Orange, please." And here is the strange thing : as soon as I was ashore I went to the nearest soda-water-fountain, and in a loud, firm voice I said, " Orange, please." I remember one man who went mad that way over tinned peaches, and who wandered over the face of the earth saying plaintively, " Have you any peaches? "

Most of the wounded and sick had to be tab-ulated and marshalled in sections and thor-oughly officialised, so that I was in time to take a position on the verandah of Chamberlain's Hotel and see my late shipmates taken to the hospital. The verandah was crowded with women in light, charming summer dresses, and with

spruce officers from the Fortress. It was like a
bank of flowers. It filled me with awe. All
this luxury and refinement and gentle care and
fragrance and colour seemed absolutely new. Then
across the narrow street on the verandah of the
hotel there was a similar bank of flowers. Two
companies of volunteers dug a lane through the
great crowd in the street and kept the way, and
then through this lane there passed a curious
procession. I had never known that they looked
like that. Such a gang of dirty, ragged, emaciated,
half-starved, bandaged cripples I had never seen.
Naturally there were many men who couldn't
walk, and some of these were loaded upon a big
flat car which was in tow of a trolley-car. Then
there were many stretchers, slow-moving. When
that crowd began to pass the hotel the banks of
flowers made a noise which could make one
tremble. Perhaps it was a moan, perhaps it was
a sob—but no, it was something beyond either a
moan or a sob. Anyhow, the sound of women
weeping was in it.—The sound of women weeping.

And how did these men of famous deeds appear
when received thus by the people? Did they
smirk and look as if they were bursting with the
desire to tell everything which had happened?
No they hung their heads like so many jail-birds.

Most of them seemed to be suffering from something which was like stage-fright during the ordeal of this chance but supremely eloquent reception. No sense of excellence—that was it. Evidently they were willing to leave the clacking to all those natural born major-generals who after the war talked enough to make a great fall in the price of that commodity all over the world.

The episode was closed. And you can depend upon it that I have told you nothing at all, nothing at all, nothing at all.

THE SECOND GENERATION

I

CASPAR CADOGAN resolved to go to the tropic
wars and do something. The air was blue and
gold with the pomp of soldiering, and in every ear
rang the music of military glory. Caspar's father
was a United States Senator from the great State
of Skowmulligan, where the war fever ran very
high. Chill is the blood of many of the sons of
millionaires, but Caspar took the fever and posted
to Washington. His father had never denied
him anything, and this time all that Caspar wanted
was a little Captaincy in the Army—just a simple
little Captaincy.

The old man had been entertaining a delegation
of respectable bunco-steerers from Skowmulligan
who had come to him on a matter which is none
of the public's business.

Bottles of whisky and boxes of cigars were still
on the table in the sumptuous private parlour.
The Senator had said, " Well, gentlemen, I'll do

what I can for you." By this sentence he meant
whatever he meant.

Then he turned to his eager son. "Well,
Caspar?" The youth poured out his modest
desires. It was not altogether his fault. Life
had taught him a generous faith in his own abilities. If any one had told him that he was simply
an ordinary d——d fool he would have opened
his eyes wide at the person's lack of judgment.
All his life people had admired him.

The Skowmulligan war-horse looked with quick
disapproval into the eyes of his son. "Well,
Caspar," he said slowly, " I am of the opinion
that they've got all the golf experts and tennis
champions and cotillion leaders and piano tuners
and billiard markers that they really need as officers. Now, if you were a soldier——"

" I know," said the young man with a gesture,
" but I'm not exactly a fool, I hope, and I think
if I get a chance I can do something. I'd like to
try. I would, indeed."

The Senator lit a cigar. He assumed an attitude of ponderous reflection. "Y—yes, but this
country is full of young men who are not fools.
Full of 'em."

Caspar fidgeted in the desire to answer that
while he admitted the profusion of young men who

were not fools, he felt that he himself possessed
interesting and peculiar qualifications which would
allow him to make his mark in any field of effort
which he seriously challenged. But he did not
make this graceful statement, for he sometimes
detected something ironic in his father's temper-
ament. The Skowmulligan war-horse had not
thought of expressing an opinion of his own
ability since the year 1865, when he was young,
like Caspar.

" Well, well," said the Senator finally. " I'll
see about it. I'll see about it." The young man
was obliged to await the end of his father's characteristic method of thought. The war-horse never
gave a quick answer, and if people tried to hurry
him they seemed able to arouse only a feeling of
irritation against making a decision at all. His
mind moved like the wind, but practice had placed
a Mexican bit in the mouth of his judgment.
This old man of light quick thought had taught
himself to move like an ox cart. Caspar said,
" Yes, sir." He withdrew to his club, where, to
the affectionate inquiries of some envious friends,
he replied, " The old man is letting the idea
soak."

The mind of the war-horse was decided far
sooner than Caspar expected. In Washington a

large number of well-bred handsome young men were receiving appointments as Lieutenants, as Captains, and occasionally as Majors. They were a strong, healthy, clean-eyed educated collection. They were a prime lot. A German Field-Marshal would have beamed with joy if he could have had them—to send to school. Anywhere in the world they would have made a grand show as material, but, intrinsically they were not Lieutenants, Captains and Majors. They were fine men, though manhood is only an essential part of a Lieutenant, a Captain or a Major. But at any rate, this arrangement had all the logic of going to sea in a bathing-machine.

The Senator found himself reasoning that Caspar was as good as any of them, and better than many. Presently he was bleating here and there that his boy should have a chance. " The boy's all right, I tell you, Henry. He's wild to go, and I don't see why they shouldn't give him a show. He's got plenty of nerve, and he's keen as a whip-lash. I'm going to get him an appointment, and if you can do anything to help it along I wish you would."

Then he betook himself to the White House and the War Department and made a stir. People think that Administrations are always slavishly, abominably anxious to please the Machine. They are not ; they wish the Machine sunk in red fire, for by the power of ten thousand past words, looks, gestures, writings, the Machine comes along and takes the Administration by the nose and twists it, and the Administration dare not even yell. The huge force which carries an election to success looks reproachfully at the Administration and says, " Give me a bun." That is a very small thing with which to reward a Colossus.

The Skowmulligan war-horse got his bun and took it to his hotel where Caspar was moodily reading war rumours. " Well, my boy, here you are." Caspar was a Captain and Commissary on the staff of Brigadier-General Reilly, commander of the Second Brigade of the First Division of the Thirtieth Army Corps.

" I had to work for it," said the Senator grimly. " They talked to me as if they thought you were some sort of empty-headed idiot. None of 'em seemed to know you personally. They just sort of took it for granted. Finally I got pretty hot in the collar." He paused a moment ; his heavy, grooved face set hard ; his blue eyes shone. He clapped a hand down upon the handle of his chair.

" Caspar, I've got you into this thing, and I

believe you'll do all right, and I'm not saying this because I distrust either your sense or your grit. But I want you to understand you've *got to make a go of it*. I'm not going to talk any twaddle about your country and your country's flag. You understand all about that. But now you're a soldier, and there'll be this to do and that to do, and fighting to do, and you've got to do *every d——d one of 'em* right up to the handle. I don't know how much of a shindy this thing is going to be, but any shindy is enough to show how much there is in a man. You've got your appointment, and that's all I can do for you; but I'll thrash you with my own hands if, when the Army gets back, the other fellows say my son is ' nothing but a good-looking dude.' "

He ceased, breathing heavily. Caspar looked bravely and frankly at his father, and answered in a voice which was not very tremulous. " I'll do my best. This is my chance. I'll do my best with it."

The Senator had a marvellous ability of transition from one manner to another. Suddenly he seemed very kind. " Well, that's all right, then. I guess you'll get along all right with Reilly. I know him well, and he'll see you through. I helped him along once. And now about this commissary business. As I understand it, a Commissary is a sort of caterer in a big way—that is, he looks out for a good many more things than a caterer has to bother his head about. Reilly's brigade has probably from two to three thousand men in it, and in regard to certain things you've got to look out for every man of 'em every day. I know perfectly well you couldn't successfully run a boarding-house in Ocean Grove. How are you going to manage for all these soldiers, hey? Thought about it?"

"No," said Caspar, injured. " I didn't want to be a Commissary. I wanted to be a Captain in the line."

" They wouldn't hear of it. They said you would have to take a staff appointment where people could look after you."

" Well, let them look after me," cried Caspar resentfully ; " but when there's any fighting to be done I guess I won't necessarily be the last man."

" That's it," responded the Senator. " That's the spirit." They both thought that the problem of war would eliminate to an equation of actual battle.

Ultimately Caspar departed into the South to an encampment in salty grass under pine trees.

Here lay an Army corps twenty thousand strong. Caspar passed into the dusty sunshine of it, and for many weeks he was lost to view.

II

" Of course I don't know a blamed thing about it," said Caspar frankly and modestly to a circle of his fellow staff officers. He was referring to the duties of his office.

Their faces became expressionless ; they looked at him with eyes in which he could fathom nothing. After a pause one politely said, " Don't you ? " It was the inevitable two words of convention.

" Why," cried Caspar, " I didn't know what a commissary officer was until I *was* one. My old Guv'nor told me. He'd looked it up in a book somewhere, I suppose ; but *I* didn't know."

" Didn't you ? "

The young man's face glowed with sudden humour. " Do you know, the word was intimately associated in my mind with camels. Funny, eh ? I think it came from reading that rhyme of Kipling's about the commissariat camel."

" Did it ? "

" Yes. Funny, isn't it? Camels!"

The brigade was ultimately landed at Siboney as part of an army to attack Santiago. The scene at the landing sometimes resembled the inspiriting daily drama at the approach to the Brooklyn Bridge. There was a great bustle, during which the wise man kept his property gripped in his hands lest it might march off into the wilderness in the pocket of one of the striding regiments. Truthfully, Caspar should have had frantic occupation, but men saw him wandering bootlessly here and there crying, " Has any one seen my saddle-bags? Why, if I lose them I'm ruined. I've got everything packed away in 'em. Everything!"

They looked at him gloomily and without attention. " No," they said. It was to intimate that they would not give a rip if he had lost his nose, his teeth and his self-respect. Reilly's brigade collected itself from the boats and went off, each regiment's soul burning with anger because some other regiment was in advance of it. Moving along through the scrub and under the palms, men talked mostly of things that did not pertain to the business in hand.

General Reilly finally planted his headquarters in some tall grass under a mango tree. " Where's Cadogan?" he said suddenly as he took off his hat and smoothed the wet grey hair from his brow. Nobody knew. " I saw him looking for his saddle-bags down at the landing," said an officer dubiously. " Bother him," said the General con- temptuously. " Let him stay there."

Three venerable regimental commanders came, saluted stiffly and sat in the grass. There was a pow-wow, during which Reilly explained much that the Division Commander had told him. The venerable Colonels nodded; they understood. Everything was smooth and clear to their minds. But still, the Colonel of the Forty-fourth Regular Infantry murmured about the commissariat. His men—and then he launched forth in a sentiment concerning the privations of his men in which you were confronted with his feeling that his men— his men were the only creatures of importance in the universe, which feeling was entirely correct for him. Reilly grunted. He did what most commanders did. He set the competent line to doing the work of the incompetent part of the staff.

In time Caspar came trudging along the road merrily swinging his saddle-bags. " Well, Gen- neral," he cried as he saluted, " I found 'em."

" Did you ? " said Reilly. Later an officer rushed to him tragically : " General, Cadogan is off there in the bushes eatin' potted ham and crackers all by himself." The officer was sent back into the bushes for Caspar, and the General sent Caspar with an order. Then Reilly and the three venerable Colonels, grinning, partook of potted ham and crackers. "Tashe a' right," said Reilly, with his mouth full. "Dorsey, see if 'e got some'n else."

"Mush be selfish young pig," said one of the Colonels, with his mouth full. "Who's he, General?"

"Son—Sen'tor Cad'gan—ol' frien' mine—dash 'im."

Caspar wrote a letter:

"*Dear Father:* I am sitting under a tree using the flattest part of my canteen for a desk. Even as I write the division ahead of us is moving forward and we don't know what moment the storm of battle may break out. I don't know what the plans are. General Reilly knows, but he is so good as to give me very little of his confidence. In fact, I might be part of a forlorn hope from all to the contrary I've heard from him. I understood you to say in Washington that you at one time had been of some service to him, but if that is true I can assure you he has completely forgotten it. At times his manner to me is little short of being offensive, but of course I understand that it is only the way of a crusty old soldier who has been made boorish and bearish by a long life among the Indians. I dare say I shall manage it all right without a row.

"When you hear that we have captured Santiago, please send me by first steamer a box of provisions and clothing,

particularly sardines, pickles, and light-weight underwear.
The other men on the staff are nice quiet chaps, but they
seem a bit crude. There has been no fighting yet save the
skirmish by Young's brigade. Reilly was furious because
we couldn't get in it. I met General Peel yesterday. He
was very nice. He said he knew you well when he was in
Congress. Young Jack May is on Peel's staff. I knew him
well in college. We spent an hour talking over old times.
Give my love to all at home."

The march was leisurely. Reilly and his staff
strolled out to the head of the long, sinuous
column and entered the sultry gloom of the
forest. Some less fortunate regiments had to
wait among the trees at the side of the trail, and
as Reilly's brigade passed them, officer called to
officer, classmate to classmate, and in these
greetings rang a note of everything, from West
Point to Alaska. They were going into an action
in which they, the officers, would lose over a
hundred in killed and wounded—officers alone—
and these greetings, in which many nicknames
occurred, were in many cases farewells such as one
pictures being given with ostentation, solemnity,
fervour. "There goes Gory Widgeon! Hello,
Gory! Where you starting for? Hey, Gory!"

Caspar communed with himself and decided
that he was not frightened. He was eager and
alert; he thought that now his obligation to his
country, or himself, was to be faced, and he was

mad to prove to old Reilly and the others that
after all he was a very capable soldier.

———

III

Old Reilly was stumping along the line of
his brigade and mumbling like a man with a
mouthful of grass. The fire from the enemy's
position was incredible in its swift fury, and
Reilly's brigade was getting its share of a very
bad ordeal. The old man's face was of the colour
of a tomato, and in his rage he mouthed and
sputtered strangely. As he pranced along his
thin line, scornfully erect, voices arose from the
grass beseeching him to take care of himself. At
his heels scrambled a bugler with pallid skin and
clenched teeth, a chalky, trembling youth, who
kept his eye on old Reilly's back and followed it.

The old gentleman was quite mad. Apparently
he thought the whole thing a dreadful mess, but
now that his brigade was irrevocably in it he was
full-tilting here and everywhere to establish some
irreproachable, immaculate kind of behaviour on
the part of every man jack in his brigade. The
intentions of the three venerable Colonels were
the same. They stood behind their lines, quiet,

21

stern, courteous old fellows, admonishing their regiments to be very pretty in the face of such a hail of magazine-rifle and machine-gun fire as has never in this world been confronted save by beardless savages when the white man has found occasion to take his burden to some new place.

And the regiments were pretty. The men lay on their little stomachs and got peppered according to the law and said nothing, as the good blood pumped out into the grass, and even if a solitary rookie tried to get a decent reason to move to some haven of rational men, the cold voice of an officer made him look criminal with a shame that was a credit to his regimental education. Behind Reilly's command was a bullet-torn jungle through which it could not move as a brigade; ahead of it were Spanish trenches on hills. Reilly considered that he was in a fix no doubt, but he said this only to himself. Suddenly he saw on the right a little point of blue-shirted men already half-way up the hill. It was some pathetic fragment of the Sixth United States Infantry. Chagrined, shocked, horrified, Reilly bellowed to his bugler, and the chalked-faced youth unlocked his teeth and sounded the charge by rushes.

The men formed hastily and grimly, and rushed.

Apparently there awaited them only the fate of respectable soldiers. But they went because— of the opinions of others, perhaps. They went because—no loud-mouthed lot of jail-birds such as the Twenty-Seventh Infantry could do anything that they could not do better. They went because Reilly ordered it. They went because they went.

And yet not a man of them to this day has made a public speech explaining precisely how he did the whole thing and detailing with what initiative and ability he comprehended and defeated a situation which he did not comprehend at all.

Reilly never saw the top of the hill. He was heroically striving to keep up with his men when a bullet ripped quietly through his left lung, and he fell back into the arms of the bugler, who received him as he would have received a Christmas present. The three venerable Colonels inherited the brigade in swift succession. The senior commanded for about fifty seconds, at the end of which he was mortally shot. Before they could get the news to the next in rank he, too, was shot. The junior Colonel ultimately arrived with a lean and puffing little brigade at the top of the hill. The men lay down and fired volleys at whatever was practicable.

In and out of the ditch-like trenches lay the Spanish dead, lemon-faced corpses dressed in shabby blue and white ticking. Some were huddled down comfortably like sleeping children; one had died in the attitude of a man flung back in a dentist's chair; one sat in the trench with his chin sunk despondently to his breast; few preserved a record of the agitation of battle. With the greater number it was as if death had touched them so gently, so lightly, that they had not known of it. Death had come to them rather in the form of an opiate than of a bloody blow.

But the arrived men in the blue shirts had no thought of the sallow corpses. They were eagerly exchanging a hail of shots with the Spanish second line, whose ash-coloured entrenchments barred the way to a city white amid trees. In the pauses the men talked.

"We done the best. Old E Company got there. Why, one time the hull of B Company was *behind* us."

"Jones, he was the first man up. I saw 'im."

"Which Jones?"

"Did you see ol' Two-bars runnin' like a land-crab? Made good time, too. He hit only in the high places. He's all right."

"The Lootenant is all right, too. He was a

good ten yards ahead of the best of us. I hated him at the post, but for this here active service there's none of 'em can touch him."

"This is mighty different from being at the post."

"Well, we done it, an' it wasn't b'cause *I* thought it could be done. When we started, I ses to m'self: 'Well, here goes a lot o' d——d fools.'"

"'Tain't over yet."

"Oh, they'll never git us back from here. If they start to chase us back from here we'll pile 'em up so high the last ones can't climb over. We've come this far, an' we'll stay here. I ain't done pantin'."

"Anything is better than packin' through that jungle an' gettin' blistered from front, rear, an' both flanks. I'd rather tackle another hill than go trailin' in them woods, so thick you can't tell whether you are one man or a division of cav'lry."

"Where's that young kitchen soldier, Cadogan, or whatever his name is. Ain't seen him to-day."

"Well, *I* seen him. He was right in with it. He got shot, too, about half up the hill, in the leg. I seen it. He's all right. Don't worry about him. He's all right."

"I seen 'im, too. He done his stunt. As soon

as I can git this piece of barbed-wire entangle‑
ment out o' me throat I'll give 'm a cheer."

"He ain't shot at all, b'cause there he stands,
there. See 'im?"

Rearward, the grassy slope was populous with
little groups of men searching for the wounded.
Reilly's brigade began to dig with its bayonets
and shovel with its meat-ration cans.

IV

Senator Cadogan paced to and fro in his
private parlour and smoked small, brown weak
cigars. These little wisps seemed utterly inade‑
quate to console such a ponderous satrap.

It was the evening of the 1st of July, 1898, and
the Senator was immensely excited, as could be
seen from the superlatively calm way in which he
called out to his private secretary, who was in an
adjoining room. The voice was serene, gentle,
affectionate, low.

"Baker, I wish you'd go over again to the War
Department and see if they've heard anything
about Caspar."

A very bright-eyed, hatchet-faced young man
appeared in a doorway, pen still in hand. He

was hiding a nettle-like irritation behind all the
finished audacity of a smirk, sharp, lying, trust-
worthy young politician. " I've just got back
from there, sir," he suggested.

The Skowmulligan war-horse lifted his eyes and
looked for a short second into the eyes of his
private secretary. It was not a glare or an eagle
glance ; it was something beyond the practice of
an actor; it was simply meaning. The clever
private secretary grabbed his hat and was at once
enthusiastically away. " All right, sir," he cried.
" I'll find out."

The War Department was ablaze with light, and
messengers were running. With the assurance of
a retainer of an old house Baker made his way
through much small-calibre vociferation. There
was rumour of a big victory ; there was rumour of
a big defeat. In the corridors various watchdogs
arose from their armchairs and asked him of his
business in tones of uncertainty which in no wise
compared with their previous habitual deference
to the private secretary of the war-horse of Skowmulligan.

Ultimately Baker arrived in a room where some
kind of head clerk sat writing feverishly at a
roll-top desk. Baker asked a question, and the
head clerk mumbled profanely without lifting his

head.   Apparently he said : " How in the blankety-blank blazes do I know ? "

The private secretary let his jaw fall.   Surely
some new spirit had come suddenly upon the
heart of Washington—a spirit which Baker understood to be almost defiantly indifferent to the
wishes of Senator Cadogan, a spirit which was
not courteously oily.   What could it mean ?
Baker's fox-like mind sprang wildly to a conception of overturned factions, changed friends, new
combinations.   The assurance which had come
from experience of a broad political situation suddenly left him, and he would not have been
amazed if some one had told him that Senator
Cadogan now controlled only six votes in the
State of Skowmulligan.   "Well," he stammered
in his bewilderment, " well—there isn't any news
of the old man's son, hey ? "   Again the head
clerk replied blasphemously.

Eventually Baker retreated in disorder from
the presence of this head clerk, having learned
that the latter did not give a —— if Caspar Cadogan were sailing through Hades on an ice yacht.

Baker stormed other and more formidable offi-
cials.   In fact, he struck as high as he dared.
They one and all flung him short, hard words,
even as men pelt an annoying cur with pebbles.

He emerged from the brilliant light, from the groups of men with anxious, puzzled faces, and as he walked back to the hotel he did not know if his name were Baker or Cholmondeley.

However, as he walked up the stairs to the Senator's rooms he contrived to concentrate his intellect upon a manner of speaking.

The war-horse was still pacing his parlour and smoking. He paused at Baker's entrance. "Well?"

"Mr. Cadogan," said the private secretary coolly, "they told me at the Department that they did not give a cuss whether your son was alive or dead."

The Senator looked at Baker and smiled gently. "What's that, my boy?" he asked in a soft and considerate voice.

"They said——" gulped Baker, with a certain tenacity. "They said that they didn't give a cuss whether your son was alive or dead."

There was a silence for the space of three seconds. Baker stood like an image; he had no machinery for balancing the issues of this kind of a situation, and he seemed to feel that if he stood as still as a stone frog he would escape the ravages of a terrible Senatorial wrath which was about to break forth in a hurricane speech which would snap off trees and sweep away barns.

"Well," drawled the Senator lazily, "who did you see, Baker?"

The private secretary resumed a certain usual manner of breathing. He told the names of the men whom he had seen.

"Ye—e—es," remarked the Senator. He took another little brown cigar and held it with a thumb and first finger, staring at it with the calm and steady scrutiny of a scientist investigating a new thing. "So they don't care whether Caspar is alive or dead, eh? Well . . . maybe they don't. . . . That's all right. . . . However . . . I think I'll just look in on 'em and state my views."

When the Senator had gone, the private secretary ran to the window and leaned afar out. Pennsylvania Avenue was gleaming silver blue in the light of many arc-lamps; the cable trains groaned along to the clangour of gongs; from the window, the walks presented a hardly diversified aspect of shirt-waists and straw hats. Sometimes a newsboy screeched.

Baker watched the tall, heavy figure of the Senator moving out to intercept a cable train. "Great Scott!" cried the private secretary to

himself, " there'll be three distinct kinds of grand,
plain practical fireworks. The old man is going
for 'em. I wouldn't be in Lascum's boots. Ye
gods, what a row there'll be."

In due time the Senator was closeted with some
kind of deputy third-assistant battery-horse in the
offices of the War Department. The official obviously had been told off to make a supreme effort
to pacify Cadogan, and he certainly was acting
according to his instructions. He was almost in
tears; he spread out his hands in supplication,
and his voice whined and wheedled.

" Why, really, you know, Senator, we can only
beg you to look at the circumstances. Two scant
divisions at the top of that hill; over a thousand
men killed and wounded; the line so thin that
any strong attack would smash our Army to flin-
ders. The Spaniards have probably received re-
enforcements under Pando; Shafter seems to be
too ill to be actively in command of our troops;
Lawton can't get up with his division before to-
morrow. We are actually expecting . . . no, I
won't say expecting . . . but we would not be
surprised . . . nobody in the department would
be surprised if before daybreak we were compelled
to give to the country the news of a disaster which
would be the worst blow the National pride has

ever suffered. Don't you see? Can't you see our position, Senator?"

The Senator, with a pale but composed face, contemplated the official with eyes that gleamed in a way not usual with the big, self-controlled politician.

" I'll tell you frankly, sir," continued the other. " I'll tell you frankly, that at this moment we don't know whether we are a-foot or a-horseback. Everything is in the air. We don't know whether we have won a glorious victory or simply got ourselves in a deuce of a fix."

The Senator coughed. " I suppose my boy is with the two divisions at the top of that hill? He's with Reilly."

" Yes ; Reilly's brigade is up there."

" And when do you suppose the War Department can tell me if he is all right. I want to know."

" My dear Senator, frankly, I don't know. Again I beg you to think of our position. The Army is in a muddle ; it's a General thinking that he must fall back, and yet not sure that he *can* fall back without losing the Army, Why, we're worrying about the lives of sixteen thousand men and the self-respect of the nation, Senator."

" I see," observed the Senator, nodding his head

slowly. " And naturally the welfare of one man's son doesn't—how do they say it—doesn't cut any ice."

V.

And in Cuba it rained. In a few days Reilly's brigade discovered that by their successful charge they had gained the inestimable privilege of sitting in a wet trench and slowly but surely starving to death. Men's tempers crumbled like dry bread. The soldiers who so cheerfully, quietly and decently had captured positions which the foreign experts had said were impregnable, now in turn underwent an attack which was furious as well as insidious. The heat of the sun alternated with rains which boomed and roared in their falling like mountain cataracts. It seemed as if men took the fever through sheer lack of other occupation. During the days of battle none had had time to get even a tropic headache, but no sooner was that brisk period over than men began to shiver and shudder by squads and platoons. Rations were scarce enough to make a little fat strip of bacon seem of the size of a corner lot, and coffee grains were pearls. There would have been godless quarreling over fragments if it were not that with these fevers came a great listlessness, so that men were almost content to die, if death required no exertion.

It was an occasion which distinctly separated the sheep from the goats. The goats were few enough, but their qualities glared out like crimson spots.

One morning Jameson and Ripley, two Captains in the Forty-fourth Foot, lay under a flimsy shelter of sticks and palm branches. Their dreamy, dull eyes contemplated the men in the trench which went to left and right. To them came Caspar Cadogan, moaning. "By Jove," he said, as he flung himself wearily on the ground, "I can't stand much more of this, you know. It's killing me." A bristly beard sprouted through the grime on his face; his eyelids were crimson; an indescribably dirty shirt fell away from his roughened neck; and at the same time various lines of evil and greed were deepened on his face, until he practically stood forth as a revelation, a confession. "I can't stand it. By Jove, I can't."

Stanford, a Lieutenant under Jameson, came stumbling along toward them. He was a lad of the class of '98 at West Point. It could be seen that he was flaming with fever. He rolled a calm eye at them. "Have you any water, sir?" he said to his Captain. Jameson got upon his feet and helped Stanford to lay his shaking length under the shelter. " No, boy," he answered gloomily. " Not a drop. You got any, Rip?"

" No," answered Ripley, looking with anxiety upon the young officer. " Not a drop."

" You, Cadogan?"

Here Caspar hesitated oddly for a second, and then in a tone of deep regret made answer, " No, Captain ; not a mouthful."

Jameson moved off weakly. " You lay quietly, Stanford, and I'll see what I can rustle."

Presently Caspar felt that Ripley was steadily regarding him. He returned the look with one of half-guilty questioning.

" God forgive you, Cadogan," said Ripley, " but you are a damned beast. Your canteen is full of water."

Even then the apathy in their veins prevented the scene from becoming as sharp as the words sounded. Caspar sputtered like a child, and at length merely said: " No, it isn't." Stanford lifted his head to shoot a keen, proud glance at Caspar, and then turned away his face.

" You lie," said Ripley. " I can tell the sound of a full canteen as far as I can hear it."

" Well, if it is, I—I must have forgotten it."

"You lie ; no man in this Army just now forgets whether his canteen is full or empty. Hand it over."

Fever is the physical counterpart of shame, and when a man has the one he accepts the other with an ease which would revolt his healthy self. However, Caspar made a desperate struggle to preserve the forms. He arose and taking the string from his shoulder, passed the canteen to Ripley. But after all there was a whine in his voice, and the assumption of dignity was really a farce. "I think I had better go, Captain. You can have the water if you want it, I'm sure. But —but I fail to see—I fail to see what reason you have for insulting me."

"Do you? " said Ripley stolidly. " That's all right."

Caspar stood for a terrible moment. He simply did not have the strength to turn his back on this —this affair. It seemed to him that he must stand forever and face it. But when he found the audacity to look again at Ripley he saw the latter was not at all concerned with the situation. Ripley, too, had the fever. The fever changes all laws of proportion. Caspar went away.

" Here, youngster ; here is your drink."

Stanford made a weak gesture. " I wouldn't touch a drop from his blamed canteen if it was the last water in the world," he murmured in his high, boyish voice.

" Don't you be a young jackass," quoth Ripley tenderly.

The boy stole a glance at the canteen. he felt the propriety of arising and hurling it after Caspar, but—he, too, had the fever.

" Don't you be a young jackass," said Ripley again.

VI

Senator Cadogan was happy. His son had returned from Cuba, and the 8:30 train that evening would bring him to the station nearest to the stone and red shingle villa which the Senator and his family occupied on the shores of Long Island Sound. The Senator's steam yacht lay some hundred yards from the beach. She had just returned from a trip to Montauk Point where the Senator had made a gallant attempt to gain his son from the transport on which he was coming from Cuba. He had fought a brave sea-fight with sundry petty little doctors and ship's officers who had raked him with broadsides, describ-

22

ing the laws of quarantine and had used inelegant
speech to a United States Senator as he stood on
the bridge of his own steam yacht. These men
had grimly asked him to tell exactly how much
better was Caspar than any other returning
soldier.

But the Senator had not given them a long
fight. In fact, the truth came to him quickly, and
with almost a blush he had ordered the yacht back
to her anchorage off the villa. As a matter of
fact, the trip to Montauk Point had been under-
taken largely from impulse. Long ago the Senator had decided that when his boy returned the
greeting should have something Spartan in it.
He would make a welcome such as most soldiers
get. There should be no flowers and carriages
when the other poor fellows got none. He
should consider Caspar as a soldier. That was
the way to treat a man. But in the end a sharp
acid of anxiety had worked upon the iron old
man, until he had ordered the yacht to take him
out and make a fool of him. The result filled him
with a chagrin which caused him to delegate to
the mother and sisters the entire business of suc-
couring Caspar at Montauk Point Camp. He had
remained at home conducting the huge correspondence of an active National politician and waiting

for this son whom he so loved and whom he so
wished to be a man of a certain strong, taciturn,
shrewd ideal.   The recent yacht voyage he now
looked upon as a kind of confession of his weakness, and he was resolved that no more signs
should escape him.

But yet his boy had been down there against
the enemy and among the fevers.   There had
been grave perils, and his boy must have faced
them.   And he could not prevent himself from
dreaming through the poetry of fine actions in
which visions his son's face shone out manly and
generous.   During these periods the people about
him, accustomed as they were to his silence and
calm in time of stress, considered that affairs in
Skowmulligan might be most critical.   In no
other way could they account for this exaggerated
phlegm.

On the night of Caspar's return he did not go
to dinner, but had a tray sent to his library,
where he remained writing.   At last he heard the
spin of the dog-cart's wheels on the gravel of the
drive, and a moment later there penetrated to
him the sound of joyful feminine cries.   He lit
another cigar; he knew that it was now his part
to bide with dignity the moment when his son
should shake off that other welcome and come to

him, He could still hear them ; in their exuberance they seemed to be capering like school-children. He was impatient, but this impatience took the form of a polar stolidity.

Presently there were quick steps and a jubilant knock at his door. " Come in," he said.

In came Caspar, thin, yellow, and in soiled khaki. " They almost tore me to pieces," he cried, laughing. " They danced around like wild things." Then as they shook hands he dutifully said " How are you, sir ? "

" How are you, my boy ? " answered the Senator casually but kindly.

" Better than I might expect, sir," cried Caspar cheerfully. " We had a pretty hard time, you know."

" You look as if they'd given you a hard run," observed the father in a tone of slight interest.

Caspar was eager to tell. " Yes, sir," he said rapidly. " We did, indeed. Why, it was awful. We—any of us—were lucky to get out of it alive. It wasn't so much the Spaniards, you know. The Army took care of them all right. It was the fever and the—you know, we couldn't get anything to eat. And the mismanagement. Why, it was frightful."

"Yes, I've heard," said the Senator. A certain wistful look came into his eyes, but he did not allow it to become prominent. Indeed, he suppressed it. "And you, Caspar? I suppose you did your duty?"

Caspar answered with becoming modesty. "Well, I didn't do more than anybody else, I don't suppose, but—well, I got along all right, I guess."

"And this great charge up San Juan Hill?" asked the father slowly. "Were you in that?"

"Well—yes; I was in it," replied the son.

The Senator brightened a trifle. "You were, eh? In the front of it? or just sort of going along?"

"Well—I don't know. I couldn't tell exactly. Sometimes I was in front of a lot of them, and sometimes I was—just sort of going along."

This time the Senator emphatically brightened. "That's all right, then. And of course—of course you performed your commissary duties correctly?"

The question seemed to make Caspar uncommunicative and sulky. "I did when there was anything to do," he answered. "But the whole thing was on the most unbusiness-like basis you can imagine. And they wouldn't tell you anything. Nobody would take time to instruct you

in your duties, and of course if you didn't know a
thing your superior officer would swoop down on
you and ask you why in the deuce such and such
a thing wasn't done in such and such a way. Of
course I did the best I could."

The Senator's countenance had again become
sombrely indifferent. "I see. But you weren't
directly rebuked for incapacity, were you? No;
of course you weren't. But—I mean—did any of
your superior officers suggest that you were 'no
good,' or anything of that sort? I mean—did
you come off with a clean slate?"

Caspar took a small time to digest his father's
meaning. "Oh, yes, sir," he cried at the end of
his reflection. "The Commissary was in such a
hopeless mess anyhow that nobody thought of
doing anything but curse Washington."

"Of course," rejoined the Senator harshly.
"But supposing that you had been a competent
and well-trained commissary officer. What then?"

Again the son took time for consideration, and
in the end deliberately replied "Well, if I had
been a competent and well-trained Commissary I
would have sat there and eaten up my heart and
cursed Washington."

"Well, then, that's all right. And now about
this charge up San Juan? Did any of the Generals

speak to you afterward and say that you had done
well? Didn't any of them see you?"

" Why, n —n—no, I don't suppose they did . . .
any more than I did them. You see, this charge
was a big thing and covered lots of ground, and I
hardly saw anybody excepting a lot of the men."

" Well, but didn't any of the men see you?
Weren't you ahead some of the time leading them
on and waving your sword?"

Caspar burst into laughter. " Why, no. I had
all I could do to scramble along and try to keep
up. And I didn't want to go up at all."

" Why?" demanded the Senator.

" Because—because the Spaniards were shooting
so much. And you could see men falling, and the
bullets rushed around you in—by the bushel. And
then at last it seemed that if we once drove them
away from the top of the hill there would be less
danger. So we all went up."

The Senator chuckled over this description.
" And you didn't flinch at all?"

"Well," rejoined Caspar humorously, " I won't
say I wasn't frightened."

" No, of course not. But then you did not let
anybody know it?"

"Of course not."

"You understand, naturally, that I am bother-

ing you with all these questions because I desire
to hear how my only son behaved in the crisis.   I
don't want to worry you with it.   But if you went
through the San Juan charge with credit I'll have
you made a Major."

"Well," said Caspar, "I wouldn't say I went
through that charge with credit.   I went through
it all good enough, but the enlisted men around
went through in the same way."

"But weren't you encouraging them and leading them on by your example?"

Caspar smirked.   He began to see a point.
"Well, sir," he said with a charming hesitation.
"Aw—er—I—well, I dare say I was doing my
share of it."

The perfect form of the reply delighted the
father.   He could not endure blatancy ; his admiration was to be won only by a bashful hero.   Now
he beat his hand impulsively down upon the table.
"That's what I wanted to know. That's it exactly.
I'll have you made a Major next week.   You've
found your proper field at last.   You stick to the
Army, Caspar, and I'll back you up.   That's the
thing.   In a few years it will be a great career.
The United States is pretty sure to have an Army
of about a hundred and fifty thousand men.   And
starting in when you did and with me to back you

up—why, we'll make you a General in seven or
eight years. That's the ticket. You stay in the
Army." The Senator's cheek was flushed with
enthusiasm, and he looked eagerly and confidently
at his son.

But Caspar had pulled a long face. "The
Army?" he said. "Stay in the Army?"

The Senator continued to outline quite rapt-
urously his idea of the future. "The Army,
evidently, is just the place for you. You know as
well as I do that you have not been a howling success, exactly, in anything else which you have tried.
But now the Army just suits you. It is the kind
of career which especially suits you. Well, then,
go in, and go at it hard. Go in to win. Go at it."

" But——" began Caspar.

The Senator interrupted swiftly. "Oh, don't
worry about that part of it. I'll take care of all
that. You won't get jailed in some Arizona
adobe for the rest of your natural life. There
won't be much more of that, anyhow ; and besides,
as I say, I'll look after all that end of it. The
chance is splendid. A young, healthy and intelligent man, with the start you've already got, and
with my backing, can do anything—anything!
There will be a lot of active service—oh, yes, I'm
sure of it—and everybody who——"

"But," said Caspar, wan, desperate, heroic, "father, I don't care to stay in the Army."

The Senator lifted his eyes and darkened. "What?" he said. "What's that?" He looked at Caspar.

The son became tightened and wizened like an old miser trying to withhold gold. He replied with a sort of idiot obstinacy, "I don't care to stay in the Army."

The Senator's jaw clinched down, and he was dangerous. But, after all, there was something mournful somewhere. "Why, what do you mean?" he asked gruffly.

"Why. I couldn't get along, you know. The—the— "

"The what?" demanded the father, suddenly uplifted with thunderous anger. "The what?"

Caspar's pain found a sort of outlet in mere irresponsible talk. "Well, you know—the other men. you know. I couldn't get along with them, you know. They're peculiar, somehow; odd; I didn't understand them, and they didn't understand me. We—we didn't hitch, somehow. They're a queer lot. They've got funny ideas. I don't know how to explain it exactly, but—somehow—I don't like 'em. That's all there is to it. They're good fellows enough, I know, but——"

"Oh, well, Caspar," interrupted the Senator. Then he seemed to weigh a great fact in his mind. "I guess——" He paused again in profound consideration. "I guess——" He lit a small, brown cigar. "I guess you are no damn good."

THE END.